GRIMOIRE

GRIMOIRE

A Wayward Tale

T A Newman

To order additional copies of this book, contact:
Xlibris
800-056-3182
www.Xlibrispublishing.co.uk
Orders@Xlibrispublishing.co.uk
670173

CONTENTS

ACKNOWLEDGEMENTS

Firstly, I would like to thank my wife who has supported me in completing this novel and everything that goes with it. She is love and understanding personified.

Secondly, I would like to thank my media-marketing guru, Jon, who is more family than friend, who believes against my constant insistence that I named that protagonist after him. He's a funny guy.

Thirdly, I would like to thank my grandmother and grandfather who are, sadly, no longer with us. They would often indulge my creative writing and story telling as a small child, encouraging my correct spelling and pronunciation. Joyce and Bill were pure examples of generosity and commitment and will always be missed.

Acknowledgements Continued . . .

A thank you to a few of the world's most generous and supportive people who made this book possible. Without you, Jon Wayward may have never had the chance to grace the pages you hold before you now.

Garrod Jon Winter
Shehan Udugampola
Jacob Seldon
Callum Douglas
Tom, Tina, Harry, Jack and Emma Graham
Chris, Lynda, David, Jill and Jack Wall

And especially . . .
Nicola Newman (the wife who makes me look good)
Nick Newman (the favourite Newman sibling)
Anne Newman (the mother who puts up with much)
Mark Newman (the father who loves without question) and Jon Wayward (for keeping me company)

P.S. A special thank you to you . . . the reader. I hope you enjoy the first of the Wayward Tales.

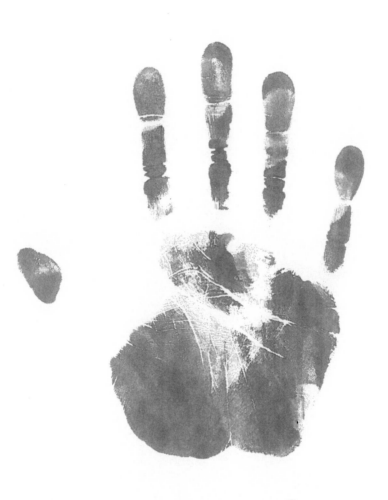

Wayward

CHAPTER ONE

Smoke and Mirrors

Magic is something that most people stop believing in around their eighth birthday. They think that the only magic in the world was in a Disney film they saw as a child or that it came from a magician for hire at one of those birthday parties that has no doubt emotionally scarred all in attendance for the rest of their lives. Well, I can tell you they are wrong. The all-too familiar man in a black-tailed coat, bow tie, and top hat who pulls a suffocated rabbit out of thin air is *not* magic. I've seen magic at its best, its worst, most beautiful, and unfortunately for me, at its most terrifying . . . but then, again, I'm not most people.

Before I go into detail about my first real tangle with magic, I think it's best if I introduce myself. My name is Jon, and I'm an Aquarius, a university classics and ancient history graduate who is self-conscious about being slightly overweight and considers sarcasm to not only be the best form of humour but also uses it as *the* go-to defence mechanism. I inherited a collector's shop in Amersham, just on the outskirts of London. I say antiques collector's shop, but I don't really tend to see too many regular antique hunters cross my doorstop, the reason being that my collector's items are all, or have some connection to, the occult and magical world. For example, I have a two-headed King George coin that always comes up tails, a vanity hand mirror that shows your death as if it were happening right there and then, which is said to be a gift from Doctor Dee to his gracious Queen, allowing her to reign a little longer than expected by most, especially those who attempted to have her assassinated, and a very rare 1602 book of secrets that keeps translating itself into different languages every time a page is turned.

You would think that this makes my life one of excitement and mystery, but the only mystery in my life is the social element that seemed to evaporate when I took over Smoke and Mirrors as a full-time business. That's the name of the shop, Smoke and Mirrors. Cool, huh? We do some face-to-face transactions, but mostly, I pay the rent with online sales, especially around the witches' festivals Samhain, Yule, Imbolg, Ostara, Beltane, Midsummer, Lammas, and Mabon. I keep the accounts on the shop and try to find new ways to promote the business by reading *The Dumb Guy's Guide to Running a Successful Business* over and over. Unfortunately, this means that the most stimulating conversation I have on a day-to-day basis is with myself, where I usually point out that talking to one's self is the first sign of madness. After agreeing with my familiar statements on insanity, I normally like to keep my head down and only deal with the supposed magical or occult antiques that cross my path in the predictable fashion. But, occasionally, something will jump out of nowhere and catch my attention. This happened when a short round man, soaked through to the bone, opened my shop door, ringing the obligatory bell and signalling it was time for me to become customer-friendly. He squelched his worn leather shoes across my Turkish rug; actually, it was my grandfather's rug. The man claimed that it was a magic carpet from the east, and he took great care in keeping it spotless, leaving great smears from one end to the other. For a man so small in stature, he really did have big feet, and it was those oversized feet that made me examine the man a little more closely.

In complete opposition to my charming yet classic brown side parting of the kind that never goes out of fashion, his thin greying hair stuck to his domed head as all comb-overs do, but it was the penny-sized rounded spectacles and button nose that gave him the appearance of a mole. It didn't help that even with his bottle-cap lenses he still had trouble making out whatever was in front of him until it was an inch from the tip of his nose. I would normally have welcomed this man to a seat and a hot drink, but there was something unsettling about him, and it wasn't just his grey tired skin hanging from his cheekbones or the fact that he had left his mark on my grandfather's rug; it was his black little eyes that stared in a trance-like state as he seemed to examine me in an inhuman manner.

There is only so long that you can pretend not to notice someone until the whole affair becomes uncomfortable, so I decided to begin the usual proceedings. "Is there anything in particular I can help you find?" I said, moving around a stack of books on Wallachian folklore. His pitch-black glare intensified as his eyes shrunk, and he focused on my face. I kept talking, which is a habit I have when I'm nervous, and to be fair, this man's beady little eyes made me exactly that. "Are you looking for bargain? Because I've just got a new order of hex bags that have come in from Haitian Central, finest quality."

"Wayward? You seem different," said the Mole-man in a rasping voice as if he were in need of an inhaler. Between his beady eyes and rasping lungs, I was surprised he had made it to adulthood.

"That would suggest we've met, and I never forget a face. I'm the owner and proprietor of this collection of fine antiquities, and you won't find a better range of occult and magical tools of the trade than right here at Smoke and Mirrors," I said with all the grace of a used-car salesman as I pulled my waistcoat back into shape and straightened my tie.

"You are Wayward, George Wayward?" he said with the same rasping voice, but before I could answer him, he exploded into a fit of coughing, struggling to catch his breath. I ran down the aisle of Hoodoo bags next to the dolls and puppets into the back of the shop where I had a basic yet adequate kitchen. Within a few more spluttering coughs, I had returned and was by his side, holding a glass of water. He made no sign to take the glass but only held out his palm, refusing the drink. He turned on the spot, and with his back to me, I saw his hand slip into his pocket followed by a flash of warm orange light and the sudden taste of sulphur. He took a large breath and turned, smiling with contentment; a long pipe now hung between his plump flaky lips.

"You can't smoke in here! Nearly everything in here needs to be kept in the best possible condition, including the fifteenth-century tapestry depicting the fall of Abramelin the Mage on the wall behind the counter, which is going to decrease in value every time you blow smoke at it," I explained with an irruptive and attempted authoritative manner.

"But, George, you always let me smoke my pipe before. Why? We always smoked together," said the Mole-man with a look of hurt, expelling his contented smile. "OK, George, have it your way, but you might change your mind when you see what I have brought you. By the way, when did you start taking Shambala sap? Didn't take you as the type to want to stay forever young? Although I can imagine the ladies appreciate a few less wrinkles," he said as he tapped out the contents of his thin pipe into the glass of water I still held and gave me a rattle of his wheezing laugh.

"Now just a minute, mate. I think you've gone and mistaken me for someone else. My grandfather was George, but I'm Jon, not George." Both of us took a minute just looking at each other. I studied him as he studied me, his face full of confusion and mine full of suspicion. A moment turned into a minute and that minute turned into the uncomfortable silence I was trying to avoid earlier. He obviously didn't believe or understand what I was saying because that same smile of contentment began to spread across his face as if old George had played a trick on him. I had to put a stop to it before he called me George again. "Wait a second. Please just listen to me for a moment. I'm not quite sure how you have confused me for my grandfather, but you have. George, my grandfather, passed away two years ago, leaving this shop to me." The Mole-man's face dropped as the realisation of George's fate became a reality. "Is there something I can do for you, Mr. . . ." I trailed off, hoping he would fill in the blank.

"I think I should return at another time perhaps?" he rasped quieter than before as water glistened in the white of his eyes. "But since you are the new proprietor, as you say, I must leave you my card." From his pocket came his business card, which he placed in my hand in such a fluid movement I wasn't sure it had happened until I saw him back across the Turkish rug and halfway through the door, braving the rain once again as he spoke over his shoulder to me. "Goodbye, *Jon* Wayward. I will see you soon I am sure."

"Can I ask . . . If you knew my grandfather, how did you miss his funeral?"

"I have been indisposed for many years, and I find it harder to keep track of time these days," he finished as the shop door closed behind him, and the bell rang out his exit. He left me with the thought of my grandfather who had raised me as his own. I was glad to recall that memory, then intrigued by the business card in my hand, which only had a name on it accompanied by his job title; it read 'Procurer', and I could see why my grandfather had done business with him and potentially had even been friends.

Surely not, I thought as I slowly calculated, without using my fingers; my grandfather had been eighty-one when he died, and the Mole-man was not a day over fifty. If he had worked with my grandfather, he would have been a child and not much help in the procuring of occult and magical artefacts. What kept my gaze firmly upon the business card in my hand was the symbol inscribed beneath his name; I hadn't seen anything like it before. It was no language I had studied within the arcane texts, and it certainly wasn't a translation of his name that stood out clearly above in swooping calligraphy; his name was Maurice, which somehow suited him perfectly.

Catching me by surprise, the bell rang out again as the shop door opened for the second time that day, and within the brief second it took for my next patron to walk through the door, I had forgotten all about Maurice the Mole-man and his quizzical ways. Standing no more than a foot away and very much in my personal space, once again dripping and marking my grandfather's rug was the most beautiful woman I had ever seen framed by my very own shop door, and the best part was that she wasn't just stopping to ask for directions. "Mr Wayward?" she asked with the fragility of an angel.

"Yes, please call me Jon." I rushed my words to make sure she knew I wasn't my grandfather.

"Jon Wayward, I need your help," she said, smoothing her dark hair down, looking as if she was almost on the verge of crying, and I knew from the moment she walked into my shop I would help her; it was just a matter of when. What can I say; I'm a sucker for a damsel in distress.

"Let's get you inside and warmed up," I said, taking her sleek black coat and ushering her further into the shop.

CHAPTER TWO

Damsel in Distress

Sitting in the client's chair in my office, which is next to the kitchen at the back of the shop's antiquarian front where I handle all my private conversations and wealthy clientele and drink heroic amounts of coffee, was Emilia. She told me her name as her dark damp tousled hair was being dried with a towel I found and was now clinging to her slender pale neck, but that's not why this damsel had me committed to her cause before I knew what we were up against. Oh no, it was her emerald eyes that seemed to glisten more with every blink or fluttered eyelash. She slurped her tea in an uncharacteristic fashion, but somehow it seemed to explain a lot about her without saying a word. She was beautiful but didn't have to use it to her advantage, even if some of us were weak willed enough to succumb to her beauty without even being asked. Her soft pale skin, emphasised by the delicate way she held herself, allowed me to further examine her slender nose, long neck, and purple painted nails. I imagined that she would look quite at home on the cover of *GQ* magazine and then quickly put those thoughts out of my mind before instinctually creating the centrefold and blushing like a little schoolboy.

Nothing was said while she took a moment to gather her thoughts, and then as she noisily put her cup of tea on to its saucer, she spoke with that faint voice of hers. "Thank you for the tea, Mr Wayward."

"Just Jon, I insist," I said with the best smile I could muster.

"Thank you, Jon," she said with growing confidence in talking to me.

"So tell me, Emilia, you said you needed help, and I would love to. But unless it's within my expertise, there's nothing I can do."

"Oh, but it is, Mr Wayward . . . *Jon*. In fact, you've come highly recommended to me."

"How highly?" I asked since I knew there weren't a lot of people in the business, let alone enough people to recommend a competitor.

"Very highly. Your family name carries with it a reputation, does it not?" She gave a knowing smirk, and if she knew my family name and reputation, then she knew I wasn't exactly keen on discussing it with anyone. We're a private bunch, us Waywards, so much so that I'm part of the clan yet I don't even know much about my predecessors.

"All families have a reputation if you look close enough, but that's not what you're here to discuss, is it?" I said as her mind flashed back to the reason she came, and she pulled from her bag, which she had carried on her forearm, a large yet thin rectangular object covered with a black cloth with red runes sewn into the material and a purple ribbon tying it all up in a bow. She placed it gently on to my desk and then sat back into her chair, staring deeply into my eyes, hers still sparkling emeralds. The runes made me think of pre-Roman priesthood in Britain, but these were different somehow; they were druidic with a twist, but I couldn't quite put my finger on it. Literally, they were just out of my reach.

As a rule, I always look and don't touch, something my grandfather said should always be a given, especially when what you're looking at and not touching isn't yours. So I asked the obvious in hope of a straight answer, "So what is it?"

"A job, part of a whole, incomplete," she said.

"And I can only imagine you want me to complete that whole for you?" I asked, trying to play her game and cut to the chase.

"Open it, Jon," Emilia said with her confidence almost radiating off her every word.

"No, thanks. Nothing personal, but you open it," I said, leaning back into my chair and steepling my fingers against each other to give the impression that I was used to this kind of thing happening every day, but it didn't, and I was extremely curious. No doubt it was some kind of book from one particular supposed magical origin that held the untold secret of power, just like every other book out there. The runes stuck with me though. *Ogham of some kind?* I thought.

"If you want the job, Jon, then you must commit to it from the start. Once you are in, you are in. I have to say that your unwillingness to explore my offer is quite the contradiction to your name Jon *Wayward*," she said, emphasising my surname with some weighted importance beyond my understanding. I hated it when people tried to use my family name as a way to get their claws into me. Firstly, because I didn't really know my family, except for my grandfather, and secondly, because it worked nearly every time. From her bag, she pulled out another cloth-covered rectangular object larger and heavier than before, but this time she uncovered it straight away and then held it up for me to see. It was obviously an old book as it was worn leather but not damaged. I couldn't tell by looking at it just how old it was and that intrigued me. In some places, it looked only twenty or thirty years old, whereas in others, it looked hundreds of years old, maybe even thousands; I'd never seen anything like it. There was nothing further I could deduce without actually having it in my hands and a good few hours to work with it and some serious magnification lenses.

"And what may I ask is that?" I asked, still trying to keep a dignified and relaxed attitude to the obvious treasure in front of me.

"Oh this? This would be your payment for helping me, all up front and above board." Her smile grew with each word.

"What would I want with that?" I asked impatiently.

"It is a family heirloom."

"Why would I want one of your family heirlooms?" I questioned, but my expression was obviously quite quizzical.

"Not one of *my* family heirlooms, one of *yours*."

"I'm sorry?" I couldn't stop my eyes from flickering between her half smug expression and my supposed family heirloom. "OK, Emilia, I think it would be best if you just explained, as you seem to have me at a disadvantage."

"You help me with my little problem, which is very much in your line of work, by tracing a rare collection for me, your paying customer, and I will, in return, give you the Wayward grimoire along with forty thousand pounds and expenses on top."

"All that?" I asked coolly and swallowing hard, which was against every fibre of my excited being that wanted to froth at the mouth with the mention of forty thousand pounds.

"All that," she confirmed.

"The Wayward grimoire?" My mind reran the deal I had been offered. "You mean a book of spells?" Shock and confusion took over my facial expression, and there was nothing I could do to stop it.

"Not just your grandfather's book of spells. This literally goes back through the ages, passed down from Wayward to Wayward right up until the passing of William Wayward, your great-grandfather. Then, for some unknown reason, his grimoire ended up on the market. Luckily for me and for you, I made the right offer." The grimoire was now on my desk with Emilia rapping the tips of her fingernails on its cover.

Without second guessing anymore, I moved my eyes from the grimoire on the desk and picked up the first cloth-wrapped bundle littered with red runes across its black surface, and a wash of warm air fell over me; it was like an adrenaline rush focused entirely through my fingertips and up into the veins in my arm. After a few seconds, the rush faded into nothing, leaving only a deepened sense of curiosity, and with that, I whipped off the ribbon and removed the cloth cover, still unsure as to what all the prominent runes meant. The ones I could decipher were key words like *protector*, *observer*, and *guardian*, which is just another way of saying 'prison' for whatever was inside. The runes would theoretically stop the package from being tracked, traced, or detected, but in my time of finding lost and obscure items, I'd never seen anything this extreme and very rarely only ever read about it, understanding half of what was legible at best.

The cloth fell to reveal a darkly varnished wooden box with three initials engraved into the lid: A.K.T. I looked from the initials to Emilia and then down to my grandfather's grimoire, wondering what secrets I was moments away from discovering if I took the job. I knew a few of the stories about our family and supposedly what the Wayward family were capable of and had done over the years, but to think that I could find out for sure was too tempting, especially when that knowledge came wrapped in forty thousand pounds.

That was the first time I realised that my stomach wasn't just in knots with my nerves but strangling every butterfly jumping around inside. I just couldn't put my finger on what it was that I had to subconsciously fight to force myself to lift the lid that bore the engraved letters A.K.T. To buy some time and, hopefully, some answers, I questioned Emilia and thought my grandfather would have been proud with my quick thinking. His number one rule was 'question everything'. So I did: "Do you have an A.K.T. in your family? Or is it an acquaintance?"

"I was hoping you could tell me," she said, now holding the Wayward grimoire to the table with the tips of her fingers; she was letting me know that until I took her job, I wouldn't see any form of payment.

A tingle ran up my fingers as I gently lifted the box's lid, and it glided open, doing most of the work for me. I was looking at the top of a tarot deck; a jester was prancing around, waving his comical implements into the air with one word printed above: Fool. It was nothing special. I had traced tarot packs before for sentimental value and obsessed collectors. I could imagine all Emilia wanted was for me to say when, where, how, and lastly and most importantly was the who. People formed attachments to the weirdest things, but who am I to judge when I let their emotional attachments pay my bills? "Tarot cards?" I asked.

"Yes, but it's not what you think."

"And what am I thinking, Emilia? That you want me to read your fortune?" I needed her to give me more if she wanted to keep me on the job.

"You're thinking that this will be a clear-cut investigation where I ask you to find the cards' origins or some such trivial act." I couldn't help but smile; she was pretty good and she knew it. Her confidence grew as she continued talking. "I can assure you that it's not and this case *will* change your life. What you will notice is that only and exactly two-thirds of this deck is there and authentic to its maker, which no one has been able to date or find the elusive A.K.T. The one-third that is missing from the deck is precisely what I am hiring you to track down. Once the cards have been located, I will send suitable funds and instructions for the delivery of the complete deck into my hands. The only discernible way of identifying the correct cards will be the . . ."

"The initials A.K.T. on each card." She gave me a mixed look, impressed that I was on the same page as her and annoyed that I had stopped her obviously well-rehearsed speech before she had finished. Oh well.

"I'm going to need a complete and full history of the deck or at least as much as you can provide and then . . ." It was my turn to give her the half-and-half look.

"There is no information held on the cards. The initials A.K.T. on the box they are contained in is all that I can give you."

"You mean no one knows."

"I mean I have no information that I can give you. But you're welcome to do your own investigation if that will help you collect the missing cards. Assuming the job is yours." Her emerald eyes now showed no sign of nervousness or uncertainty, only fixed with a definite and intrusive will to get what she had come here for. I guess she was lucky she had something I really wanted.

"And my grandfather's grimoire?" I asked, trying to mask the anticipation in my voice.

"As I said earlier, Jon, you take the job and you get the grimoire now," she said, her eyes still sparkling with hunger. I was amazed how she had changed since she first walked through my door.

"Then it looks like we have ourselves a deal, but there is one last thing I'm afraid we must discuss before you leave." Emilia's eyes turned soft again, knowing that she only had to concede to a few basics and I was hers. "I want a reason. Why do you want this deck?"

"Ours is not to question why. Ours is but to do or . . ."

". . . die." Cutting each other off was becoming a habit. "Is Tennyson the preferred reading of the tarot collector?"

"Just get in touch with me when you've found them or need my help – financially or otherwise." Her pale hand slipped into her bag once again, and I couldn't help but wonder how that one bag could hold so much. Then, unsurprisingly, she pulled out a thick envelope and passed it to me. As I took it from her, one of my fingers brushed hers, and an image flashed in front of my eyes for the briefest of moments. I could barely recollect what I had seen moments before; it was as if I had felt it and imagined it. "This is the first payment. The rest is on delivery of the whole deck. And this . . ." She slid the grimoire across the table, and it nearly dropped into my lap. ". . . this is for you. Be careful, Jon. Every family has a few skeletons in the closet, and yours has more than its fair share."

After that, she got up without saying a word and left. I had the feeling that those tarot cards were more important to her than she was letting on, especially since I was getting my family grimoire, forty thousand pounds, and expenses thrown into the bargain just to track down the missing ones. This would officially be the best-paid case I had ever been offered and a family heirloom thrown in the mix to boot. Business was good, better than good, business was miraculous.

I spent a moment gathering my thoughts and then hooked the 'closed' sign on to the door. On the way back to my office, I caught myself in the seventeenth-century wall mirror, and I looked worn out. My eyes were tinged with red, and my clothes were creased to buggery, so I stood sorting myself out as best as I could in case any more eccentric wealthy clients wanted to throw money at me. Smoothing the creases in my shirt and re-buttoning my waistcoat, I managed to catch a glimpse of something in the mirror. It was the same something I caught a glimpse of when I touched Emilia's finger, something watching from behind a purple haze and a dark hood, waiting, watching, the same something that I had seen when I first saw my death in the mirror. Every year on my birthday, I would watch my death so that I could try to avoid it when it came, and now I *knew* that Emilia would be the death of me. Literally.

Whatever the hooded thing was or whatever it wanted, it was going to have to wait until I had a chance to rediscover my family and my past, regardless of how many skeletons I had to dig up to get there. I was about to discover what being a Wayward was all about.

CHAPTER THREE

Revelations

I was taking my grandfather's grimoire to my inner sanctum, which was his personal lab hidden within the flat upstairs I now lived in, where he cooked up all sorts of potions and supposed remedies that were popular with the young and wannabe witches and wizards of our time, who had no clue as to what real magic was. Even though I was no more than six steps away from the sliding bookcase leading to my inner sanctum, I couldn't take my eyes away from the *W* engraved into the worn leather cover. It was exactly the same way he, my grandfather, and any other member of the Wayward family had signed their names, allowing that extravagant *W* to stand out as if it needed to. It was almost instinctual.

With no lights in the lab, I lit the several candles I had dotted around the room for maximum illumination. It had never been wired up, and modern electrical appliances and potions weren't exactly a healthy mix. It always made me think of the age-old 'nature vs. science' battle and which side I was on. I didn't like choosing and always found it hard to come down on one side. That's why I subscribe to the 'ignorance is bliss' method of choice. The warm glow danced along the stone goblets that sat in the centre of a circular table, looking as if it had seen more than a few hundred years of use. The walls, pictures, and mirrors lit up and left slithers of shadows between the raised wooden panels and the frames of the wall. I placed the grimoire in the middle of the table, and as I leant over it with anticipation, I lifted the cover to reveal a handprint with a title written above it in a very expressive and old italic scrawl. The handprint was designed with the same ink as the italic title and looked as though it must have taken a long time and had no room for error as I saw the acute attention to detail in every curve and line the palm could offer. It was like looking at a labyrinth hiding its true path with the walled lines of the hand, but for some reason, the path it led to had something familiar about it, something I should recognise in it.

I moved my palm over the inked hand as I read the title, and I felt a tug from the open grimoire to my hand, almost as if gravity had changed its rules. I pulled my hand away uncertainly, but curiosity got the better of me, which was the habit of a lifetime and completely contradicted my *ignorance is bliss* method. I laid my palm on the imprint, and instantly, I was amazed at how perfectly my hand fit the ink; it was as if the page was hugging my hand, and within a heartbeat, I realised I had been saying the title of the page over and over, intoning the words like some religious nut. I'm not ashamed to say that I was scared. "Way-ward, Way-ward, Way-ward, Way-ward." I pulled my hand away from the grimoire, and a mist was pulled from around me, a mist I had never seen before, never noticed it creeping up on me. It was then for the first time in my life that I saw not only my grandfather's inner sanctum for what it was but also the world.

On every panel of every wall glowed a different symbol or rune of blue flames burning but causing no damage or creating any smoke. I followed them down the wall as they were in vertical lines, burning from ceiling to floor. Whichever one I looked at seemed to burn a slightly lighter shade of blue than the one before. On the Wayward family tree, framed and hung opposite my grandfather's root-and-herb collection, only one line of family stood out with the same blue fire highlighting it from the rest. I reached out and traced the bloodline of blue fire with my finger only to notice something even more disturbing. The entire inside of my right palm, stretching all the way down my fingers, was covered with the ink-designed handprint from the grimoire's front page; it had peeled off and stuck to my hand. I followed the detailed prints with my other hand, but the black dips and contours of each fingerprint or lifeline were tattooed on my skin. I hadn't noticed until just that moment that there were lines, dashes, and crosses in the same tattooed black markings leading away from my palm and up the inside of my wrist across my beating pulse and spiralling beneath my sleeve. I tried to read what the symbols said, which struck me as odd only as an afterthought as I had never seen those particular markings before. "*Fyarn-loos-AE-luhm-mwin-EH-duth.*" I immediately felt a burst of wind force itself from behind me as the candles in the room took on a life of their own, each dancing high up into the air with a roar, touching the ceiling. They were no longer just burning gently; they were fiercely fighting to stay as big and as alive as they could. So much so that I could feel the heat lapping over my face and neck, wave after wave, as if the flames were showing off, and with each wash of heat, I could feel a heaviness falling over me until I fell faint, reaching out for the edge of the table. I was out like a light before I cracked my head on the floor and split my lip. But let me tell you this: passing out and nearly burning down my laboratory, apartment, and place of business in one fell swoop was the least of my worries, especially with the kinds of friends I was going to be making over the next few days.

Before I had travelled anywhere near consciousness again, I had a dream, or nightmare, played out in my mind's eye with yours truly cast in the leading role. *I walked down a wood-panelled corridor with my feet lightly padding on the floor as I looked up at the pictures framed either side of me. The pictures all had me in them, but I was in places that I had never been to, doing things I had never done. It wasn't just an "Oh look, there I am at the Eiffel Tower or Stone Henge and Big Ben". No, it couldn't have been a normal kinda dream because in each of these photos, I was surrounded by a swirl, which sometimes looked like inky water flowing around me in blue, green, and black, dispelling as it swam, and followed me, and I even saw one where I was holding flames in my hand! It wasn't burning me because my face in the photograph was calm and focused; the fire sat in my open palm as if it were coming from me, from my own hand. In each photo, I could see* him *lurking somewhere – the hooded figure I saw when my hand touched Emilia's. He wasn't really doing anything but was just there, waiting and watching as those inky colours swirled around me.*

Looking down at my hand, I could see the unique markings across my wrist and the inked handprint; the ink bled up my arm, forming new symbols and dashes. The black beads of ink trickled up my arm, defying gravity and leaving tracks in its wake. My heart began thumping within my chest at such a pace I felt giddy for the briefest moment, and when I noticed that the black trickles weren't stopping, my heart beat broke into a gallop. I heard my blood racing with each beat of the pulses echoing in my eardrums. The ink quickened up my arm, my heartbeat urging it on to finish covering my skin in its runes, leaving nowhere unclaimed. I reached over with my hand and gripped my forearm, trying to block the ink's path by covering the inside of my elbow, but the path seemed to be blocked, and I hoped it would pool around my hand, forming some sort of dam. As you can imagine, it didn't quite have the effect I was after. At first, I thought that the ink had just stopped on its own accord with those harshly inked symbols finishing just under my left hand. That's when I felt the effects on the inside of my left palm, in and under my skin. Instantly, the ink became ice-cold, racing up my arm and reaching over my shoulder and on to my neck. I tried to brush off the ink making its way to my face and chest; my breathing sped up, and I saw the ink had rapidly increased in speed and infected the clean hand and begun the same attack from this arm as well.

I fell against the wood-panelled wall as panic set in, and my balance abandoned me. My face was up against a photo of a mountaintop that showed a vast storm almost attacking the peak itself. I could see the shadows of people standing at the top being thrown around in the storm like rag dolls. I just hoped I wasn't one of the ones in the middle.

A shiver rippled over my entire body, and I closed my eyes and dropped to the floor as if an electric current had run through my muscles without warning. I thought for a moment I could feel the wind from the storm quickly whip through the corridor. Gentle taps stroked my cheeks and one directly on to my eyelash, which forced me into an instant flickering of rapid blinking, leaving my eyes open to see where I found myself. Outside! How did I get outside? I pulled myself up to sitting as snowflakes fell from the skies. I must have been here for hours. I looked at the floor around me in this very unfamiliar street and saw that there was a good inch of snow on the ground, and it was still falling, obscuring the street lamps' glow. Finally pulling myself to my feet, a lone flake found its way on to my bottom lip with the gentlest of kisses, and as I had done when I was younger, I licked it from my lip, but unlike my childhood days of playing out in the street with my grandfather, I knew instantly that two things were wrong. Firstly, the taste of the snowflake was more like dust or dirt and made me spit it out the second the taste registered. If anything, it was the absolute opposite to what pure white snow should have tasted like. Secondly, there was a silhouette standing further down the road bathed in the night's darkness. The only reason he came into my sight was because of the ravens at his feet, screaming in turn for my attention as his breath misted in front of his mouth as it said my name – 'Wayward'. Then my skin rippled again across my body, and I dropped to the ground.

My heart was now beating like a runaway locomotive and pounding in my ears with my blood pulsing through my body. In no small part due to the ice-cold ink trying to consume me, I felt like I was going into shock and found it harder and harder to catch my breath like an asthmatic in a vacuum. I could not only feel the ice-cold symbols burning their permanent residence on my skin, but I could also feel it inside me, on the inside of my skin, consuming me. I tried to keep my eyelids closed, but it no longer felt like I had control, and suddenly, the ink on the inside of my skin had taken over and was forcing my eyelids open. My vision started to blur as the ink ran into the whites of my eyes, and I could feel drops tipping over the edge and trickling down my face as black oily tears. It didn't sting like I thought it would, but it was so very, very cold. And that was the last I remember as I dropped into a very dark and very cold place. Falling into this dream within *a dream or nightmare within a nightmare, all I could hear was that voice and the call of my name becoming a distant whisper as I fell into the abyss.*

That and the splitting headache from nose-diving the floor.
Good times . . . well . . . times.

CHAPTER FOUR

A Well-Dressed Truth

I started to feel myself coming back to reality with the comforting screech of a whistle engraining its hurtful tones into my frontal lobe forever more. With every nail across a chalkboard of a note, my eyelids flickered to the offbeat as if I were having a mild yet traumatising fit. I decided that the throbbing heat and pain surging through my delicate grey matter was enough on its own, without the very real feeling of someone weighing around sixteen stone kneeling on my neck, so I peeled open my eyelids which only managed to show me a blurred orange glow lost in a swirl of greys and blacks. Instead of his horrendous whistling, I heard his voice for the first time, all melodic and smooth, as if the words danced their way through his cigarette and out into the twists of smoke floating between us.

"Wayward? There hasn't been a Wayward for a few years now." He sounded as if he were royalty taking the day off from elocution lessons to come into my shop and browse the rare and exotic antiques with a dark past in occult magic. It was the slow dawning of my next thought that whipped my vision back into its focus like a slap across the face.

Firstly, there was a man sitting above me, watching as I lay in my semi-conscious state, and secondly, and more importantly, we weren't in my shop but in my secret laboratory where I had gracefully nose-dived the stone floor. I did manage a glimpse at the stonewalls to see that the glowing blue runes had gone. *Not sure how I'm going to explain that one.* No one was supposed to know about the laboratory – no one except my grandfather. Let me rephrase: except my *dead* grandfather and the *dead* Wayward clan that came and went before him.

"Evening, Wayward," he said. "I'm so glad you could find the time to join me after I came all this way at your request."

I managed to mumble half-formed words. "Who raer ooo?" Communication wasn't my strongest tool at that moment. It was by this point that the laboratory began to take some kind of shape, and I realised the gentleman sitting in front of me not only spoke like a royal but also held himself like a prince in his pressed white suit and ocean blue shirt hidden beneath a white large knotted tie looking like something out of the Great Gatsby. Very similar to my own style except that my charcoal three-piece suit was at least four years old and sporting the modern look of lighter patches on the knees from close inspections of floors displaying low-laying antiques such as tapestry rugs, engraved messages into slabs, burial sites, and hopefully one day, buried treasure. My other classic look which hadn't really helped with the upper-class intimidating stare I was receiving from the man in white was my bottom waistcoat button, salvaged from a dying jacket and sewn on using dark red cotton. Classy I know, but business had been slow, and I hadn't won the lottery.

"Charming, I can see we are going to be best chums, you and I. We'll get along swimmingly." The sarcasm in his voice was not lost on me as I pushed myself from the cold hard slabs that had acted as my temporary bed. He looked only a year or two older than my good self, and now that I got to study him on a more even keel, the details were coming into shape. "Sebastian Dove is my name." He contrived to look at me as if it should mean something to me, but all I could do was look back at him in confusion and impatience.

"Is there something I can do for you, Mr Dove?" I asked, getting myself up from the floor, groaning as I could feel my bruised body forcefully remind me of its fall. I knew that I had at least some control of my limbs, and that was a help. "I mean there *must* be some reason why you have not only appeared in my secret laboratory But also have obviously been prying into whatever you were able to see, and why? To keep an eye on me while I was passed out in case I what . . . passed out *some more*? Popped round to see if I dropped into a coma never to return, to see if I would die so you could loot my shop and do God knows what to my body!" I wanted to come across as someone not to be messed with, someone you never took advantage of or pushed around. Due to the natural unsurprising white gleam of straight teeth glaring back at me from behind Sebastian's smile, I guess all I managed to do was to come across as irritable and a flustered individual who didn't like being treated like a mushroom. For those of you who have never grown mushrooms, let me tell you the best way to care for them: keep them in the dark and feed them crap.

"My dear Wayward, ask not what you can do for me, but what I can do for you," said Sebastian, smiling through his smoke, which flashed the memory of that dirty snowflake from my dream to the front of my mind. I breathed the smell in for the first time, and from then on, it was all I could taste. That and the bait I took. "OK then, what can you do for me?" I asked.

"Not nearly as much as you can do for me. Ha!" He began giggling as if he had just told a classic one-liner and somehow we were old pals laughing as we always had at his rapier wit, but I can assure you that I was not laughing; if anything, I was scowling.

"Enough of your bloody riddles! Why are you here?" I was almost shouting in his face, and once again, he showed no signs of discomfort or any other chink in his armour that I could see.

"I'm here to help you, Wayward," Sebastian said, dropping his cigarette butt to the floor and crushing it with the heel of his handmade Italian leather shoes. Everything about Sebastian Dove rubbed me the wrong way; ever since I had woken up in his presence, I had had a niggling sensation in the back of my mind, and now I knew that that feeling was my instincts warning me. I wasn't used to my instincts telling me anything apart from *feed me*, so when they told me to 'beware this man', I was obliged to listen.

My nerves and my temper finally got the better of me, and I fired my next question at Sebastian like a man possessed. I prodded his chest with my finger and got right up into his face. The smell of his cigarette clung to my nostrils like an overheated vacuum cleaner. "What exactly are you going to help me with?"

"This," Sebastian said calmly as ever. He grabbed my wrist with both hands, and immediately, they seemed to be burning my skin through my shirt; they were so hot. He slid one hand up my arm towards my elbow, turning my shirtsleeve to ash beneath his palm, cindering orange with white sparks falling to the floor. I was silent and confused and not just by my shirtsleeve turning to ash and falling away but due to the ink on the runes running up my arm that should have disappeared with my nightmare.

"Holy crap, these things are real?" I felt weak in the knees and buckled, but Sebastian caught me and held on to my arm, forcing me to stay standing.

"Easy there, Wayward," he said, steadying my sleeveless arm in front of me, forcing me to look on to the swirling black symbols and minute lines. Staring at the markings of circles over triangles laced with miniature runes running through a number of languages I could use, there was no end to the secrets in forgotten words and letters. My world fell into the cracks beneath, reality just waiting for me to catch up.

"What is all this? I've never wanted a tattoo, especially anything like this." I lifted up the crispy and charred edge of the remaining shirtsleeve to reveal each line of seemingly random symbols running all the way up to my shoulder. "This is too much!"

Another wave of shock washed over me in a very unfriendly and sobering thought. *What if this ink trailed over my shoulders? Is it on my face?* With that, I was attacking the buttons on my waistcoat, starting with the golden-coloured odd one out with red cotton and moving up to the smaller and easier silver ones that were actually made for the waistcoat. I was stroking my face to see if I could feel whether the ink was on my skin. When the waistcoat came off, I spared no mercy for my already half-burned shirt and began pulling it off, popping buttons and ripping thread as I went. Sebastian gave me a comforting, if not annoying, piece of advice. "Just keep calm, and I'll explain what happens next." My shirt came off in a spectacular struggle with my intact sleeve, revealing my entire upper body covered in a thousand intricate little designs that half looked familiar and half like gibberish.

It started with the black-inked print on my right hand, which had infected my arm all the way up to my neck, poking out over my collarbone, right across my chest, stomach, and back, all in a variety of sequences and patterns. My heart beat rose, and not for the first time that day, I clenched my teeth and asked Sebastian a question. "Is it time for you to stop treating me like a mushroom and bring me into the light?"

"You've been marked," he replied.

"Marked? Really? How could you tell?" Once again, my anger decided to poke its sarcastic head out.

"Wayward, listen to the words I am saying. You have been marked and not just by those symbols imprinted upon your flesh but also by an order of men and women from your own bloodline. You have been given a gift, or rather you have been *chosen* for a gift, but nonetheless, it's yours to use, however you see fit." I could see that Sebastian paused for a moment to see if I was actually listening to what he was saying; he didn't have to wait long because I was completely enthralled by his blatant bout of insanity. After smoothing his hair on to the side of his face, he continued his ramblings. "There is a small choice you will have to make, but the important thing is that you embrace your gift and the new opportunities it will provide, whilst occasionally representing our kind."

"OK, Sebastian, I think we have indulged your crazy discursive nonsense for long enough, but I reckon we should call you a taxi and get you somewhere safe." *Now he was telling me what to do. OK, too much. It's time to end this bad dream that started with this well-dressed stranger,* I thought as I walked over to the back of my sliding bookcase. That's right; I said *sliding* bookcase. It was stacked with all sorts of vials and herbs on this side rather than books on the other. Even though the sliding bookcase was on a mechanism that helped it move open to shut, it didn't explain how he played his next trick.

"Wayward, I fear you are not taking me seriously," he said as I caught the slightest flick of his wrist from the corner of my eye. Luckily, I was still facing the bookcase as it slammed shut inches from my face; otherwise, I would have jumped across the room. Watching the vials and bottles rattle, I had a second to remind myself that I didn't trigger the sliding door, and Sebastian was behind me . . . I realised I hadn't jumped across the room, but from where I was looking, I could see that I had fallen back on to the cold stone floor again, with Sebastian standing over me. His white suit hummed with an orange glow borrowed from the surrounding candles melted and flickering erratically. "Nice trick there," I said, pulling myself up by the table leg.

"It was no trick, Wayward, but I believe you already know that."

"Really? So what exactly am I supposed to believe? That you appeared in my secret laboratory, then incinerate half of my shirt with the touch of your hand and slammed the bookcase door from five feet away without even touching it? Not to mention you claim to know what my new body art means!" I huffed a few breaths out, trying to judge his reaction. Once again, he just stood there, beaming with a calming confidence that few people ever really achieve in their whole lives.

"You need more proof?" Sebastian asked as if he were offering me a cup of his finest earl grey.

"Proof of what?"

"Of what you already know, of what you are, of what you have become, of what you will be, and of what you have always known in the deep recesses of your mind." He stroked his hair back again.

"It's nice that we cleared that up, but since you offered, I think proof would probably be the best way to go." I couldn't believe it, but I actually wanted to know more about what this bloody lunatic had to say. I obviously knew he was some type of clinically insane miscreant, but there was something about him, about his aura or presence, that I couldn't put my finger on. And he was still standing in my secret laboratory with the grin of an inspirational speaker or serial killer; either way, I wanted to get him out of here, and this seemed like the best way to get him to leave.

And yes, I know that the only people to have secret laboratories are either super villains or super geeks. I like to think of myself as a mixture of both with a dash of James Bond and a sprinkle of Batman. Seriously.

CHAPTER FIVE

Show of Power

I had insisted that I at least change my shirt before Sebastian showed me his *proof*, which wouldn't shock me all that much if it turned out to be a large bag of dried mushrooms coated in LSD.

He told me that his proof was in the alley outside and as I finished buttoning up my new shirt and throwing my waistcoat back on over my burn-free light blue double-cuff shirt, which was a bit excessive as I could only imagine he wasn't taking me out for a fine dining experience, I prepared myself for the worst. I followed him out through my not-so-secret sliding door down the metal spiral framed staircase into the shop and out into the street just as I flipped over the sign in the window from OPEN to CLOSED.

I reasoned to myself that outside with crazy was better than inside with crazy, and at least I could run away outside. It wouldn't come to that anyway, I was sure. I followed a couple of steps behind, thinking Sebastian would try to show me his proof, and when it failed, I would threaten him with the police and a restraining order and anything else I could. *I wonder how easy it is to have someone you don't know committed to an institution.* Once again, there was something niggling away, and it wasn't in the back of my mind or a second guess but was more instinctual, and that worried me. My instincts had always been trustworthy when they rarely reared their heads, and they had gotten me through more scrapes than my brain had even been aware of.

The street we walked down was empty except for a drunken tramp humming to himself. He was taking a leak up the wall of the local pawnshop, which I occasionally did business with – the shop not the tramp – whilst trying to find his long-lost balance. Luckily for me, it was the adjoining side alley that Sebastian turned down as I didn't fancy wading through a stream of recycled triple strength discount larger. "Tell me, Wayward, what do you see?" he asked.

"What do I see?" I repeated sceptically. There was nothing to see but a muddy and overgrown path with puddles running down either side, two high brick walls flanking us, and a smouldering fire in a bin. I presumed the tramp had been using the remains of it at the other end. Apart from that, Sebastian was the only piece of the puzzle that really seemed to stand out. His back was still facing me with his white glaring suit that somehow seemed to be spotless in this filth-infested alley. My shoes and the bottom of my trousers had already been splashed as we came around the corner, and somehow I'd even managed to get some specks of what I could only hope was mud on my new clean shirtsleeves. "I see a normal everyday alley with a bat shit crazy man wearing too much white and another man who is a complete fool by letting himself be taken on a wild goose chase just to appease his own curiosity, and we all know how that ended for the cat who tried the same thing, don't we?" I spat out in a flurry of words. To be perfectly honest, I was disappointed. I think I half expected there to be proof of some kind in this dark and dingy alley.

"You are no cat, Wayward," Sebastian said in his matter-of-fact way that made me feel like I should have been wearing a dunce's hat and sitting in the corner.

"Well, that's cleared that up then. I guess you're not crazy at all!" I wasn't sure if sarcasm had a limit, but if it did, I was getting close. "It's all been one great big misunderstanding."

"You didn't answer my question," he said.

"What?"

"What do you see?"

"I told you! I see you. I see me. Mud. Puddles. A burnt-out fire and my life slowly slipping away."

"And what are these things to you?" he asked calmly.

"I'm sorry, Mr Dove . . . Sebastian. But what does this have to do with a book full of symbols ending up using my skin as their canvas, you almost setting me on fire and the chance to get my life back into some semblance of normality? You told me we were coming down here for some proof, and if I'm not mistaken, there is none. So unless you can give me one hell of an answer, I'm going back to my shop where I will lock the door behind me and ask you never to darken my doorstep again or, in your case, brighten my doorstep with your crazy white suit." I was pleased I had gotten my rant finished but also a little worried. I had never been around a crazy person before when their bubble of imagined reality had popped.

Sebastian turned on me, his eyes pale blue and swimming into the colour of his shirt, coming alive with only the pupil as a fixed dot that looked deep into my own. He threw his hands out to his sides, which made me jump, and muttered something under his breath as if he were getting ready to dance or launch a karate move at me. "You want answers, Wayward? Here they are," Sebastian said in what I felt was a threatening manner. He began to raise his hands, outstretched either side, towards the sky and murmured a word I could just hear: "*Tenebris*". As he did, the alley we stood in actually seemed to be getting darker. "Every time your soul aches, every time you experience déjà vu, every time you feel a shiver down your spine, or the hairs on the back of your neck stand up, it is because of one simple and undeniable truth . . ." His hands were almost touching above his head, and the alley had become considerably darker. I literally couldn't believe my eyes as Sebastian was stealing the daylight around us. ". . . Magic. Is. Everywhere." He sounded as if he were enjoying himself as his hands finally reached each other, and dusk fell over the alley like a table cloth being laid out across its surface. Beyond Sebastian, at the other end of the alley and behind me, where we had walked in, bright sunshine still shone as naturally as ever but unable to enter into the alley. I had never seen anything like it; he was *literally* breaking the laws of physics.

"Magic?" was all I could manage to say. I was half in shock and half in a dream in which my mind kept shouting, *This can't be real! Seriously!* My eyes, body, and soul somehow knew it was; they all knew on some instinctual level that he was telling the truth.

"I can see you need a little more convincing before you are able to take my word as the truth of the matter," Sebastian said with some relish in his regal tones, then muttered so I couldn't hear him this time. Everything around us went still, the air moved slower than I ever thought possible, the puddle of rain water moved in a heightened slow motion as a ripple curled outwards, and the embers of the dying fire glowed their soft orange glow without fading. It was as if someone had paused time with the exception of Sebastian and myself and then played with gravity. The lack of movement made me think of being a child and climbing around my grandfather's shop, pretending I was on the moon or a distant world with low gravity, making me take overly big and slow steps as I climbed up over a chair or display stand. Sebastian began speaking again, but now he had the attitude and inflection of a teacher or a performer making sure that his audience, me, understood. "Basic magic consists of five essential elements that have ruled our worlds since the dawn of time. Earth," he said with a curl of his hand and sweeping flick of his forefinger as he whispered under his breath. "*Terrae*."

The ground beneath my feet began to shift, and I almost dropped to the mud-plastered pavement. I was held in shock and disbelief, which was now only being added to by a circular wall of mud, gravel, and weeds rising behind me and being moulded into a wall from the ground. When the wall steadied itself and I could stand up without fear of falling or being consumed by the earth itself, I saw that the wall of floating earth and debris had stretched out from the two opposing buildings, completely blocking off the alley's exit behind me.

"Fire," he said next, then whispering, "*Ignis*" as the tramp's poor attempt to keep warm exploded from behind Sebastian and engulfed him like a million wasps swarming. I let out a little scream, which was slightly more feminine than I'd like to admit. He exploded into flames and spoke again. 'Water,' he commanded as clear and as calmly as he did before he whispered, '*Aqua*', and amongst the fiercely dancing flames around his body, the puddles of rainwater lying at either side of the alley rose up and leaned in over Sebastian as he held out his flame-engorged arms. The occasional droplet that escaped his grasp hissed into vapour as it fell into his burning mass. The image stayed with me for a long time after that day. It was biblical; a man stood unharmed by flames with two walls of water parted like the Red Sea on either side of us.

The water swelled in over our heads where they touched, and as soon as they did, the rainwater came crashing down upon us. I was forced back against the wall of mud and weeds, knocked to the floor on my hands and knees, and by the time I was upright once again, I could see Sebastian standing with his arms and hands outstretched. A smile flashed across his face as he spoke his next words. "You might want to brace yourself for this. Wind! *Ventus*." Straightaway, I was knocked against the back wall, but I managed to keep my balance and lean forward into the blast of freezing cold air. I could actually feel my soaked clothes drying from the wind as I judged how far forward I had to be without getting blown off my feet. The sound was incredible, like two high-pitch whistles blasting into my eardrums with a million people screaming in time beneath it. I could feel my cheeks and lips being pushed back around my face, and as quickly as it had started, it stopped, and once again, I found myself on the floor.

I stood to find Sebastian in front of me as if nothing had ever happened, or what had happened was so normal it didn't need all the protestations and disbelief that I had given it. "OK then. Magic is real, and that was proof," I said in awe of what I just experienced.

"I am glad we are finally on the same page, Wayward."

"Magic." I giggled to myself for a moment, which was a true sign that my nerves had suffered. "You can use magic."

"I'm not the only one, Wayward."

"There's more of you?" I asked.

"More of us." He pointed out.

"Us?" I asked as I realised my nerves were about to go another ten rounds in a new world where reality was comparable to a very strong hallucinogen.

CHAPTER SIX

Magic Is Real

We ended up in my office instead of my secret laboratory, which was a long dazed and confused walk to the back of Smoke and Mirrors. A half-remembered view of the various herbs and concoctions I had made and stored following old family recipes stood out to me. I hadn't noticed the walk back from the alley, and I wouldn't have been able to tell you if I had walked into the oncoming traffic due to my inflated state of shock and confusion. I realised where I was after Sebastian placed a cup of tea in a Han Solo mug next to me. He sat opposite me, staring through the rising steam of his own hot drink from my Chewbacca mug with his unmoving, unblinking ice-blue eyes hooked into my own hazel and undilated ones.

"Tell me," Sebastian said.

"Tell you what?"

"What you are thinking. I imagine you have some questions you would like answering," he said in a lower tone, almost in a caring way, which he must have found hard as his cutting accent made him sound uncaring and harsh.

"Questions!" I snapped out of my shock-induced trance and let my mouth run away. "Yeah, I got questions, like who the hell are you? What do you mean by *us*? Why does nobody know about magic? And how in the name of all that is holy do I get a thousand tattoos off without a huge laser and thousands of pounds to waste on tattoo-removal surgery?" I finished with a splutter as I ran out of breath.

Sebastian took a moment for himself as he smiled over his cup, making me wait for my answers. To be perfectly honest, I don't like to play mind games; I often say what I mean and call a spade a spade, or a shovel. And if it was anyone else in front of me, clients included, I would have told them to stop wasting time and tell it to me like it is. Trouble was, Sebastian wasn't a client. He was someone who had the answers I needed, and if he wanted to take his sweet time and make me wait, then there was nothing I could do about it.

"Answers I have," he reassured me, although his calm manner was beginning to grate on my sensibilities. "Some I can give you, some I am forbidden to reveal, and some you must find for yourself."

"I knew you were going to say something stupid." I rubbed my eyes to wake myself into paying attention. "But as we're here, I suggest we start with the answers you can give me." I said rather matter-of-factly, trying my hardest to get down to business.

"Magic is as real as you or I," he said, leaning forward. "It is older than time itself. It created time, an energy that all life supports. It is life! It can only be manipulated or used by a select few beings. Over the centuries, those who use magic have been known by many names – Priest of Samaria, Healers of Tribes Pagan, Wizards of the Crown, Witches of Europa, Alchemists of Life, Mages, Grimoires and many, many more, depending on religion and tongue."

"So what are you? Wizard? Priest?" I asked.

"In modern magical society, we are commonly referred to as Magi or Mages, allowing the magic we use to imprint a small part of its power on to us. Mages mainly come from three schools of magical application. I am one, you are another, and we all work together for the betterment of our magical understanding.

"The symbols that have bonded themselves to your flesh are the marks of your ancestors and the magical disciplines they have studied. You are a very interesting case, Jon Wayward. Magic has been in your family bloodline since before the 'Ignorance of the Masses,'" said Sebastian with a hint of superiority in his tone.

"Ignorance of the Masses?" I asked.

"How do you think magic has stayed out of the public eye? How do you expect us to use magic without anyone noticing and telling the rest of the world that the myths and fairytales of old are true?"

"What myths and fairytales?"

"You've heard of Grimoire Merlin?" he asked with a smile.

"As in King Arthur? Round table? That Merlin?"

"Real Grimoire, real magic."

"Come on, surely you're pulling my leg?"

"Surely not. How do you explain miracles?" said Sebastian as he raised his eyebrows to wait for my answer with a knowing look on his face. I was beginning to hate that face.

"Magic?" I said in a defeated tone.

"Absolutely, the bread, the wine, the fish, parting the Red Sea, curing leprosy and blindness. Every culture on the planet has its own version of a miracle and their own justification of how it happens, but we know better, don't we, Wayward?" His face, mouth, and eyes were smiling; everything was smiling.

"Magic." I paused for a moment, really trying to take all this as seriously as I could, realising that the only word I had said in minutes was 'magic'. Time for a change. "Are witches . . ?"

"Real," he answered.

"Monsters?" I asked, trying to throw him off his trail.

"Real. Well, most of them anyway," he said, shrugging off my question. "Importantly, you must recognise that you are of a magical bloodline, strong enough to open your ancestors' grimoire and take their knowledge into you."

"The tattoos?" I was trying to put the pieces together.

"Those symbols are a sign of natural power and ability," he said, looking at my wrist where a few runes crept on to the back of my hand, and then flicking his fingers up to my shirt collar, he revealed a triangle motif that sat encircled by foreign letters from an ancient language. "Those symbols contain every spell and potion ever used by the Wayward bloodline. Those spells have now become a part of you, who you are, and most importantly, who you will become.

"I am a Mage of a different ilk. My knowledge is founded from the Alchemists and from the "Pillars of the Blackened Earth" who can help you become a true Grimoire and user of the mystic arts. My magical disciplines have been mastered through years of study and practice." Sebastian's voice wavered, and his eyes lowered to his now empty cup as he spoke his next few words. "You, Wayward, will not have to study these ways, for your markings will transfer your ancestors' knowledge to you through your blood like an ink and red-celled osmosis. The Pillars can show you this path if you listen to my instructions."

"Are you saying I will just learn it?"

"It's not that easy. It's a subconscious knowledge at the moment. Words will come to you as a reflex or a reaction. Words have power, or why else do you think they call it *spell*-ing?"

"Words? Can I not just think it or wave my wand? Do I get a wand?" I perked up as my desire to have a wand took over my normal state of confusion.

"Wands?" Sebastian spat the word at me as though I was insulting his mother's virtue. "Wands are for trashy tales and repulsive television. Any true Mage, Shaman, or Grimoire needs nothing more than his knowledge of the mystical arts. I suggest you start using your magic as much as you can. You will get a stronger understanding of what power you have." He looked at me, waiting for my agreement to his rant about wands. Considering what I had seen him do earlier, I wasn't going to disappoint. Shame though, as a wand would have been interesting.

He described a few of the magical disciplines, explaining how the elemental magics work for him – earth, fire, wind, water, and the spirit – although he was very vague about Spirit magic and just compared it to the others as a conduit for our powers.

I noticed that Sebastian became very relaxed in his language as he began to tell me that there were people he wanted to introduce me to. I got the feeling that they were persons of interest as he said he would have to arrange a meeting and would be in touch, but most importantly, he told me that I would have to be ready. He told me that the Pillars of the Blackened Earth were a secretive organisation and didn't like to draw too much attention. Like most magic using orders, I imagined this was the norm. I didn't push him to tell me more, as tiredness fell upon me so strongly that my eyelids were fighting to stay open. He saw how exhausted his student had become and told me he would be in touch soon. Trying to hold on to my concentration, I heard him talk of magic as a living thing and how the Pillars of the Blackened Earth spent their lives trying to serve magic and how there were people out there who wanted control over *all* magic. My eyes dropped, unnaturally heavy with his warning of these greedy magic users who were relics of a time long ago.

What seemed like seconds later, I was forcing my eyes back open, and there was no sign of Sebastian. He had obviously let himself out, but before he did, he had written a note, which he attached to the wooden box with the A.K.T. engraving. In his delicate writing, which was a beautiful calligraphy, was a message of a slightly worrying nature. It read thus:

Keep your mind busy and full of newly inherited knowledge; brush up on your Latin, which will follow suit. Speaking of suits, you may want to occupy your time with A.K.T. and his split deck of cards. If you hit a dead end, call this number.

At the bottom of Sebastian's note was a six-digit number with an area code that was completely foreign to me. Below the number, it said, '*Call and ask for Maurice*'. The Mole-man instantly came to the front of my mind with his bottle-cap glasses and thin greasy hair. His whole appearance seemed older than it should have been. His short stature and tweed jacket gave him the appearance of a professor or a 1950s teacher, but those thick black eyes told a different story, a darker story.

I hadn't noticed how late it had gotten and decided that I would begin my A.K.T. investigation in the morning. I got out of my seat, and as I made my way around the desk, I traced my fingertips over the engravings on the box. To this day, I couldn't tell you what it was, but there was a tingle of pleasure through my fingertips. It was a guilty pleasure, reminding me of smelling petrol when filling up the tank. Nothing too serious, although tangible enough for me to register it as a guilty feeling.

Shaking off the influence of the A.K.T. tingle, I headed up the spiral staircase, which is completely off limits to everyone. It leads up to my fortress of solitude, my hidey-hole and my home. I have a small bathroom with a lopsided sink and shower, lacking a shower curtain, a bedroom big enough for a double bed – I like to sleep in style, and a walk-in wardrobe running the length of the room, with a removable floor panel hidden at the end, containing my super-secret safe, not that there is anything in there. Opposite the bedroom is my living room. It's a big room sitting at the front of the building with a sofa, couple of stools, TV, coffee table, and rocking chair. My super-secret sliding bookcase that led to my evil genius laboratory was next to the TV. If and when I ever had company, I would wait to see if anyone noticed that the dimensions of the room were smaller than downstairs. No one ever did, and I loved having that secret all to myself, and now Sebastian.

Ignoring the living room, where I would usually spend an hour or two reading before going to sleep, I headed directly for my bed. A potential slumber weighed heavily on me, forcing me to shed the majority of my clothes and leave them in a discarded pile at the bottom of the bed. I lay half-awake for what seemed like an age, replaying the events of that enlightening time with Sebastian. He showed me wonders beyond my imagination. I began tracing the symbols and hieroglyphic runes that clung to my flesh in the dim glow of the streetlight as if they had always been there, claiming my flesh as their own. I was careful not to utter any of the translations lest I should ignite my bedclothes and ruin a truly deserved night of rest.

Chapter Seven

It Was All a Dream

I woke to find my bed sheets clinging to my chest and not through a normal cold sweat, if you can say a cold sweat is normal. My stomach muscles were taut and aching in simpatico with my arms and legs. My sweat-covered white chest bled the remaining colour from my skin as thin white slithers behind my tattoos of magic. My teeth chattered so hard that they reminded me of the wind-up pair I had as I kid, but I worried over my current health, as I had never felt like this in my whole life. My first thought was that I was dying; my second was that a severe hypochondriac needed to calm down.

Forcing myself up in bed and peeling the sodden sheet from my chest, I could only just feel my fingers as I clenched and unclenched my fists. Every joint or muscle in my body creaked overly tight and begged for some form of warmth. After rolling off the side of the bed to save my legs from having to do all the work, I managed to stumble into a standing position and cover the length of my bedroom and half of the hallway. This I can only imagine resembled what the beginning hours of the zombie apocalypse might look like as I climbed, very carefully, into the shower. The moment I turned the hot tap and the water blasted at my shoulders, I felt like I was being shot at by a hundred ball bearings. My arms flew up instantly to take the brunt of the heat as I twisted to face the evil showerhead. The room seemed to instantly get darker, and a memory or a dream flashed back with a vengeance.

Standing on a grass-and-mud-patched mound, I could see myself. I was only an observer because the other me kept the real me in his eyeline. He made no sign of acknowledgement or recognition. He stared past me, looking out into the nothingness of the night sky. He listened to the sound of the not-too distant ocean lapping wave over wave. His clothes were different; he wore a pair of black trousers, no shoes, and a light grey shirt unbuttoned and blowing gently in the wind, showing his – my – tattooed torso. He rolled up his sleeves past his elbows with a deep concentration on his face. Then he threw out his arms either side of him and pointed straight up as if he were posing to show off his biceps. He slowly began to bring his arms together, whispering words to himself over and over, 'dehr-AEluhm-roosh-kuhl'. His arms got closer and closer as a raven flew overhead and let out a scream, and as it did, the light drew in lower and lower. His, the other me, forearms were almost touching now, struggling against an opposing force, so much so that his arms shook. His muscles twisted as sweat trickled from his brow into his eye. The light dwindled, hiding the world around us.

When I came to, I was sitting at the bottom of the shower, the room full of steam, and my shivering slowed from the blanket of heat pouring down from above. I got into some clothes and threw a forgotten and cold coffee down my throat. I paused as I noticed that the clothes I wore were the same black trousers and grey shirt I had had on in my dream. *Wow! Twilight Zone.* I tore off my shirt and pulled out a blue-and-white striped one, deciding I would put on the suit which I wore the day before – no point in tempting fate. There were no burn marks on the shoulder of the waistcoat as far as I could see, so I threw caution to the wind and hoped that no one would notice the smoky smell. If anything, I just wanted to give déjà vu the middle finger and make sure that I wasn't about to relive a dream that forced my body into a state of panicked convulsion.

The next half an hour was spent in my office with the shop door hooked on to the bell so I could run down if any customers arrived out of the blue. I flicked through my grandfather's rolodex, picking out some of the more favoured contacts, only discernible by the faded number on the corner where the cards had been removed and replaced numerous times. I called to quiz them subtly on the A.K.T. deck of tarot cards. After more than a few dead ends and acute memory loss, I spoke to a fellow trader of rare antiquities, although this fellow was based in Wales around the Aberystwyth coastline. "Hello, Mr Pryce?" I asked hopefully.

"Yes, hello," he said with a hint of friendly Welsh twang.

"Mr Pryce of The Charmed Pot?" I asked, relishing the name of his shop, which I thought was brilliant.

"Yes, that's right. How can I help?" His cheer at the prospect of a customer was palpable.

"My name is Jon Wayward from Smoke and Mirrors, and I was calling in regards to tracking down a specific item. You were in my grandfather's list of contacts, so I thought I'd give you a call. I hope you don't mind."

"Not at all, my boy. I worked with your grandfather a few times over the years, even got into a few scrapes because of his wild whims." He chuckled to himself as he clearly reminisced a few of the alluded-to scrapes. "You'll have to pass on my regards to the old man and tell him I have a present for him. He'll know what I mean."

"I'm afraid George passed away. It was quite sudden, and the funeral was a quiet affair. I'm sorry to introduce myself with such bad news."

"Oh dear, that is terrible news." He sounded genuinely upset. "Although I do believe we have met before, but you were only a little lad. How are you holding up? I know he was like a father to you." I could tell he was concerned for my well-being, which warmed me to him and his affectionate elongated vowels of Welsh positivity.

"I'm OK. Actually, I've been very happy keeping his legacy running. It seemed the right thing to do. I grew up in this shop, receiving my antiquarian education, but I'm quickly coming to grips with the cut-throat business attitude after being at university for so long." I was momentarily distracted thinking about my tattoos after catching a glimpse on my wrist.

"I am glad that Smoke and Mirrors has stayed in the family. It wouldn't be right without a Wayward smile from behind the counter." There was a lingering pause in which I can only imagine we were both thinking of my grandfather's heart-warming smile that could put even the most nervous of customers at their ease. "Down to business then, Jon," he said, bringing my mind back into focus and in line with my reason for calling. "You're trying to find something?"

"It's a six-by-three-inch hand-carved oak box, engraved with the letters A.K.T. Inside it is a partial set of tarot cards like no others. Is any of this sounding familiar? Because I could really use all the help I could get."

"No, not at all. No alarm bells ringing here! Can't say I deal much with tarot cards or the like." Mr Pryce's voice had lost its helpful caring quality, and his Welsh accent had become clipped and thicker as he tried to sound overly casual.

"Right, well, if you happen to hear anything from the grapevine, a quick call would be muchly appreciated. I'm trying to find the missing cards and put the full deck back together. If there were anything I could do to return the favour, then don't hesitate to ask because I'm sure I can help." I tried to keep it as friendly as possible as I'd obviously crossed a line that he wasn't prepared to step over. It sounded as if he wanted to say something but couldn't.

"I'll be in touch, Jon. You take care of yourself, boy, and remember, one job is just as rewarding as another, and oftentimes, it's best to just move on."

With a riddle of a goodbye, I was holding the phone receiver in my hand, listening to a dead line sing its lonely tone. Mr Pryce wasn't hanging around to chat about any type of cards, let alone tarot cards. I have to admit that my interest was piqued. Unfortunately, it was in the same manner as the day before when I was standing in an alley with a magical Alchemist surrounded by the manipulated elements. It was then that Sebastian's words came back to me: *If you hit a dead end, call this number.* Along with a number to a man I had already met, the tired little Mole-man with those searching black eyes who insisted I was my grandfather, a man who called himself Maurice.

I opened the top drawer of my office desk and pulled out the card he had given to me. It had his name accompanied by a series of runes beneath, lots of little lines similar to the ones taking residence upon my flesh, but no number. I turned over the business card to find a bizarre foreign-looking sequence of numbers that had no area code I recognised, and once again, I picked up the phone receiver, hoping that this time I might get some answers, whether I wanted to hear the truth or not. *Let's be honest,* I thought. *They're just a pack of cards.*

CHAPTER EIGHT

Unexpected Guest

I called for Maurice, but there was no answer. There wasn't even a personalised message, just the company woman spouting the usual spiel about how sorry she was that the owner of the phone was not available and that if I would like to leave a message, I should do so after the beep. "Hello, Maurice, this is Jon . . . Jon Wayward from Smoke and Mirrors. We spoke the other day, or was it yesterday? I'm not sure, a lot has happened since then, and everything has been a little crazy." I paused for a moment, looking for the right words, but all that came to mind was an image of the oak box engraved with A.K.T. on the front, and it came crashing into my mind like a finger in the eye. "I need your help with something, and obviously, I am willing to pay. I just figured, since you had worked with my grandfather, that you might be willing to do some business with me." I picked up the card he had left me and inspected it as I spoke into his answer machine. "You did leave your card with me, and a procurer of rare antiquities is exactly the kind of man I need help from right now. Please call me back at Smoke and Mirrors when you can. I'm in the book." I put the phone receiver back and spared a few thoughts as to whether Maurice would actually bother calling back or just let me twist in the wind. I wasn't the most welcoming when he came in, although he was blowing smoke at my tapestries and walking mud all over the shop. I looked to the tattoos creeping on to the back of my hands, and I could swear that some of them had moved. I lost a good ten minutes of the day watching to see if I could catch them, and I tried to read the rune markings. Some looked like Druidic Ogham and some were ancient Latin; there was even a splash of Demotic Egyptian, I think, but there was definitely no dominant language I could see.

The bell on the shop door exploded into life, and someone called "Hello" in a rough voice. Jumping up from my desk, I jogged across the shop, catching a split-second glance to find the man standing just inside the doorway. He stood at least half a foot above me, and I'm not exactly short for my height. I slowed as I approached him, and he stood with his hair pulled back over his scalp, his forehead shining in the light from the shade less bulbs that hung from the high ceilings. He ground his teeth together as I walked over, and a gut feeling washed into me. As many times as I have heard people comment "Oh, I grind my teeth when I sleep", I had never seen or heard of anyone grind their teeth quite like this. It was on par with nails down a chalkboard, squeaky styrofoam, whilst listening to Bjork sing out of tune on purpose.

"I was hoping you could help me find a few things. I was looking for a particular collection you might have." His voice was scratchy and sounded as though it hurt him to speak. "I've heard there is an open market for cards of a certain nature." His smile turned from a grimace to a worrying set of broken and yellow teeth that would have given a dentist a cardiac arrest. As he continued to talk, I could feel the room darkening around me and the warmth all slowly seeping towards the increasingly hideous form that stood before me. "Cards can be extremely revealing about one's self, their knowledge, and nature." His voice was now cracking and wheezing as if his vocal cords were tearing further with each new word.

My eyes widened with fear, and my hands began to tense into balls as I took an instinctive step away. The longer I looked the more my fear grew, allowing uncertainty and panic to settle in my mind. I gripped my hands tight as if I were to never let go again. The temperature dropped in my body as I felt my blood turning into ice water. It pumped around my heart and up to my brain that still hadn't really come to terms with what I was seeing.

"What the hell are you?" The words fell from my mouth without my brain realising, and the moment I asked the question, the broken yellow facade of a smile stretched even further across this creature's face.

"I am your immediate future, Jon Wayward." Its voice was somewhere between a cry of pain and a growl of anguish. Its breath had gone beyond rasping and was torturing its master as it fought to pull in clean air and push it back out as infected oxide. "I am the choice that lies before you, life or death, depending on what you do next."

A shiver rippled up my spine as the tattooed grimoire slithered over my skin beneath my shirt, rearranging itself, but this time, the runes and symbols felt different. They felt familiar in the way they were reacting to the monstrous creature in front of me, guiding me, like the reflex reaction with the candles in the lab, but different as the words began to take meaning, not too obvious, but for some reason, they were beginning to make sense. The creature's tortured voice broke my concentration as it spat Its words out at me. The distance between us had grown while I slowly backed away, and he centred himself between two aisles. "I want the cards. It's either you or them."

"What cards?" When I'm nervous, I actually can't help talking, which usually forms itself as constant questioning. Honestly, it's a disability and something I have to live with.

"The tarot cards. I WANT THEM!" His voice exploded across the room, and I dropped to the floor, holding my hands over my eardrums as if it would help the brain pulsing shriek. He began screaming the words over and over, thumping against my sanity, bringing me to the point of tears. "I WANT THEM! I WANT THEM! I WANT THEM!" Opening my eyes, I found myself curled up in a ball behind the Witch Finder General's chair, still squirming away from the broken and howling scream the creature let loose. I wasn't exactly sure how I had managed to escape from the creature's gaze, but somehow I had, and he didn't know where I was. "Jon Wayward, there is no point in prolonging the inevitable. Give me the cards, or I will take them along with your life!" he hissed.

"Why don't we just calm down? We could settle this in a much more gentlemanly fashion, not that you're a gentleman, or even a man." Like I said, an invisible motor linked my nerves and my mouth. "But I can look past that simple nightmarish fact and offer an olive branch. A really long and distant friendly olive branch, but I believe it could be a start."

"What do you mean, Jon Wayward?" Its voice seemed momentarily relieved as though a great burden had been lifted off.

"I don't know. Maybe we flip a coin," I said.

"A coin?"

"Yeah, y'know, heads you leave the shop, tails I do. Everyone's a winner," I said, trying to sound as hopeful as possible. I could hear him shuffling around the shop floor, dragging his feet. His momentary release was over, and his laboured torturous breathing came rasping back, echoing off every cabinet, display case, and windowpane.

"Show yourself, Jon Wayward, you wouldn't want it known that one of the great Waywards met his fate crawling around on the floor, would you? I assume *cowardice* must be in the blood and a trait of your family." He chuckled to himself, coughing between every other breath out. I forced myself to peer around the panelled side of the Witch Finder General's chair and caught a glimpse of what this un-supposing customer had turned into.

His eyes were shaded the same repugnant yellow of his broken teeth as if they were rotting simultaneously, the jacket he wore had patches missing, and where the remainder of the material was left, it had dried hard and began cracking and flaking off with each shuffling step. What rekindled the bottomless pit of enduring fear within my now overly sensitive guts was the way his skin had melted like heated rubber, dripping and bubbling from his nose, ears, chin, and fingers, leaving pools of human fleshy puddles all over the shop floor and revealing a gangrenous smelling set of scales beneath. They looked like a thousand tiny black-coated shields flecked with red blood.

"Don't mind me, ugly. I'm just keeping an eye out for your puddled face so I don't miss any later when I'm mopping up what's left of you." I couldn't help myself; bad-mouthing a genuine monster wasn't something you got to do every day, or outside of a film set for that matter. But he wasn't leaving me a choice; even if I gave him the tarot cards, he was going to kill me. There was something in the way he kept saying my name that made me think he would be happy to see me dead, and that rang more than a few alarm bells.

"You like to play games, Wayward? I think it only fair that we play by the same rules, Wayward," he spluttered, but then began mumbling, and I heard the same word three times over: "*Obs-cur-um, Obs-curum, Obscurum.*" He clapped his hands, and the room dropped into pitch black, which was hardly encouraging as it was the middle of the day outside in the picturesque town of Amersham, and for once, it was sunny as well. *Obscurum? I know that word!* I thought as I realised that had been what my dream self was saying but in another language. An overwhelming pride washed over me in this most unfortunate turn of events, and I remember thinking, *At least I'm starting to connect the dots.*

He may have turned off the lights in the shop, but an extra-large, super-powered, Wayward-friendly bulb came on in my mind: '*Obs-cur-um*'. I knew it, and I knew what it meant. More importantly, I knew which language it was in. Obscurum was the Latin command for darkness, but in my mind, I saw it as the Druidic *dehr-AEluhm-roosh-kuhl*.

When subject options had come up at school, my grandfather let me choose almost anything I wanted, although he did insist upon one specific subject, a dead subject for a dead language – Latin – a language now very alive and being used by some hideous monster killer maniac with a penchant for magical imbued items in my possession. Unsurprisingly, coincidences never ceased to amaze me, not that I believed in them any more.

CHAPTER NINE

Guardian Shaman

"*Loos-IHduth-gohrd-hOOuh-TINgyuh!*" I shouted my words of magic for the chance of light, hoping that my level of noise would compensate for my lack of practice with spoken Druidic spells. The room brightened up a touch, which meant that my eyes struggled to follow the dragging footsteps and laborious breathing of the first customer of the day. I wasn't sure where he was, but I felt that he was getting closer, sensing his presence moving around the shop with one intention – possibly two if you count my demise.

You'd think I'd have been able to find my way around the shop in near pitch black, but it's not as easy as you think it is. Blindfold yourself, go to work, and see if you can find your way around whilst a killer demon threatens your life and your sanity. Honestly, you'll love it. I, on the other hand, wasn't overly keen on the whole scenario.

I padded around as quietly and gently as possible with each breath shallow and controlled, praying to any and all the Gods that would listen. I kept thinking I could try to make it upstairs, sneak through my living room, and hide in my laboratory. Either that, or attack the demon monster head-on and hope he makes any number of mistakes. Neither idea won outright, so I decided to make a run for the shop door and then coolly burst on to the street, screaming "FIRE!" or just the old classic "HELP!" I hoped that the killer thing following wouldn't want to be seen by the general public who didn't know about magic and monsters. I hoped he would think they might react badly to their worlds crashing down around their now cracked and fragile minds, as they would insist on calling the police and accusing aliens or drugs or aliens *on* drugs.

Crawling on my belly, I pulled myself to a sitting position at the back of a glass display cabinet holding various hoodoo charms I didn't want my customers accidentally imprinting. I was also accompanied by a Shaman spell book and beautifully crafted voodoo dolls which were still anonymous, just waiting for their future owner to identify their intended victim and attach some hair or clothing as a representation of the physical body. Leaning against the cabinet next to my leg were two genuine, like all my products, ritual staffs that resembled oversized walking canes. They were twice the thickness and height, of a walking cane with a circular wooden ball at the top carved with Shamanic runes on each one. The first and only thought that came to mind was to jump out and bludgeon the monster, screaming something like "DIE, YOU EVIL SPAWN OF LUCIFER'S EXCREMENT!" and if it dies, it dies, but if it didn't, then I could fall back to my running and screaming plan.

My conscience took hold of me. *Was I really going to kill this thing? I mean, it is still a living creature, monster or not. Could I really kill it?*

"WAYWARD!" screamed the monster accompanied by the sound of thick wood crunching under an extremely heavy force that was being applied.

"Why do you want the cards?" I said loud enough for the creature to hear but hopefully not loud enough to give away my position. "Do you even know what's so special about them?"

"Come out here and I'll tell you," It said with what I can only imagine to be a *killer* smile.

"You don't know, do you? Are you working for someone else?" I said, and the only answer I got was its rasping, hissing, wheezing laugh.

"If you're not behind that chair, you must be behind another. I just have to keep destroying the Wayward's life work collected in this mausoleum of magic until you stop being a coward, a selfish pathetic coward and you decide to bring me what I want," he said, almost enjoying every insult, knowing that he had more than a fair point.

Trouble was that the Witch Finder General chair that he had turned into firewood was never for sale; it was purely for show, a part of the personal Wayward collection that had been a growing matter of pride for generations. That one act of mindless vandalism swept my conscience off the board. He was about to become a *dead* demon, monster, hellish, beastly thing.

I wrapped my fingers around one of the Shaman ritual staffs and raised it above my head. Just as I did, the shop door opened wider than I knew it could, letting the unaffected sunlight from outside pour into the imposed magical darkness within. There was someone standing in the doorway whose silhouette I couldn't make out; in fact, I couldn't have told you if it was a man or a woman. All I do know is my vision was impaired by the sudden change in light, which I was hoping was the case for my monstrous friend as I was going to use the momentary distraction to attack him.

From the corner of my eye, I caught a glimpse of the demon turn to face the open door, and I threw myself behind him and brought the Shaman staff crashing down on to the crown of Its skull, using the solid spherical wooden ball. It hit the floor with an impressive crack, pulling the Shaman ritual staff from my hands as it was lodged into Its skull, crushing Its grey matter to grey mush. It was what I would call the desired effect.

CHAPTER TEN

Dead Scaled Monster

It took me a moment to remember that the only reason I had gotten the jump on the demon was that someone had walked in through the shop door. I stood with the Shaman's ritual stick still in one hand, dripping with what could only be described as an oily sludge that smelt like burnt sulphur. I couldn't think of anyone who would have been comfortable walking in on the scene that lay before them unless they were another demon or in cahoots with this demon, or the employer of this demon . . . Turns out I could think of a few people who would be in the realms of 'comfortable' walking into this mess. I was hoping none of the above had opened the shop door and distracted the pungent mess now lying at my feet. Luckily for me, it was the Mole-man himself, Maurice.

"Mr Wayward?" His curious and squeaky voice floated towards me, slowly bringing me back into the room as my adrenaline bottomed out and panic set in.

"Yeah?" was all I could manage to say.

"I was about to ask if you had a moment to talk, but I can see you are otherwise occupied," he said, looking around the room and finally bringing his eyes down to the intruder lying on the floor. He took a long pull on his pipe and slowly let the smoke unfold around his drawn face as he spoke. "What happened to the Witch Finder General's chair?"

"Our new acquaintance here thought I was hiding behind it and decided it was better as kindling." Once again, I was using my poor excuse for humour as a defence against the reality of what had just happened. "Shut the door, Maurice."

53

"Are you unhurt?" he said as he closed the world out and waddled back over to my side where I still stood holding the ritual stick in my hand.

"I'm fine, Maurice."

"Are you sure?"

"We . . . At least I'm better than this guy," I said as I prodded the dead demon with the tip of my shoe. The demon twitched involuntarily, forcing me to scream and bring down the ritual stick on the stump of its head once again. Pulling myself together, I suggested a distraction. "I think we need to get rid of this mess and clean up. I suggest that we start with . . ."

"You don't have a clue, do you?" Maurice asked.

"Not one."

"When disposing of a magical being, I would advise fire, and lots of it."

"Really?" I asked as Maurice gave me a look of *I suppose you know better*. "Well, OK. I guess we can take him down into the cellar and use the furnace. It's an old building, and we still have all the eighteenth-century modicums you would expect."

"Perfect."

It had taken my grandfather's flying carpet and a slow trip down the spiral stairs at the back of the shop to make sure that our killer demon pal was well and truly stuffed into the furnace. As Maurice was about to bring him to his fiery end, I stopped him and asked if I could be the one to introduce him to meet his Maker, to which he once again gave me a look of puzzlement. As I attempted to bring the creature's remains to combust, I thought of the words I needed, not actually knowing what they were from when I had nearly brained myself in my laboratory. I felt a small patch on the back of my arm just above my elbow begin to warm and then it struck me and made perfect sense. The heat was forming the word on my upper arm, spelling it out, and this brought it to my mind with immense clarity, the word flashing up before my eyes, urging me to say it.

Before I said the word out loud, I pulled at my shirt and smiled a big smile of certainty that hadn't crossed my face in a long time. Maurice seemed fixed with a look of curiosity and amusement whenever he was near me, and as I unbuttoned my right cuff and rolled up the shirtsleeves, he was the first to see the tattoo glowing orange like a candle's fiery core. The other tattoos wavered as if they were shimmering from the heat.

"Can you see it?" I asked.

"Yes. Your tattoo is burning."

"I know!" I exclaimed. "Check this out." The excitement was too much. Without having to utter the incantation, I thought it and saw in my mind's eye the tattoo burn away from the flesh on my arm. With that thought and my hands slapped together, as if I knew it was the right thing to do, sparks burst from between my fingers like a flint hand been scrapped across stony palms, and those sparks twisted into the air, dancing towards the fallen hell spawn. It wasn't long before there was only ash and remnants of burnt bone in the furnace, which meant that I had not only begun to understand these tattoos of magic that decorated my flesh, occasionally flaring up and vanishing into the recesses of my mind as Sebastian Dove said they would but also had managed to get rid of the body of the first *whatever* I had killed. Never a dull moment.

I turned back to smile at Maurice and ask him just how awesome he thought I was for creating fire with my fingertips, but when I looked at his face, I saw that he was scared and not of me. His eyes were looking past me into the corner of the crowded and dust-covered cellar where a few lifetime's worth of storage and unlabeled, uncatergorised collecting had found its resting place. It wasn't the mountainous and unkempt boxes he was staring at but the shadowed figure rising from the darkness of the unlit corners where the shade had been at home for so long that it had become a part of the fabric of the walls.

When my eyes fell upon the living shadow, I'm not ashamed to say that I screamed again. Luckily for me, I was so terrified and so very much at the end of my nerves being in survival mode that no sound came through my open mouth. I looked like I was reacting quickly by directing the sparks from my palms that had just incinerated the monster's scaly corpse at the incoming darkness that had opened Its arms wide. It was stretching out, allowing the gathering darkness to flow around It like a hooded cloak. Flames shot out in a line, and the shadow man didn't even flinch as the flames burst right through him and slapped into the wall behind, scorching a black circle into the red brick work. The shadow ghost-like being swirled around the line of fire from all sides, reforming as a whole in front of me when my magic failed me. I could feel it watching me, looking deep into the core of my being. It found my fear and used it to hold me frozen to the spot I was standing in. Just when I thought that it was game over for the charming and handsome Jon Wayward, the ghostly darkness threw itself at me, screaming one word with the intensity of an old steam train's high-pitched whistle: "W-A-Y-W-A-R-D!" The darkness exploded on to my chest as it hit, sending my name echoing out in a hundred directions around the cellar. Like I said before, never a dull moment.

After pulling me upstairs and slapping me across the cheek, Maurice told me he would take care of the shop whilst I made a cup of tea for us both. It was the first moment I had had to myself, and a few things were beginning to sink in. I'm not really someone who poses much of a threat to anyone, which makes it even harder for me to come to terms with the fact that something tried to kill me. Two somethings actually. I needed answers, and I had two people in mind who could offer some.

"Maurice, do you take sugar?" I yelled out to the shop floor. It was the first thing that popped into my head when I heard the kettle boiling and realised I had been staring at my novelty Sherlock Holmes and John Watson mugs, indulging in my new plan. I needed to gain information for my personal survival, and if I could get the tarot cards as part of the process, then I would come out on top.

"No sugar for me, Jon. Thank you," Maurice squeaked back. I quickly made up two teas, and when I reached the shop front, I was flabbergasted. Smoke and Mirrors had never been so tidy. Not only was the black gloop of demon brains mopped off the floor, leaving no visible stain, but the whole shop was clean, really clean. It hadn't ever been so clean since I had first come in and sat with my granddad, playing with harmless trinkets. I thought of this shop as a maze of intrigue and curiosity forgotten by time.

"This place is amazing!" I said, handing him his Watson mug – because the Sherlock mug was my favourite – and gazing at the polished wood, display cases, and antiquities.

"It does have a fine selection to browse around."

"The chair!?" I was shocked at seeing the Witch Finder General's Chair all in one piece.

"It was one of George's favourite party games," Maurice said with some fond memory, allowing him a smile. "With the incantation hidden in the confessor's commandment, which would be read aloud from the engraving on the back of the chair, it forces the occupant to tell the truth. We had great fun with that one. He unofficially borrowed it from C.O.V.E.N."

"What is C.O.V.E.N.?" I asked.

"They're the Mage's version of the police force. Best kept at arm's length, if you ask me." He giggled to himself with quick rasping breaths. "You know you look like your grandfather," he said, leaving me a little bemused.

"Well, I'm not sure what to say apart from thank you and I need your help."

"I thought as much. That's why I popped in when you called. Although I wasn't expecting a Lamiac to shed itself and attack you in your own shop. That is just rude."

"Lamiac? What *pray tell* is a Lamiac?" I asked over a few sips of tea.

"A Lamiac is the spawn of Lamia, half woman, half serpent. She was said to have been cursed by the gods of Olympus and, over time, transformed and changed her diet to cannibalism. A lovely woman, by all accounts. I've heard it told that she doesn't really get involved in the world of man any more, but she does have offspring left to survive on their own. They often find themselves working for anyone who can tolerate their presence and that usually tends to be within the Mage community – not Mages who you would cross paths with on a daily basis, you understand. They would only be drawn to those who abuse their power."

"Wait. There are *Olympian* gods?"

"No one has seen hide or hair of them for thousands of years. They were probably self-proclaimed gods who were men and women using magic to further their own needs. They wouldn't get away with it now, not with the Court's rules. Neither will this Lamiac."

"So why would a Lamiac want to get his hands on the cards and kill me in the process?" I asked.

"He wouldn't. He must have been working for someone. Lamiacs are known for their ruthlessness, not so much for their strategy and intelligence."

"So the Lamiac thing was sent here by someone. Who?" I asked.

"I'm afraid I do not have the answer to that," Maurice said with the last few slurps of his tea.

"I guess we add it to the list of growing questions. Firstly, what the hell do these tarot cards do that make them so important? Secondly, who would hire someone to kill me with a snaky reptile demon? Thirdly, what is a shadowy ghost doing in my cellar? And lastly, why was Mr Pryce so reluctant to tell me what he knows about these cards?" I asked, speaking my thoughts out loud.

"Mr Pryce of The Charmed Pot in Aberystwyth?" Maurice asked with a higher squeak than usual.

"Yeah, I called him, and he said he had nothing for me, but he sounded as if he was hiding something because he wanted to get off the phone pretty quick," I said with my most convincing detective summation. "Maybe we should pay Mr Pryce a visit."

"We?" Maurice almost choked on his tea.

"Yes, we. How do you feel about a road trip?"

CHAPTER ELEVEN

Dropping In on Mr Pryce

A long car journey was not what Maurice considered a fun time, especially in my 1984 classic cobalt blue Mini in which he wasn't allowed to smoke his pipe. I love my Mini; I spent all my spare time working in a local bookshop whilst studying for my degree to save up for the third-hand machine. Hence my classic car rules: no food in the car and no smoke in the car. Done.

If Maurice wasn't staring out of the window annoyed with my rules, with his squinted eyes exaggerated by his thick black glasses and mumbling to himself about all cars needing seat belts, then he was telling me his thoughts on long-distance travel. "There are easier ways to traverse the land, and hopefully, it won't take you too long to come across them." I didn't reply to his niggling because I made an educated guess that travelling by car or any conventional vehicle wasn't the norm for Maurice.

We pulled up on the sunlit seafront, and before I could tell Maurice we were here, he was out of the car and standing next to the white railings overlooking the pier and out to sea. Immediately, he was packing his pipe and lighting it with what seemed like a never-ending pack of invisible matches. I locked the mini, both doors, and stood next to him, hoping he would say something, rather than continue to mumble to himself. "Are you OK?" I asked tentatively.

"Just taking it all in."

"What? The ocean?"

"Yes, Jon Wayward, the ocean and its raw power."

"Power?"

"I believe you know something of the elemental powers within this world. Otherwise, the disposal of certain assassin Lamiacs would have been harder to take care of than previously demonstrated," Maurice said with what I assumed to be a hint of interest in how I had come by this knowledge so fast.

"I had someone tell me a little bit," I said.

"Someone?"

"Yeah, he called himself Sebastian Dove. He's an Alchemist."

"Never heard of the man."

"Well, he's heard of you. He told me to call you if I got stuck with the cards. So I did, and you arrived just in time to see me bludgeon a lizard monster to death."

"How interesting," he squeaked and turned to look at me. "Did he say how he knew me or where from?"

"Nope, just that I should call you if I needed help. I thought you two must have worked together. He stopped by the day after you, claiming that he could show me how to unlock my potential."

"That is the purpose of an Alchemist ordered by the Court."

"The Court? I keep hearing about this Court."

"The Court must have assigned him to you to develop your magical knowledge and ability safely and productively. He must be quite special if they are assigning him to a Grimoire."

"Grimoire? Wait, who makes up this Court?"

"I think we should have a talk with Mr Dove," Maurice said. "If he hasn't told you about the Court, then what else has he failed to mention?" His voice sounded odd in a protective tone, if you can find a squeak protective. "But for now, we have a reluctant dealer to introduce ourselves to," he said, knocking the contents of his pipe over the railing. I was enjoying watching Maurice taking the lead and allowing me to process for a moment. I had had some welcome thinking time on the long drive up there, but every second was a luxury.

"Quite right," I said as we turned in synchronisation back towards the town and began walking away from the sea. Neither of us said anything until we got to his front door; it was as if the tide brought with it a hypnotic sound, calming both of us into a state of readiness. It only broke when I read the shop's name out loud: "The Charmed Pot".

Maurice looked at me with his normal goggle-eyed stare as his glasses enlarged his pupils to extraordinary proportions. "After you."

I stepped into the shop after Maurice and found that it was well kept. Most of the display cabinets were quite new, and the whole place was immaculately cleaned. For my personal tastes, it was a little too clean, too sterilised, which surprised me. I didn't think that that would have fit the clientele, but what do I know about the magical world? I'd only just found out that magic is real. It's quite feasible that all magic users are clean freaks and won't buy herbs and various concoctions from a vendor where contamination is possible.

"Hello?" I called out and waited for a reply. Nothing. "Hello?" I called again a little louder. This time there was a rustle and the sound of a something being snapped shut somewhere behind the counter and the door that lay behind. Both Maurice and I waited as silently as possible. We were both still and a little on edge and were trying to expect the unexpected. A long bony-fingered hand clawed around the door followed by a gaunt man in a navy suit. His smile showed most of his teeth, even though he was missing one or two, and his eyes were sunk into his head. He looked like the walking dead, and I probably would have tried to set fire to him if it hadn't been for his first words.

"You must be Mr Wayward, a pleasure," he said with his Welsh lilt pushing most of his vowels to an exaggerated inflection.

"I am, yes, and this is my . . . friend Maurice," I said as Maurice nodded at Mr Pryce with a suspicious smile forming upon his face.

"I would ask how I can help, but I have a feeling you are here about those damn tarot cards. Am I right or am I wrong?" he quickly said with his toothless smile plastered across his face, missing the occasional tooth.

"I hope you won't be offended, Mr Pryce, but you seem very different than you were when I spoke to you earlier on the phone." I wanted to see what Mr Pryce's reaction would be if I asked about his sudden personality change.

"I'm not sure what you mean?" he asked as his smile became stretched and a bead of sweat trickled from his temple. *What is wrong with this guy? Something is going on.* I knew that Pryce was hiding something and so did Maurice from the look on his face.

"Nothing. It's been a long drive. I guess I'm just a little tired," I said, giving my best fake smile, which also happened to be my best "How can I help you?" smile. "You mentioned the tarot cards."

"I mentioned the *bloody* tarot cards, yes."

"Well?" Maurice joined the conversation, as he was as eager to get to the point as I was.

"Like I told you before, Mr Wayward, I don't know anything about those tarot cards, or where you might be able to inquire . . . about . . . them," he spat the last word or two, forcing it from behind gritted teeth that sounded as if they were cracking. Another bead of sweat ran down Pryce's forehead, although this time it found a path between his eyebrows and down the one side of his nose, curling off at the corner of his lip. He didn't seem to notice this. He was intently focused on holding back for some reason and he appeared as though it was causing him significant pain.

"Are you OK, Mr Pryce?" I asked.

"Oh yes," he said and then gave a nervous laugh. "I'm completely fine." His stretched smile pulled even further. "Is there anything else I can help you with before you go?" A tear fell from the corner of his eye, running into the sweat that was now soaking into his shirt collar. A sharp breath was heard from behind Pryce as if someone were trying to stop themselves from laughing.

Maurice looked at me and tried to gesture something to me about the door that Pryce had come through. I looked at it, even moved slightly, but the only thing I noticed was that Pryce was now locked in place and wasn't even following me with his eyes. He looked as if he had died but had forgotten to fall to the floor; apart from the sound of his clenched teeth, he stood as frozen as a statue. He was tensed to the point where something was going to have to give or snap and the smart money was on snap. Maurice moved closer to the door behind the counter that Pryce had come through, and I noticed something poking out of Pryce's breast pocket on his suit. I pulled and began to slide it from him and saw that it was a tarot card, but not just any; it was a chariot card with the word *Messenger* written on it. The second it left Pryce's body, he dropped to the floor like a marionette with its strings cut, and he hit the overly clean tiles with a crack. This was accompanied by what can only be described as an incredibly loud breathe-in and a moment's silence that hovered in the air.

Looking from the tarot card in my hand to Maurice, I had just enough time to see him turning away from the door and half forming a sentence that looked like 'Hit clown!' But I couldn't work out why he would say that, until the counter was smashed by gale force winds coming from the back of the shop across to the front and out through the display window, ending in the street. It was then that I realised Maurice wasn't discussing clowns and his need to have them beaten, but a warning for me to 'Get down'.

Obviously.

Chapter Twelve

Dropping Out on Mr Pryce

Fighting for my life was not something I was used to, although I could imagine that it was something I would become familiar with given enough time and regular contact with the people within the magical community.

Pryce still lay on the floor at my feet and made nothing more than a whimpering when the front of his shop was blown across to the other side of the street. Some of the debris hit the pier's rusted white rails and catapulted into the ocean. I gave what could only be described as a blood-curdling scream and dropped to the floor next to him. Once again, my natural manliness didn't fail to impress. From the hole in the wall where Pryce had originally come from stood two silhouettes. At first glance, they looked like they could fit the casting call for Lenny and George in a sharply dressed Victorian retelling of *Of Mice and Men*. When they stepped through the destruction that they had created and the daylight found them, I quickly changed my opinion and thought that they would be much more comfortable being associated with Al Capone and Lucky Luciano by the clothes they wore and the pure look of pleasure they were getting from the destruction. It seemed that three-piece suits were all the rage with Alchemists, Mages, and the magical folk as a whole; in the minor experience with those I had met, I had always felt underdressed.

I lay in the rubble, still looking up at them, as they stared at the broken relics that lay in their path, the ocean lapping over any other sound as the ringing faded in my head. The bigger one was a muscle-bound monster of a man who had a horseshoe moustache with eyes so dark that the irises looked as black as the pupils. The other man, who was a little shorter than me, had the same eyes as his friend but with a different style of moustache. He was sporting a Clark Gable, needless to say that as much as these two looked like they were out of place; they also looked like they belonged together from the pages of a twisted noir thriller.

"Wayward!" shouted the smaller one. "Where are you?" he said playfully. Turning to his companion and looking up to his face, he said, "I hope we haven't killed him." This brought a smile to the big fella's face. At least I knew that they didn't want me dead, or at least they didn't want me dead yet. I took a chance I normally wouldn't take, because normally, I would play dead and wait to see if I came out of this craziness alive. There was something within that urged me to stand up, and when I realised it was those tarot cards and how they wouldn't leave my mind, I knew I had to do what I could to get them and me out in one piece.

"I'm Wayward," I said with as much confidence as I could muster. Obviously, it wasn't that much because Tweedle Dee and Tweedle Dum looked at each other and laughed. The big one made no sound when he laughed, but the little one giggled in a childish manner.

"Well, hello there, Jon Wayward," said the smaller one. "You'll have to forgive our rudeness. It's just that we were expecting someone a little more . . . impressive. A little more worthy of the name *Wayward*. I guess what they say about your bloodline is true, and the apple doesn't fall far from the tree. Disappointing."

"You never know, I might surprise you," I said, feeling a little more confident in myself as I brushed off the dust from my shirt and waistcoat. I made a mental note to find out what people said about my ancestors and why everyone seemed to know.

"Surprise us?" His grin grew larger as he took a few steps closer. "That's good, I like that. Before we go any further, we should introduce ourselves. I am known as the Poet, and my companion here is known as the Bard, and we have been looking for you, Mr Wayward." He spoke as if he had an audience.

"Really? You didn't try very hard. You know I'm in the phone book?" I said with a bit of cheek that wasn't really needed.

"Between you and I . . ." Poet said as he closed in the last few steps between us and began a whisper that was more for effect than to actually whisper to me. ". . . we were very keen to meet the next generation of Wayward, see what you were made of, if you know what I mean. So please don't take it personally when I do this."

"Do what?" was all I could manage before Poet whipped his hand up in the air and spoke under his breath and then the floor beneath my feet took off, with me hanging on for dear life. Everything went by in a complete blur, and when I hit the floor, I didn't feel the pain but just heard the crack of one of the ribs on my right side. I hauled myself to my feet, groaning in pain, and turned, hoping that I could use the inferno I had used in the cellar, but when I stood facing Bard who had stepped in front of his smaller companion, nothing came to mind except 'Bugger'.

He opened his mouth to shout and what came out were ripples in the air aimed directly at me. Before I knew it, I'd shouted back in my subconscious Druid tongue to block his magic, "*bayh-loos-onn-kuhl!*" I felt the warm trickle across my shoulder blade. Bard's ripple of power reflected off whatever I had created, and I knew that I had used another word of power from my body art and that it was now lodged in my mind, allowing me to reflect magical attacks. Even through the ripple bouncing back at him, I could see a face of surprise as it took him off his feet and threw him into the back of the shop through the door he had previously blown a hole out of.

"Wow! Did you see that?" I blurted out with amazement. What I didn't realise was that I was saying it to Poet who came through the shop, now looking as if he wanted to rip me in half. Instinctually, I dived into hiding.

"You *are* full of surprises, Mr Wayward, I'll give you that," he said with anger, stepping through the rubble of the shop and out on to the street to get a clearer line of sight on me. He stood in the middle of the road and waited for me to stand and face him. I was about to get up from my hiding spot and douse him with fire, now that my mind was calm, and I could remember how to, but I lay still for a second to make sure I could recall how to do it. *Hold out my hand, click with my thumb and middle finger and see the whirl in my mind.* This immediately turned into a ball of fire that I held in the palm of my hand, which rolled anticlockwise on its axis. *Magic!* It had become a matter of visualising what I wanted my magic to do, and I knew that my imagination and willpower were going to come into good practice. That's when I heard his voice again, cutting through the air like an ignored child who needed attention. "Let me ask you a question, Wayward. Are you a coward like your grandfather, or are you worthy enough to pull your family name out of the mire it now resides in?"

It took me no less than a second to stand and face Poet after the slight he had made to my grandfather's name. Luckily for him, Maurice had crept up behind, and just as I made eye contact with his black little mole eyes, Maurice laid a finger on each of his temples, saying one Latin word "*Somnus*" and then Poet's pupils widened as he let out a horrifying scream as he crumpled to the floor without using his hands to brace the impact.

"What did you do?" I asked, jogging over to Maurice.

"I put him to sleep."

"Forever?" I was shocked to think he'd been put down like a stray cat or a rabid dog.

"No, just for a couple of hours."

"Oh, OK then," I said, not really caring about Poet's well-being any longer.

"Where is Mr Pryce?" Maurice asked as if the magical skirmish we had just survived hadn't happened at all.

"Over here," I said as we ran over to where he was. He had a few pieces of his shop lying near and next to him, and he looked like he was catching up on his sleep. I leant down and poked him in the arm. "Pryce, wake up." He stirred slightly, and I poked him again. "Pryce!" I shouted in my impatience.

"Don't hurt me," he whimpered through tears.

"I'm not going to hurt you. But I do need to get you up." I nodded to Maurice to grab his other arm, and we pulled him up. We took him through the rubble of his shop and led him to a bench on the seafront a few yards away. Once we sat him down and the realisation dawned on him that he wasn't in any immediate danger, he managed to stop crying and look at us for the first time, although I'm sure that he was in deep shock.

"Thank you, Mr Wayward. Thank you so much for setting me free." He looked like he had been starved to death and brought back to life by some twisted magical defibrillator, which no doubt probably existed.

"Setting you free?" I asked. Maurice kept looking back over to Poet, who lay in the street, and the shop front, which currently remained Bard-less.

"Those men were controlling me. They had a hold over me with a card. They didn't want me to tell you anything."

"A card? Like the type of tarot card I called you about and you said you had *no idea* and that I should stop looking?" I said full of pointed questions.

"The very same," he answered regardless, with his emotion emphasised by his accent.

"I need you to tell me everything that you can about those men, the tarot cards, and whatever else is going on that you think I should know about," I said full of persuasiveness.

"Those two men came around to my shop and told me they were looking for some tarot cards. They went on saying they were a specific type of cards, very old and very rare. They said they're not even sure if the cards were one of a kind, but it wouldn't surprise them if they were. I asked them if they could describe those cards to me, and the only information they could give were three initials . . ."

"A. K. and T.," I interrupted.

"Quite right, Mr Wayward! How did you know?" Pryce seemed shocked that I knew.

"Lucky guess. Please carry on." I waved my hand in small circles to help him understand I wanted to know everything as quickly as possible.

"I said exactly the same to them that I have said to you. I don't know anything about those cards, and I don't know anyone else who does," Pryce said.

"But you were lying," I interrupted again.

"Yes. I was lying. I had come across a few cards from a collector back in the early Eighties who had held on to them, and she told me that I should never let them out of my sight. She said they are the type of magic that can change *things* that shouldn't be changed."

"Who was this collector?" Maurice squeaked up with his pipe in hand, dropping tobacco into the bulb of his pipe and getting ready to light it.

"She was a Scottish collector. Isobel Gowdie." Pryce looked back and forth between Maurice and me as if to check whether he should continue. Maurice nodded to me as he lit his pipe to let me know that he had heard of her, and Pryce continued his tale. "So I took the tarot cards from her and kept them in a safe place, never telling anyone about them, including you."

"So what happened when these two turned up?" I asked.

"They knew I had them and began to torture me, with my wife." A tear formed in Pryce's eye once again. "The small one got inside my head, and I wasn't strong enough to stop him. He took memories of my wife. He was trying to erase my wife from my memory! She passed six years ago now. He kept taking them one by one until I told him where the cards were." His tears were in full flow now, and he had to take a minute before he could continue. "That's when you two turned up. They plucked out one of the cards from the deck and then placed the card in my pocket. I froze, and they had control of me." Pryce had started to become angry at the end of his story about how he had been treated. Even though I was amazed at all the magic I had seen, especially the spells meant to kill me, this was too much, far too much.

"You know me, Pryce. You can sense the kind of man I am. I'm not like them, but I do need those cards," I said in a sympathetic yet controlled manner.

"I know. Oh, I know. You can have them. I want them out of my life, and since you saved it, you can have them. The big one put them in his trouser pocket. Help yourself," he said with a clear conviction and distaste for the tarot cards. Maurice headed off to the shop remains to find Bard and sneak the cards from his pocket.

"Lastly, I need to know where I can find the rest." Pryce looked warily at that. "Pryce, I wouldn't be asking if it wasn't important."

"Yes, I understand. The only other person, apart from Isobel, who has had an interest in the cards over the years, has been Edward Kelley. Last time I had correspondence from him, he was based in Devon, staying at the hotel on Burgh Island. He's a part of some cult down there," he said all this with a straight face, which was impressive, especially if he didn't know who Kelley was. I mean come on, even I knew who Kelley was.

Maurice returned holding the cards in his hand, and he placed them in mine straightaway as if he didn't really want to be holding them at all. "Looks like we nearly have a full deck," squeaked Maurice as I realised I was getting used to the pitch of his voice.

"Almost, but I bet you can't guess who has the rest?"

CHAPTER THIRTEEN

Faded Splendour

We had decided to split our efforts, our leads, and our skills. Maurice seemed to think he could make some headway with the Scottish lady Gowdie, and I was intrigued to see if Kelley was *the* Kelley my grandfather had told me about. I had read about him as a devoted Mage and tuning fork for the spirits, or as a charlatan, depending on whom you believed. He had always come across as someone who flirted with magic and talked to spirits in the aide of man who got all the attention, the more famous Doctor Dee, bearing in mind this was all during the sixteenth century; it would be an interesting conversation and one I had no idea how to start. Over the following night, I ran through many potential conversation starters, but none of them stood out as clear winners. I decided I was going to play it by ear and just hope that I didn't just stare and look like a lobotomised mime artist.

After a well-deserved night's sleep back at Smoke and Mirrors, I racked up even more miles when I took my Mini down to South Devon. It took a fair amount of time and was the best way to get there without delay or interruption. I knew I could use the thinking time since I was only just coming to grips with my new lifestyle and how small the country had begun to seem. There was a lot going on that I either didn't understand or was still being kept a secret from. I knew the latter was more likely. Firstly, I wanted to know who Poet and Bard were and what they wanted with the tarot cards. Secondly, I was beginning to question Emilia's part in this, what her motives for wanting those cards were, and why she wasn't going after them herself. Thirdly, I wanted to know why Maurice, who I now trusted enough to follow a lead, and Sebastian were so keen to help me in my efforts to find the tarot cards and expand my use of magic. Sebastian knew Maurice, but Maurice had never heard of Sebastian. *Interesting, isn't it?*

These thoughts haunted me for the whole drive down, although Emilia popped into my mind for other reasons once or twice, and it wasn't anything to do with the job. It was about the way she had sat in my office, and I had found it hard to do anything apart from look into her emerald eyes and nod to everything she said. Beautiful women walking into my shop and asking for help wasn't really a situation that had ever crossed my path before. I was understandably nervous and extremely on edge, but it was enough to set my mind running over every word she said, crazy.

It was only when I had seen the signs for Plymouth and Exeter that my attention had really begun to wander. My thoughts were so lost in the questions I had, along with the bizarre events of the last couple of days now burned into my memory for good, that I caught myself looking into the rear-view mirror as in a spy movie with shady Russian accents, just in case I was being followed. Hoping that no one had spied me, I shook off my gumshoe daydream and murmured something to myself about 'paying attention or paying the price'. An image stayed in my mind, consuming my concentration; I allowed my eyes to flash back up to the rear-view mirror, but instead of looking out at the car's behind and falling back into my detective fantasy, I looked at the tattoo creeping up my neck from my shoulder. These words of magic tattooed across my body were still hard to get my head around, especially since some of them had begun to slither around my skin and disappear from view, finding themselves a permanent home in my memory. Magic is a funny thing, and whether I wanted to or not, I was going to find out more than I wanted about what it can do.

After winding through a tangle of country roads, the motorway, and the rest, civilisation seemed to be a distant memory. There was a level of peace and serenity that came with being in the backyard of the nation. Weight lifted from my shoulders by just being out of the rat race. Being surrounded by something completely natural was a breath of fresh air, literally, especially when I pulled up to the car park sign posted 'Bigbury-On-Sea'. I got out of the Mini and walked to the edge of the car park. I could overlook the beach down below as it wrapped itself around the coast for a mile in each direction. I felt the push and pull of the tide and knew that there was magic in it. It was something I didn't have to learn; I just knew it and had felt it before on Aberystwyth pier.

The waves rolled in three at a time, each set adding to the hypnotic beauty of the place that seemed to stretch on as far as the eye could see. I wasn't alone though; there were a few other cars in the car park, and I could see one or two people walking across the beach in the gentle calming breeze as the tide was out, but the beach was so long and the tide was so far out that even the people appeared as dots on the landscape. As I looked along the beach from the high vantage point at the edge of the car park, I found what I had driven all the way for. The beach curved in along the coastline and lay at the bottom of the wooden stairs built into the slope down to the sand where a path of wet sand, sometimes covered by the sea if the tide was in, led across to a small island-like peninsula. This is known as Burgh Island.

Burgh Island was what I had imagined a Bond villain's island would look like. It had a small path, which led up from the wet sand, when the tide was out, to one of the smallest pubs in the country called 'The Pilchard'. Behind the pub and the winding path leading further up the island was 'The Burgh Island Hotel' in all its art deco splendour. I made my way over and got the chance to stretch my legs, walking with my hands in my grey coat pockets and my suit jacket unbuttoned and flapping gently over my waistcoat. Looking up at the island and the hotel, I could see why Agatha Christie had spent a lot of time here and written at least two of her books on the island about mysterious and vengeful murders. After crossing the beach, I stepped on to the concrete of the path leading up to the Pilchard and had a worrying thought: if Agatha Christie had stayed here so she could write her murder mysteries, then this island must seem like a good place for murder. I hoped that Kelley hadn't had the same thought or that he would be willing to act on it. Small graces.

I stopped outside the Pilchard for a moment and looked at my watch; I was early for my presumptuous meeting and thought maybe a moment to gather myself and some Dutch courage would be a good idea before I met *the* Edward Kelley. As I stepped in the pub, all three people in there turned to stare at me. The barman and two patrons of an older age, who looked like the term *tourist* was an insult, glanced at each other, then fixed their eyes back to me. The two older men who sat at one of the three small tables in the pub watched me walk up to the bar and give an awkwardly nervous smile to the barman. He seemed to study me without the desire to hide his intentions. "Drink?" the barman asked with his countrified Devonshire accent.

"I was about to ask you the same thing," I said but realised that my humour wasn't really welcome. The barman was now staring at me with his mouth open and his eyebrows raised, waiting for another wisecrack. "What have you got?" I quickly refocused to the idea of a drink.

"What d'you see?" he snapped back.

"Not much, but I guess a pint of your best would help open my eyes." I realise that my day-to-day communication probably needs some work, but hey, no one's perfect. The barman poured my drink for what seemed like an eternity and pushed it across the bar, spilling a good gulp or two and taking more money than I would have said a pint of anything would cost. After taking a sip of the incredibly strong beverage, I sat at the table furthest away from the two old men with my back to the bar so I could face the door and look out of the window at the path across the beach. *Paranoia is my friend, people creeping up on me are not.*

One of the old men sitting across the incredibly small room began speaking to his friend in a whisper, but since we were in such close quarters, I could hear everything that they were saying. "I reckon e's one of them," he said in a gruff Devonshire voice that sounded as if he had been smoking since before he was born.

"What else would e be doing 'ere?" the other asked almost as a rhetorical question.

"E don't look like much though, do 'e?"

"E's probably just 'ere to 'elp set up the ritual."

"Aye, probably right."

I had to jump in and see if I could get a grip on whatever they were talking about and potentially whatever I was walking into. After hearing the word *ritual*, I wanted to dig deep. "Are you young fellas here for the ritual?" I asked as politely as I could. They turned pretty quickly and locked eyes on me for a good thirty seconds before anyone said anything else.

"Do we look like your kind?" the one with the less raspy voice threw back at me.

"My kind?" I asked as casually as I could whilst taking a couple of sips of my drink.

"Yeah, one of you bloody wizards who come to the island for your meetin's and ritu'ls. Every year you lot come up here and book out the hotel for days at a time," the lifetime smoker growled.

"Actually, I'm a Grimoire . . . not a Wizard," I said, still not really sure of the difference. The two older men looked unimpressed and then burst out laughing. I decided I wasn't going to stick about for more of their social niceties, so I finished off my alcoholic concoction and walked out of the pub to the sound of belly laughter, the occasional uncontrolled spluttering, and cough, and I swear I heard one of them say *abracadabra*.

After walking up the path towards the hotel, I could feel that the wind had picked up at the same time as the evening had started to turn dark, and I was pleased that I had brought my big grey coat that looked like it should have come from some trendy First World War pilot. I had only taken a few steps as I wrapped my coat tighter around my body and stuffed my hands deep into my pockets when I stopped and saw three men, all wearing the same dark purple robe with their hoods down. They were leaving the hotel through the cast-iron gates at the front. *Now I really feel like a spy*, I thought. They didn't notice me standing further down the hill, because they went straight up the path further up the island. Obviously, I followed, what with me being the curious fellow I am.

They made their way around the 1920s tennis courts at the back of the hotel. I followed marching up the muddy path that led up to the top of the island that had an abandoned stone building with the walls intact, but nothing else. As the three men reached the top, I was clumsily climbing up behind them. I was just far enough for them to not notice that I was following like a second- or even third-rate sleuth and not the super detective I was imagining myself to be. I saw them meet another three people at the top, standing inside the stone-walled hut. They were also wearing the same purple robes but were obscured by the remaining broken walls. As the three I had followed entered the building, I crept up to the edge of one of the ridges of ground about six metres out, poking up enough from the surface to give me a hiding spot to peek at them from.

From what I could tell, they didn't exactly look like the friendliest of Mages, but I was pretty sure that one of them was Kelley. It would just be too much of a coincidence for him to be here and not be with these other magic users. They all looked relatively normal, apart from the purple robes. One had a sharp widow's peak of thin black hair and sunken eyes, another was completely bald with swirling facial tattoos, and the third had silver hair whipped over in a side parting. The three who were already in the hut were harder to see, but as they greeted each other, I could see that one was a woman with dark hair, another had cropped brown hair, and the last had already had his hood up. The one with the hood up was obviously in charge. I could see the others watching and listening intently, almost to the point of fear. That was not a man I wanted to meet, especially when he had all his pals around to do his bidding.

The hooded one was pointing with a black-gloved hand and making gestures that looked like orders, which wasn't easy to see as it was beginning to turn even darker. He spoke in a strong voice and not one that I recognised; he told his fellow robed acquaintances, "A time of change is upon us. We are nearing *full circle*, and the old ways are no longer old! It is time that we begin taking on apprentices as we will need more numbers in the nights ahead." He then dropped his voice and whispered something to each of the robed figures individually who pulled up their hoods after their leader had moved on to the next.

When he had finished the rest of the group, all sprang into action. They immediately moved to five different points of the stone hut and began laying their arms across themselves diagonally, holding themselves in place. They then looked up into the sky above them as the hut was missing its roof and started a low chant. "Night's black mantle covers all alive."

They each balled their hands in front of them as if they were trying to crush an egg end on. It looked like they were using the same amount of pressure that they would need to rupture a blood vessel in their eyes, and I remembered how that felt. The hooded leader spoke his words of ritual low and intoned. I knew it was his whisper throughout the ritual because of his deeper voice and slow pronunciation I had heard earlier. It stood out.

Then as if by magic – I know I said it – light started to shine from each of their balled hands, and it leaked through the minute gaps, sending a glow through the thin stretches of skin between fingers and thumbs. It was a spectacle to behold as they opened their hands, letting the pure light shine out. As it did, the brilliant white flare began to drink in the last evening colours, turning the ball of light into a ball of dusk. They were all enchanting beneath my ability to hear and then after a few words from the hooded leader, which I clearly heard – "Consume the light", each of the hooded figures pushed their hands to their mouth and forced themselves to swallow their ball of dusk, stretching their jaw as wide as they could go and then some. I'll admit that I was intrigued . . . And scared. Very, very scared.

CHAPTER FOURTEEN

Hide and Seek

Crouching in the dark and listening to them join in with the leader's chanting, getting louder with each repetition, I could have sworn that the night was getting darker and surrounding us with increasing speed. You would think that I would be getting used to this by now, but I still find it deeply disturbing. It seemed like the night was drawn to Burgh Island alone and that those six robed Mages were channelling the night towards them. I could no longer see into the stone hut, as there wasn't enough light to see who was doing what in there now that they had swallowed their light and had begun to move around the remains of the building. Before I realised it, they had stopped completely still, and there was a purple glow that showed outlines of one of the robed figures.

"Night's black mantle is upon our sister," said the leader of the group, which brought the others in closer to the centre of the hut. One of them was kneeling in the middle, and purple light was seeping from her mouth and eyes. I couldn't believe what I was seeing; I could tell it was the woman because she was staring straight up, and the light revealed her delicate face. That's when I saw her clearly for the first time, and I knew it was Emilia. *What the hell is this?* I thought as she began talking to the others, but it was not *her* voice that was coming from within.

"The Servants of Night must break the hollow peace," she said with three or four voices overlapping each other, sounding as if she was possessed by multiple spirits and of multiple ages and genders. Creepy, huh?

"What is going on?" I whispered to myself in shock more than anything else. Unfortunately, it was enough for six Mages to hear and follow Emilia's purple light pouring from her eyes and mouth, illuminating my hiding spot. She turned to look at me just before I ducked down, and I was quite sure that they had seen me. "Bugger, bugger, bugger!" I rolled on to my back and slid down the ridge I was hiding behind, slipping into a panic about being found by robed men and a possessed client.

"Someone intrudes upon the night's ritual!" came the many voices out of Emilia's mouth. I could hear them moving, as they must have broken from their ritual and left the stone hut behind to come out and look for me, all shouting out to call to each other. I slid even further down the ridge to hide, but it was now getting darker, and I could only see a couple of feet in front of me.

"Get out there and find them," one of the men spoke out. I wasn't sure if it was their ever-hooded leader, but I knew by his quick tone they weren't waiting around.

I pushed myself even further down the ridge, which wasn't the way I had come up, and apart from being in sheer panic at having a group of strange Mages find me and do God knows what to me, all I could think about was the island's cliff face and how loud the waves smashing on to the rocks below was beginning to sound, heralding my potential demise. I continued to slip away, and looking back, I could see a flash of light from the top of the ridge.

"*Lux-lu-cis!*" one of the men shouted out as he reached the top of the ridge. This illuminated the entire lip of the ridge, and I could see the silhouette of three figures standing there, looking down with a fourth joining them. My mind raced as to what I could do. I was sure that if I were caught, it wouldn't end well for me, so I raced through the jumble of magic that had found its home in my mind and on my flesh. Just as another purple-robed Mage repeated the spell of light, I realised I was also speaking.

"*Dehr-AEluhm-roosh-kuhl.*" This, to my amazement and surprise, counteracted the Mages' light spell, keeping me hidden from their eyes. Darkness was my friend. His light illuminated the ridge and over, *just* giving me away. My darkness encompassed his light to the sound of their protestations.

"*Lux-lu-cis!*" he repeated with anger.

"*Dehr-AEluhm-roosh-kuhl,*" I repeated with panic. Not just because they were close to finding me but because with every flash of light I knocked back, I could see how my feet were inches away from the tip of the cliff edge, dropping straight off into the sharp rocks and beating waves a long way below.

"Who is it?" one of them called out.

"I can't see him!" another shouted back.

"Do you think *he* sent him?" another asked in the movement up above.
"Who?"

"Who else? The omens of his return are piling up!" The panic in this one's voice was noticeable.

"That's not possible. No one has seen or heard from him in centuries!"

"Forget about *him*, and find whoever is spying on our coven!" shouted the hooded man who had being running everything until I so stupidly revealed myself.

I realised that I couldn't just sit between a watery death and the Mages that had taken a serious dislike to me. *Who knew privacy and Mages were so fond of each other?* So I did what I do best: I got up and ran. I jumped over a small ridge not far to my left and planted my feet on to the floor, noting how slippery the ground had become, and kept moving forward without looking back. Behind me, I heard them shouting to each other as they spotted me and the sound of them all running towards me, as a group was just audible over the waves smashing into the rocks below.

I had only gotten fifteen yards down one of the paths I had managed to find by the luck of my boots' landing in the right place and a word sprang up in my mind so suddenly it nearly knocked me off my cowardly retreat, and I halted in mid-run. I could feel the glow of the tattoo on my ribs like too much deep heat left on for too long. It had become instinct that when one of the Wayward words of magic came to mind, I said it and hoped that whatever came out would see me through: "*Peith-IHduth-TINgyuh-kuht-hOOuh*". Almost instantly, darkness fell on me, a darkness that was darker than the night but allowed me to see through it into the normal night sky just a few inches around me. This wasn't just a shadow falling upon the island before like it had with *dehr-AEluhm-roosh-kuhl*, the Druidic spell for darkness. This was my personal shield of the night's cloak hiding me from my pursuers as if I were a pitch-black shadow dancing through the night.

The Mages were getting closer, so I stepped off the path and on to the grass verge and let them run right by as I tried to make out their faces. The first to disappear into the darkness below was the man with the widow's peak, who didn't really look like he wanted to catch anyone; he had the look of someone who just wanted to get out of dodge and quickly. Next were the other two men, baldy and the silver fox, who were searching as they went checking as many different little hide-y-holes as they could find. They didn't hang around long. I turned to double back on myself and found I was nose to nose with Emilia who no longer had purple light pouring out of her emerald eyes. Bathed in the moonlight, she looked more enchanting than ever, but she didn't repay the favour of looking longingly into my eyes. Instead, she said one word as she put her hand over my brow, blocking out the world before me: "*Som-ni-um*". Then everything turned black, and I fell into an abyss of sleep.

"*There are no more than a hundred Grimoires left in the world, and Wayward is the newest of them all," said a man sitting in front of a desk in one of the two guest chairs. He was in his early thirties and had cropped brown hair; unfortunately, I couldn't quite make out his face. He was blurred by something, almost like those reconstructions on crime watch, but not as blatantly obvious. He was talking to the woman next to him, who I knew was Emilia. She had on a green dress that showed the curves of her hips and chest, making me think back to that first time when she had come into my shop. Her face was blurred too, but I was beginning to see that their faces were almost liquid or smoke pooling in on themselves to continually hide the faces.*

"*There are only a hundred for a reason. They've been hounded and chased to the ends of the earth for longer than I can remember, bound to the fate of their ancestors," Emilia replied to the man's statement.*

"*He could be the one!*"

"*Any of them could be the one, that's the problem.*"

"*Does he know?*"

"*No more than anyone else. Why would he?*"

"*You haven't told him then?*" asked the man.

"*No, I would not paint a target on him just for the sake of conversation," Emilia scorned.*

"*Enough," came a controlled voice from another behind the desk, who was out of sight. Both Emilia and the cropped-haired man sat in silence in the front. The voice sounded familiar but as if it too had been distorted like the faces of those who now sat in silence, waiting to hear from their mysterious friend. "We must know for sure as to Wayward's progeny and authenticity. There can be no mistakes this time," he explained whilst slowly turning his chair to face his human pawns and then in true fashion, everything started to go black. I fought as hard as I could to see his face, even kicking and screaming to pull myself to face the dark entity sitting behind the desk; I could make out curly hair, but my body was pulling me back into it so that mental and physical being could once again be simpatico.*

Sucking air into my lungs, I was surprised to wake up in what looked like a hotel room; to be honest, I was surprised to be waking up at all. It took a while before I could open my eyes and look around the room, nursing what seemed like an unfair and unholy hangover, since I hadn't even drank the drink to earn it. There were lots of dark red in the furnishings – the curtains, carpet, and bedclothes, which I thought might be more suited in a house of ill repute as a muzzy, half-drunk consciousness held me in its grip as I tried to make out more details within the room. It must have still been night as there was barely enough light to make out the figure sitting across the red carpet in the cracked red leather chair.

My eyes fixed as I willed them to focus on the shape that appeared to be looking back at me.

"*Lu-min-ari-um*" said the familiar voice I had heard in my dream with the use of Latin words of magic.

"You!" I forced out, trying to sound angry and in control of myself, which was far from the truth. I tried to sit up at the end of the bed only to fall back down flat and again try to push myself back up to a respectable position. Every part of me still felt distant and lost. I was actually relieved that it was Emilia and not one of her strange fellow robed Mages, especially not the entity behind the desk in my dream whose face was still a mystery.

"It wasn't a dream."

"What! What wasn't a dream?" I fired out, slurring most of my words.

"What you saw, your vision. It wasn't a dream," Emilia told me with such confidence I immediately believed what she was saying.

"And I suppose everyone gets visions in the magical community? Why wouldn't they? Obviously, everyone who has ever won the lottery was a Mage cashing in on their visions."

"Actually, Wayward," – I loved the way she said my name; it just seemed to roll off her tongue – "Mages can't see visions of the future or past."

"So I'm special?" I managed a cynical eyebrow raise.

"Not special, a Grimoire."

"Grimoire? I've heard that before . . . As in the grimoire book of spells left by my grandfather?"

"There are only . . ."

"One hundred!" I interjected.

"Yes, approximately one hundred Grimoires left in the world, who have received their magic from an ancestor's influence. There used to be over a thousand Grimoires created by the Courts of the world in the spell of ascendance, using the power of the lay lines that cross the earth's energy over the crust of the land to synchronise the Chosen few to become Grimoires and serve as magic's protectors and guardians.

"And before you ask me, yes, there is a difference between a Mage and a Grimoire. You are a Grimoire as you have inherited your family's magic that has been practised, evolved, and recorded over the centuries in their book of shadows. There are those who have the touch but are not from a magical bloodline, and these are your commonplace Mages. There was a time when some of these Mages would attempt to steal the Grimoire's knowledge for them to gain instant power. The written grimoire would then change allegiance to this new Mage, where they would consume an entire family tree of magic. This happens very rarely, but when it happens, everyone in the magical community, as you put it, feels it. The same way that everyone knew *you* had taken in the Wayward grimoire, allowing it to become a part of who you are. The same would happen if a Grimoire's book of shadows is destroyed, forcing that particular bloodline's knowledge and power to fade from our grasp back into the world to be rediscovered and tamed by one who finds himself worthy."

Silence hung in the room as I took a moment to digest what Emilia had said. Then I knew there were some things I wanted to know from her that weren't about my family; they were about hers, but first . . . "I'm going to need a minute."

CHAPTER FIFTEEN

Partner in Crime

It had taken a good hour for my *special nature* as a Grimoire and reasons why people may want me dead to sink in properly. More than anything, I couldn't stop myself from thinking about the predicament the mysterious beauty sitting across the room had gotten me into. I was hired to acquire a rare and enviable pack of tarot cards, by her, but in the process of trying to lay my hands on them, my life has changed in unimaginable ways. I've nearly been killed three times, found out that magic is real, and the only thing I've nearly sold from my shop since this whole thing began was false interest. The customer turned out to be a half-man, half-lizard, half-demon-killing machine. Yes, I know that makes three halves, but hey, it's magic.

I suggested that we go out for a coffee, and when Emilia mentioned we could have a drink in the room, I made it clear that having a drink in the room was the problem. I wanted to be out in public, where it's harder to conceal magic and to at least allow me the illusion of safety from her or anyone else who wants to take a potshot at me for some unknown reason. We left the hotel and found ourselves walking along Kingsbridge high street, leading downhill. The town was very old and looked exactly like you would imagine a small town to look like in South Devon that depends on tourism: lots of independent butchers, bakers, and grocers wafting their produce's tempting smells to wash over the unsuspecting public as they stroll by. I say stroll because no one in the town seemed to want to get anywhere at any normal speed. It was almost as if the locals were under some hypnotic trance in which they thought they had all the time in the world. I realised that there was no magic at work here and that this was just what happened to people in small west-country towns when the biggest shop they have is a WHSmith that doesn't even sell films, not that I was looking.

Halfway down the hill, our awkward silence became too much, and I stopped outside a café that caught my eye. Coincidentally, the place was called 'The Meeting Room', as I was going to suggest a meeting that my new companion would have to arrange. Firstly, I had to set some ground rules.

We sat at a table in the window away from the only other customer in the café. I ordered a latte for me and a hot chocolate for her, which I explained she would be paying for.

I took a long slow gulp of my latte and then went straight in for the kill. "Tell me about being a Grimoire."

"Grimoires are the protectors of us all . . . until they're not."

"What does that even mean?" I asked.

"It means that a Grimoire can be as powerful or as weak as the rest of us. You just get to be what you choose a lot quicker than the *run of the mill* magic users. You're a celebrity among the magical community whether you like it or not, and you have a thousand years of your bloodline's secret recipes tattooed across your skin by the looks of it."

"Celebrity, seriously?"

"Afraid you'll have to get used to it," she said.

"Get used to it? Do I need to get used to you putting me to sleep and kidnapping me as well?" I asked agitated at her smugness.

"Not if you behave."

"If I behave?" I asked and stared at her, allowing a tangible silence to grow between us. "Let's get a few things straight," I finally said.

"Just a few?" she asked with a playful smile.

"Number one, you don't use magic on me any more – not if you want to find your bloody cards."

"As you wish."

"Number two, you tell me exactly what is going on and who the main players are. I don't appreciate being used like a pawn is some magical game of chess with no rules. I especially want to know who your boss is, the one with the curly hair and a penchant for hoods." At this, Emilia's face dropped for the smallest second and then she quickly regained her composure and her smile.

"How do you know about him?" she asked, trying to look as casual as she could but not too successfully.

"You were talking to him."

"When?"

"In my vision."

"I was talking to Doctor Dee, could you see . . ."

"I think you'll find that I am the one asking questions," I said, trying to give off an air of authority as I interrupted her.

"Then ask," she gently replied. I'm assuming she saw this as the path of least resistance rather than bowing down to my whispered commands, as so many have done before in my dreams of being a bad ass. Then again, they do say that to *assume* makes an ass of you and me.

"What are these tarot cards really?"

"They are a magical conductor of sorts. They work in the same way as an electrical current passing through a metal pole. You can place a card on someone, and given that you are in possession of the majority of the pack or you can throw a hell of a lot of power into it, you can influence a person to act on their given card."

"You're going to have to give me an example," I said, needing it spelled out for me a little more. Hey, I'm a newbie to this magic game, real magic at least.

"If I placed the fool card in your pocket and had possession of all the other cards, or the majority of the cards, I could make you dance around the café, making a fool of yourself however I see fit. You would be under my control. If I placed a messenger card on you, I could influence you to tell someone, or a crowd of people, whatever I wanted you to say, with you as my personal messenger boy. You would feel the most intense desire to complete the task I had given you because my magic is channelled through the cards, meaning you would rather die trying than not achieving your goal. If you fought the magic, then your own body would turn against you, using every fibre of your existence to torture you with your own power."

"Can you channel back?"

"If your magic is strong enough, you can try, but a channelled magic tends to be supported by the channelling objects that are charged with the original enchanter's spell."

"Surely there has to be easier ways of using magic and getting someone to do something for you?"

"There are, but if you cast a spell on someone directly, it can be traced right back to the caster by other Mages."

"How do you trace it?"

"You just have to open your eyes to it and you can sense it. Even read it if you become skilled enough."

"Why would a Mage trace your magic?" I asked out of reflex rather than curiosity as I slowly began to come to terms with what Emilia was telling me.

"Why wouldn't you?" she fired back flippantly, getting tired of explaining what appeared to be the basics in magic.

"OK, point made. If you want those tarot cards so much, then why have you asked me, a complete newbie, to this fantastical magical world hidden in plain sight?" I asked in one long breath, waiting for an answer. Emilia hesitated, and I could see in her face that she was deciding what or how much she should say. Her mouth stayed closed except for a delicate yet slurpy sip of hot chocolate in the same way she had made when drinking tea in my office. "If you won't explain things, then I will," I carried on. She looked at me with a hint of interest, impressed no doubt that I was taking over the situation. "You're going to get your mate, who I'm pretty sure is one of your purple-robed buddies, to give me the cards you've sent me after. A little bit of give and take. Even though I'm not quite sure why you can't get them yourself since he's one of you occult buddies, but it will probably come to light soon enough – it always does."

"Excuse me?" she asked in surprise.

"Your mate has got some of the cards we need."

"Which one?"

"I don't know the deck off by heart."

"Which colleague? Or *mate* as you put it?"

"Kelley."

"Edward Kelley has some of the tarot cards?" Her anger grew.

"I'm pretty sure if you just repeat what I'm saying we're not gonna get very far."

CHAPTER SIXTEEN

The Summoning

Emilia wasn't best pleased when she found out that one of her purple-wearing magic monks had a few of the tarot cards she was after and obviously wasn't willing to share. She hadn't even thought that one of her own might be playing their own game. We had made our way back to Burgh Island, which was apparently the best spot to call him back to, as we knew he had been there and had a living connection to it. By the way she was pulling bits of things from her purse for her summoning spell, which I didn't know at the time, I could see she was beyond the simple curiosity of asking Kelley why he had those cards and that she was clearly blinded by her desire to force some home truths out of him by any means necessary. I, on the other hand, was admiring her work and making a mental note of what she was using for this summoning spell, until I decided that she was literally pulling together the most random objects. I was standing by ready to see how this one played out. More than anything, I was trying to keep my big grey coat wrapped tight as the wind was picking up on the top of Burgh Island, making this one of those bizarre days that actually seem to becoming the norm rather than the exception.

After our coffee break, Emilia had gone back to the hotel room as soon as I had mentioned Kelley's name and had begun packing what appeared to be whatever came to hand. A hefty leather-bound book was included. I thought it could have been a grimoire, if she was Grimoire; the thought

crossed my mind that I really didn't know much about Emilia at all. I had
followed by her back up the Kingsbridge high street. Not only because she
had told me to follow, in quite a stern voice, but also because I wanted to
see how this was going to pan out. I did panic for a moment and wondered
if she had placed a tarot card on me to enchant me into following her. I
couldn't find anything in my pockets or on my person and realised I was
a bit lost in this sea of magical craziness, and Emilia was someone I could
hold on to whilst Maurice was gone.

As these thoughts swam around in my head, Emilia seemed to have
packed everything that she needed and was ushering me out of the hotel
room and back towards my trustworthy Mini. I remember leaving it in the
Burgh Island car park, but apparently, it had been driven back to the hotel
whilst I was under her sleepy spell. We got in, and I was under no illusions
that asking Emilia why I was sitting in the passenger seat of my own car
would be a bad idea. I kept my mouth closed and my eyes open. It only took
me three to four minutes of sitting in silence as we drove out of Kingsbridge
and headed along the roads with signs for Plymouth before I plucked up the
courage to ask where we were going.

"Back," she said with her thoughts focused on someone else.

"Back where?"

"To Burgh Island."

I could see that she wasn't joking or in any kind of mood for a discussion.
Instead, I thought about being dragged out with the tidal pull and allowing
myself to indulge in her plan since I didn't really have one of my own.

We arrived at the car park overlooking Bigbury On Sea. It led up to
Burgh Island, sticking out of the water as a tiny paradise of seclusion kept
at arm's length from the world. Either that or a perfect place to indulge in
magic without worrying about the masses of onlookers you would get in
Covent Garden. Emilia parked in the exact spot I had parked in the last
time I had come to find Kelley. She wasn't in the mood to hang around. I
quickly jumped out of the car, slamming shut the squealing Mini door, and
followed her down the wooden stairs. They were built into the cliff face
leading to the beach where we crossed over to the island on the temporary
peninsula; luckily, the tide was out, so we didn't have to swim. I thought she
must have timed it well, with the tide being out, but then again, her magic
may have had something to do with that.

We climbed straight past the Pilchard Inn and the Burgh Island Hotel
and made our way right up to the top of the island next to the Huer's Hut.
A squared-off hunk of concrete sat, its former use forgotten in the mists of
time and tide. Immediately, Emilia set down her bag and began to get to
work. She was pulling things out and passing them to me. She pulled out a

little carton of lighter fluid, which she opened and then moved around the concrete hunk, sketching out a pattern with the spraying liquid. It was then that she told me to place the items she had given me at the points of the pattern. The first was a ripped piece of purple cloth that looked as if it had come from one of their order's robes, the second was a metallic ornament of a crescent moon, the third was a tuft of hair that I weighted down with a small stone, the fourth was a vial of what I can only assume was blood, and the fifth was a pack of tarot cards. This last one caught my attention.

"These aren't *special* tarot cards, are they?" I asked, hoping Emilia's obvious anger wouldn't spill on to me.

"No. They're just tarot cards. In this case, it's not the object but the power of the object as a symbol. The tarot cards symbolise what we all want," she explained as calmly as she could.

"And what exactly do you want with them?"

"They're for my employer, and that is all I will say on the matter. For now, we are meeting with Kelley."

"Using a spell?"

"A summoning spell," she corrected.

"Of course, and I suppose he'll just pop up and be happy to chat.' Sarcasm defence, check.

'Not quite. As soon as I summon Kelley, I will be trapping him inside a magical bond to make sure that he is as willing to answer my questions as quickly as possible. The pentacle is a powerful system of runes and symbols, allowing us to bind Kelley to his prison with the elements we are all drawn from. The most powerful spells are often bound with the five elements." My face must have been a sight as Emilia went on to explain further. "He won't be able to get away from answering questions he will clearly not want to give answers to. And before you ask, yes, he will be in pain, and no, I'm not planning on killing him." She emphasised the word 'planning' as if it was likely to change depending on Kelley's cooperation.

After the quick explanation of what was about to go down, I could see that she was no longer in the mood to share her magical knowledge and moved around the concrete hunk, checking what I had done and muttering words under her breath, which I rightly assumed were a part of the spell. She was speaking a variety of Latin words and phrases that all sounded bizarre when she said them. I realised that I recognised some as they mentioned summoning and appearances such as "*Si vocare te audire*". As Emilia was speaking her words of power, I could feel a familiar warm feeling growing in its intensity on my stomach just above my belly button.

Even in this cold wind, I opened my big grey coat and lifted up my shirt to reveal one of my Grimoire tattoos glowing white-hot, blurring its clarity to the eye with its heat and pulsing as if the word was being dragged out from my skin. I'm not gonna lie to you; it began to hurt, and I was beginning to panic.

"Emilia!?"

"What?" she managed to fit in-between her words of spell craft.

"My tattoo!"

"What?"

"One of my Grimoire tattoos – it's glowing!" I couldn't hide the panic in my voice.

"What are you talking about?" She turned to look at me and noticed that I had what could only be described as a halogen torchlight beaming out from above my belly button where the word had once been. "Whatever's happening to your stomach? You need to stop it – now!" she barked.

"I would if I knew how!" I said at the exact moment the light disappeared, and we stared at each other in confusion. "It's happened a few times before but never with Latin words of power."

"What is it?" Her attention was on me for the first time since she decided she wanted Kelley in her hands.

"It happens when I learn one of the spells from my grimoire. The word erases itself from my body once I know how to use it and finds its way back to the grimoire book of shadows. Cool, huh?" It was nice to be the one who knew what was going on, for once.

"Should you be using you magic like this?" She didn't pause long enough for me to answer. "What did you learn?"

"What?" I asked.

"What spell did you just learn?" Her face took on a cautious look.

"Urm, summoning someone, maybe. In Latin rather than Druidic words of power."

"Who did you summon?"

It was at this exact moment that I was lifted off my feet and thrown over the Huer's Hut, landing in mud and grass as my breath was forced out of my body on impact, and I lay winded on the ground with spittle and mud hanging over my face. The good news is that I didn't die, but the bad news is I thought I lay in the mud and grass long enough to miss what would have been an opportunity to see how practised Mages fight when they have to.

Scrambling across the muddy banks, I reached the side of the Huer's Hut and leaned around it to see who was winning. From what I could tell, they both looked like they were winning and losing. One moment Kelley was rippling the ground beneath Emilia's feet with a shout of *"Atrox Terrae!"* and then Emilia was knocked down and retaliating with a scream of *"Unda Redundo!"* bringing down a wave of ocean on top of Kelley and slamming him into the ground. I could see that Emilia was actually hurt from Kelley's attack and knew that I was about to risk my life to do something incredibly stupid.

"*Mwin-IHduth-SOLyeh-TINgyuh!*" I shouted before I knew I had even finished having the thought. It was my ancestor's magic working with me, instinctually trying to protect me from others and even myself when I was stupid enough to get into these life-threatening situations. I threw out my hands to pull the spell together; out at my side I brought my palms in front of me until they slapped together, bringing with them a mist so thick we all lost sight of each other. For a moment, I thought back to Sebastian and how he pulled darkness over us in the alley by my shop, and I knew I was beginning to really understand my magic and explore my potential the way he had advised me to.

CHAPTER SEVENTEEN

How to Play the Game

Pulling myself to my feet, I trod as carefully as I couldn't see what was happening, but that was OK, because I was assuming that Kelley couldn't either, but then, again, neither could Emilia. This is what happens when you *react* and not *act*. The point was that if no one could see anyone, then we all had more chance of living a little longer, especially me. The uneven and wet floor beneath my shoes squelched and was far too slippery for me to move at any speed, so I snuck off in the direction I thought I'd last seen Emilia in, and as quietly as possible, I called out for her. 'Emilia? It's Jon. Where are you?' I waved my hand in front of my face as if it would help swipe some of the mist away, but it had no effect. The mist seemed to sit perfectly across the top of the island without moving; honestly, it's amazing what you can do with a bit of magic. 'Emilia?'

'Here!' I heard her call from the indistinguishable white swirls off to my right. I changed my course and slowly moved in that direction, trying to listen for any other noise, anything that might tell me where Kelley was. I tried to comfort myself with the thought that he had most probably scarpered by now. *Why would he stick around? He doesn't know what's happening or why we've, I've, summoned him here*, I thought as I called out to Emilia again, and this time her voice sounded fainter as if she were hurt or unable to muster the strength to call louder. I sped up and pushed my way through the mist I had created. I called louder this time. For some reason, it was as if I knew time was running out. I stepped out into the mist, and my foot came down on to nothing, and the further it went, the less it met. I was falling, and as it registered, my arms whipped out to try to grab on

89

to something. My mind wasn't working but, luckily for me, my instincts and magic were. I heard my voice *"werna-IHduth-nihn-gohrd-SOLyeh"* and then I was pulled up into the air. The weird thing was I didn't drop back down to the ground.

I was floating in the mist for a good minute as I got used to the idea that I was actually floating, *seriously floating*, and I couldn't see where I was, and that worried me. I had an inkling that I was no longer directly over the island, which meant if I dropped, I would be heading into the ocean and the jagged and broken rocks below. "Wayward!" I heard Emilia shout from my left. "Where are you?"

"Up here!" I shouted back.

"What? Where?" she called. I could tell she was now shouting up into the sky that I was held in. "I can't see you!" she called.

"I'm just . . . around," I said. It was then that I saw an orange glow form in front of me, a ball of glowing light illuminating the mist that it sat in. It moved towards me, and my gut shrank to the size of a marble as it came closer, which it did at an extreme speed. I could clearly see it was a ball of flames about the size of a football, propelling itself towards my chest. I have no shame of the impressive scream I made as I added to the word coming out of my mouth; *"Terra,"* my Grimoire magic said from my mouth. *"Firma,"* I added from my schoolboy Latin. I was pulled out of my floating limbo and thrown on to the wet mud once again; even though I was glad to be back on the ground, I knew that this meant that I had to face the fireballs and the Mage behind them, and I was pretty sure it wasn't Emilia. Whilst this was going on, I couldn't help but be impressed with myself as I was manipulating Latin words of power as well as my Druidic ones.

"Emilia? Are you still there?" I asked.

"Yes. Where are you now? And who's throwing fireballs?"

"I'm back on the ground—" I got cut off as another fireball came glowing through the mist in my direction. I jumped out of the hole I was in and landed near the entrance to the ancient Huer's Hut. I pushed myself up against the cold stonewall. The sound the fireball made as it came past reminded me of bonfire night when I was a kid and my grandfather would take me to see the bonfire being lit at the bottom of Parsonage Wood. The bonfire covered in petrol and lighter blocks being consumed in flame within a second, creating a whoosh that comforted and terrified me with the same split-second thrill.

"I'm definitely not throwing any fireballs. If I were you, I would find a place to hide and quick!" I shouted over the wall to Emilia.

"I am a Mage and a *true* Servant of the Night, and I will not hide!" she shouted loud enough for anyone on the island to hear. Then what I heard next could only be described as Emilia's war cry, and it scared the hell out of me.

I peeked over the rubble that was still recognisable as a window frame in the Huer's Hut, and I couldn't see anything except for the mist. I knew that if any of us were going to get out of this alive, then we needed to be able to see Kelley and our surroundings. I dived into my mind and focused on the magic it now held for something to undo this misty cover, first trying to find the word that fits, then the Latin or Druidic counterpart. *See, clear, de-mist, wipe, vision, sight . . . Sight! That's it. OK, the Latin translation is . . . Os and the Druidic translation is SOLyeh-IHduth-gohrd-hOOuh-TINgyuh. Take your pick.* And they say Latin and Druidic languages are dead; from where I was sitting, they were very much alive and kicking. "*Os*," I said, choosing the short option, and waved my hand in front of me as if I were moving the mist myself. I couldn't believe it; the mist was swept from the top of the island and was disappearing on to the water's surface below. Finally, I could see what was in front of me. Outside the Huer's Hut, I saw a very different side of Emilia. She was shouting words I had never heard of, and a collection of elements all in brick-sized chunks were forcing themselves against Kelley who tried to block her magic with his own. He was still wearing his purple robe, but his hood had come down, and I could see his face illuminated in magical light with each new savage attack from Emilia.

There didn't seem to be an inch given from either of them except that they were both tiring and quickly. Magic was a power and knowledge you could call upon from within, but that also meant that with each use of magic, the body, the mind, and the spirit tired. I crawled out through the missing window and dropped to the mud beneath. I needed to end this, but every time I used my magic, the outcome was far too unpredictable, and I didn't want to do anything to hurt Emilia. Before I had even come up with a semblance of a plan, I was creeping up to Kelley as his attention was on Emilia and the rocks, sea, air, and flame she was throwing at him. I was crouched no more than three feet away, waiting for something – a plan maybe? Nothing came to mind, so I searched the ground around me and scanned the devastation lying at my feet. I saw a good-sized stone. I picked it up and shouted out over the screams of attack and defence from these well-tested battle Mages, "STOP!" I was surprised to see that they did. Emilia just looked at me standing next to Kelley like I had lost the plot. Kelley was more surprised to see me standing next to him than my attempt to stop their battle. He was about to say something to me when I brought the stone against the side of his head and saw him twist on the spot and hit the floor like a sack of spuds. Emilia came running over. "Wayward, are you OK?" She was catching her breath from the battle.

"Yeah, I'm OK. Could do with a sit-down and a cup of tea," I said, half joking and half serious as I felt relieved that Kelley was out for the count.

Emilia leant over him and checked that he was unconscious and not dead. "He won't be causing any trouble for a while," she said as the adrenaline in my body was burning on vapours and my legs gave out, plonking my bottom quite hard on to the ground for what seemed like the hundredth time that night.

I almost pleaded with Emilia. "Can we just take a minute to pull ourselves together?"

"You can. I'm going to make sure that Kelley is bound tight so that this time we can actually question him without been burned alive."

"Good idea," I said absent-mindedly. Shock waved over me like the tide below, making its way to the cliff face over and over. It wasn't because I was scared but because I was confused and didn't fully understand what had happened and also didn't have a bloody clue as to how to process all the information that was just forced into my mind, and to be fair, it probably wasn't over.

I was only really taking in some of the smaller details of what was happening around me, and afterwards, I felt a bit bad for not helping. Emilia had dragged Kelley's unconscious body over to the summoning ring she had created before and then physically tied his hands and feet together with his own shoelaces, then magically tied those bonds together with some sort of binding spell. Whatever it was, it looked like nothing I had ever seen before, and I made a mental note to work out how to do it myself. She did explain what she was doing as she was doing it, but I think that was as much for her as it was for me. When she was done, she came and sat down by my side and took a deep breath. We both sat there and just stared out at the tide rolling in for a while. It was nice. It was peaceful.

"You know you shouldn't be abusing your magic like that," she spoke to me in a way I hadn't really experienced before. It sounded like she was worried; the only other time I heard her sound even remotely caring towards me and my well-being was back at the hotel in Kingsbridge. "It's dangerous for a Grimoire to use their magic without training. It always leads to disaster."

"Are you scared of me?"

"You should be scared of yourself."

"Should I be scared of you?"

"Yes." She smiled, which was nice. I remember thinking she should smile more. "But not because of my inability to control my magic. I am a Mage and have studied the ways of magic my entire life. You are not a

Mage. You are a Grimoire, and your knowledge of magic has come to you all at once. That's too much for anyone, even a Wayward."

"What do you mean *"even a Wayward"*?" I asked.

"You Waywards are famous. As a Grimoire, you are bound to keep the balance between all those who practise magic and aid the Court in their hour of need."

"Are you serious?" I couldn't believe what I was hearing. Not only is there magic in the world and I'm one of the few people who can use it, but also, I am a Grimoire who inherited generations' worth of magic directly into my body, and now I find out that I'm also some kind of magical sheriff. "So I'm a magic cop? Do I get a shiny badge and a gun? Probably a wand, pointy hat, and beard in our case." She laughed and that was the first time I heard her laugh truthfully, and I hoped it wouldn't be the last. I was finding it hard to take in what she was saying and concentrate on not finding her so . . . enchanting.

"You don't get a wand or a pointy hat, and I wouldn't recommend you grow a beard. It wouldn't suit you. But you do need to regulate how you use your magic. I can't believe your Alchemist hasn't explained this to you?"

"My Alchemist?" I thought of Sebastian.

"You should have an Alchemist. Each Grimoire has an Alchemist on hand to help the transition and ease the Grimoire into their new lifestyle, shall we say." She sounded as if she was trying to find the right words. "So who is your Alchemist?"

"I don't know, maybe Sebastian. Although he never actually told me he was *my* Alchemist."

"Sebastian Dove?" she asked with a definite sense of shock in her voice.

"Yes, Sebastian Dove. He came to my shop and showed me his magic, showed me magic for the first time and explained who I was, kind of. He told me I should be using my magic, getting used to my power and pushing the boundaries." I wasn't sure what to believe here. I wanted to trust Emilia, but Sebastian had been there from the start. I mean, he showed what magic really was!

"Why would he tell you that?" she asked herself as much as me. "Wayward, he should be making you control your magic, showing how to develop it over years and not just letting you go wild. That is an easy path to Blackened Earth."

"Wait, he said that. He told me he was a Pillar of the Blackened Earth."

"That can't be."

A voice came from behind us. "I'm afraid it is. Who do you think is controlling all the pieces in the merry game of chess?" Kelley had finally decided to get back into the game.

Chapter Eighteen

Hint of a Prophecy

"You could just be saying that. How do we know you're not one of these Black Pillars?" I said, getting to my feet and taking a step over to Kelley still trapped in his magical bindings, with Emilia by my side. He didn't respond and just sat there smiling to himself. He had a certain look about him that made me feel agitated. He always had a smirk on his face and a card up his sleeve that he was waiting to play, and it annoyed the hell out of me. Speaking of cards, I wanted his and this over with, both Kelley and whatever it is I'd gotten myself into. This job was a weight hanging around my neck, and if I couldn't drop it, I knew it was going to take me down with it, but I really wanted to collect my pay cheque. "Before we go any further, I'm just going to tell you a few things and then I want you to think about them before you give me your answer," I said and then I waited to see if he would show me any sign of talking. He didn't. "You're going to give me the tarot cards that you have. Do you know why?" He looked away from me, trying to avoid eye contact. "I know, but I want you to work it out for yourself." Emilia didn't really know what to do with herself; I could see her shifting from one foot to the other, presumably uncomfortable with not being in control of the conversation, but she let me play my hand. For curiosity more than trust, I suspect. "No? Nothing? Then I'll give you a hint."

I took a deep breath and said what was on my mind. 'Over this last week, I have found myself the recipient of certain items and events. Some people may see this as a miracle, some as a new beginning, but personally, I see it as a threat to my existence. Not once has this magic you all fawn over brought me any luck or good fortune. If anything, I've had my life put

at risk of death over the last few days more than any person should have in their entire life! I nearly drowned in an alley, only after nearly burning to death, a snake lizard demon monster attacked me, which I bludgeoned into an oblivion, two Mages attacked me in Wales and almost killed a colleague and then I was rumbled by your purple-hooded Servants of the Night and taken hostage, only to work with one of you and summon Edward *bloody* Kelley! At which point, I somehow made myself fly or hover or whatever that was, and the worst one of all is that my body is covered in tattoos! I've never wanted a tattoo! Even when I was a teenager, I never wanted a tattoo! And this is all because of those cards! So if you decide to keep hold of your card, which we know you have, then I will be forced to enact all that has happened to me on to you. Fair is fair, right?" I stood over him, panting from not taking in a breath after finishing my rant. It felt good to clear the air.

"I will give you my cards, but you *will* heed my words, Wayward. Deal?" He sat there, looking up at me. His pale eyes were locked into mine, and I could see he was serious; even his casual smirk had vanished, and it hadn't escaped me that he said cards, plural.

"All right, Kelley, I'll listen," I said.

"Untie me," he commanded.

At this, Emilia sprung to life and interjected. "There is no way we're untying you. You'll attack us again."

"I only wish to stand and deliver to you what you desire. You have bested me, in your own way, and I do not wish to restart the conflict." He seemed very calm for a man still tied up on the floor with nowhere to go now the ocean had rolled in and had surrounded the entire island.

Emilia looked at me to make the decision; due to my hissy fit, I had taken control of the situation and was now calling the shots. *How bizarre*, I thought as time was running out and I was bloody cold up on the unsheltered island top. I nodded and added my own interpretation. "The magical bindings stay." He stood up, and the shoelaces tying his hands and feet fell from him; he looked at me curiously to see if I was taken aback as his non-magical bindings fell away as if they were nothing but a mere inconvenience.

"Come on then, Kelley, the cards." I held out my hand, pretending not to be impressed by him dropping the laces that tied his hands and feet and waited to see what he would do next. I could feel Emilia on guard next to me, ready to burst into action if she needed to, which allowed me a small reprieve, and the ability to keep the butterflies in my stomach held down momentarily.

He slipped his hands under his jacket, as they were still bound together with Emilia's magic, and pulled out three of the tarot cards and spread them as if he were about to perform a magic trick. He held on to them and began to speak. "You have no idea what these are, do you?"

"Tarot cards," I answered.

"Really? Is that the best you can do?"

"They are imbued tarot cards that can make the holder do certain things and act in certain ways if you use them right." I was searching my mind for the explanation Emilia had given me.

"They are much more than that, Wayward," he said condescendingly.

"Not this," Emilia interrupted like she was embarrassed by the turn in the conversation.

"Yes. This. The cards are powerful on their own, but in comparison with their real purpose, this is nothing." He was excited.

Emilia turned and spoke directly to me. "Don't listen to this nonsense."

"What nonsense?" I asked.

"He's trying to fool you with an old tale told to Mages when they're children." She then turned to Kelley and addressed him. "Do you really think a Wayward is going to be tricked by children's stories?"

"It's not a story! These cards are not just mere trickery, and he will know I am telling the truth because he *is* a Wayward!" He had moved past excitement and into concern; it worried him that Emilia didn't believe him and that I might not. I could see it in his eyes.

"If you don't give us the cards, we'll just take them. Simple as that," I said, hoping to scare him into handing them over. But calmness fell upon him; it was as if he had realised his situation and accepted it, only thinking of what he needed to do now, or more accurately, what he needed me to do now.

"I'll give you the cards as long as you agree to listen to what I have to say, deal?" he asked with no sign of his smirk. I looked at Emilia to judge her reaction. I thought that as long as we ended up with the cards, then Emilia had the outcome she wanted; I've heard a Mage's bedtime story, and Kelley had dropped from a red alert to a yellowish type threat. Now that's what I call a win-win.

"OK then, Kelley. Hand me the cards and then I will hear what you have to say." He passed me the cards carefully, which I took and put them in my waistcoat pocket until I could add them to the box where they live. "Go on."

"These cards *are* tarot cards, and yes, they have magical properties, but where did these properties come from? Who imbued them with the power they have? And most importantly, why?" He looked at me with an expression of wonder, waiting for me to join him.

I didn't understand why he was so impressed with what he had said, so I took the bait and followed him down the rabbit hole. "So?"

"So each imbued item has had magic introduced to it for a purpose, and given enough time and resources, you could theoretically trace who has had possession of an imbued item and who introduced it to magic in the first place, regardless of how long ago it was. Magic holds memories of everything – how it's used, what it's used for, and who uses it. Each time magic is employed, the user leaves behind an elemental signature."

"A signature?" I asked.

"Everyone is different, but you can train yourself to see it. And once you do, you'll start to see it wherever you go, and maybe you'll realise that magic isn't hidden from the world . . . it is the world."

"What does a magic signature look like?"

"I've seen minute atoms blazing as a trillion tiny suns circling Shakespeare's quill. I've seen dark smoke trickling from the bullet that finally killed Grigori Rasputin after numerous attempts."

"I'm still not sure what this means," I said confused.

"It means the deck of cards is different."

"Why?"

"Because it has no memory! No signature!"

"So?"

"So where did it come from? What is its purpose? And who created them?" He raised his voice with this, making his point hit home.

There was silence, which we all stood through, thinking our own thoughts on what Kelley had said and what it meant for each of us. I had a feeling that this made a lot more sense for Kelley and Emilia than it did for me, but I wasn't about to let that particular cat out of the bag, again. Emilia was the one to break the silence, and I started to get the feeling that there was some unfinished business between these two because of the sharp and unforgiving way they spoke to each other. "He's talking nonsense. Mages have been using the Seals as an excuse to act however they want to for hundreds of years and justifying their actions."

"The Seals?" I asked. With this, Emilia realised she had been the one to say it and not Kelley; this was when his smirk reappeared, and he began to talk again.

"The Seals were put in place to keep an old and ancient magic locked away from the world. Sometime in the 1400s, this magic tried to break out and changed what the world was. Heinrich Kramer and Jacob Sprenger and their crusade to hammer the witches, the *Malleus Maleficarum,* was a reaction to this magic seeping out from behind the cage it was locked away in."

"What kind of old magic?" I asked.

"Not old, ancient." Kelley looked at Emilia and saw that she was as engrossed in his story as I was, so he continued. "The type of magic we're talking about has the power to ruin us all and destroy our way of life. But there are some," his brow furrowed, showing his disapproval, "some who want to unleash this magic and let it infect the world and bring about the Reformation of the Mages."

"What's that? The Reformation?"

"That is the new beginning, or the end of magic, or the descent of Mage kind and mankind alike. No one really knows for sure."

"You see! It's a child's story and an excuse to take what is not yours." Emilia pointed at the cards in my pocket.

Then Kelley finished his story. "What we do know is that there are Seals to keep the cage locked. Some of us believe that these Seals are objects imbued with magic like these tarot cards."

"Why these cards? What's wrong with a key or an actual lock?" I asked quite taken with Kelley's tale of the unimaginable.

"It's all they had with them when they hid this power from the world. Supposedly, there were nine needed for the ritual, and each one of them had to offer something imbued with the magic of their bloodline,' he explained.

Bloodline? I thought to myself for a moment; why had he used that specific word? Then I realised that he wanted me to know; he wanted to tell me the truth without actually having to say it. I called him on it, half out of curiosity and half out of personal safety. "They were Grimoires, weren't they? The ones who created the Seals?"

"Yes. They were the first Grimoires, and that is why I'm talking to you and not attacking you," he replied.

"No," Emilia corrected him. "You're talking to us because you want to keep breathing and you're telling us this children's tale because you're trying to buy time. Or you actually believe it, and a Grimoire is in possession of nearly all the cards creating one of your precious Seals."

"So what does that mean?" I asked, trying to comprehend what we had heard and what, if anything, it meant I needed to keep an eye out for. "Should I be careful?"

"Being careful won't be enough. If the magic wants to find you, it will find you. But as a Grimoire, you have a responsibility to the rest of us to not go down that path. Leave the Seals as they are, and never think on them ever again."

"You would have me give up?" I asked.

"I would have you stay alive and keep the Seals intact."

"Are you trying to scare me?"

"No, I'm warning you."

"Warning me?"

"Don't go down that road. Otherwise, everyone you know will turn against you, and the darkness will surround you so much that your own shadow will want you dead. This could lead to the Reformation!"

"You're not really in a position to give warnings, are you, Kelley?" asked Emilia rhetorically.

"The Servants of the Night give these warnings, not me," he said directly to her as if he were scorning her. "The Servants helped the Courts gather the original nine, it is said, and aided the Grimoires in the task of hiding the ancient magic from the world back before the Romans invaded this island."

"It's not possible, I would know!" Emilia growled at Kelley.

"It has been kept secret ever since it happened to stop anyone from seeking out the objects for any reason or rhyme, hidden in plain sight for all to ignore, especially our *beloved* Grimoires." He paused and let us stand in front of him, thinking on what he said; if this was all true, then was this the reason why Emilia wanted the cards? "Now I must report back to my master and inform him on what has transpired between us," he said with his usual smirk growing across his face once again.

"And how will you do that?" I asked, trying to retaliate against his cocky facial expressions that were really beginning to rub me up the wrong way.

"By serving the night, as I always have and will," he finished with a hiss, stepping backwards and looking up at the night sky, which seemed to consume him in darkness as he faded completely from our sight. I waved my hand through the air to convince myself that he had gone.

I stood in the darkness on the top of Burgh Island with a hundred questions that neither of us could answer, except for one: *Why does Emilia want the tarot cards?*

CHAPTER NINETEEN

No Place like Home

It took us awhile to come to our senses and even longer to make our way back to the car parked on the mainland. We took the Mini, and I drove in silence for a time until Emilia asked where we were going. That woke me from my daze, or daydream or whatever you call it when you're driving on the motorway and your mind travels faster than you do and leaves your body behind to run on automatic. I told her we were going back to Amersham and back to Smoke and Mirrors. Emilia wanted to know what the plan was, and all I could tell her before falling back into silence was that I wanted to go back to the shop, get my head down, and get some well-deserved shut-eye. I explained that I was going to meet Maurice back at the shop, and before I stopped myself, I had told Emilia that she could stay as long as she wanted. I guess I was feeling generous, and for some reason, I felt comfortable with her around. Even if we were not on the same side, I felt like I could firmly say that we were both considered the opposition to a common foe, something about my enemies' enemy and all that malarkey.

We had further conversation on the M4 as the day turned into night, but no matter what trivial topics we discussed, we systematically avoided discussing the prophecy Kelley had told of and what it could mean. I doubt that Emilia thought on what he had said any less than I did, which meant that it was all she was thinking about.

When we pulled up outside Smoke and Mirrors and got out of the Mini, the car door screamed on its hinges before slamming shut. That painful squeal reminded me of how tired I was; the car sounded like I felt. Before going any further, I stretched out, leaning my hands on the roof of the car. My back ached and hinted to me of how much I was looking forward to some sleep and something to eat. A desire that was delayed.

"Who's that?" Emilia asked, nodding up to the window of the apartment above the shop with a light on. She read my mind. "Maurice?"

"I hope so. I'm not sure I can deal with any more surprises." I smiled a tired smile and dragged my feet over to the shop door. I heard Emilia fall in behind me and guessed that she was feeling as wiped out as I was.

We walked in through the front door, and I called out to Maurice to make sure it was him. "Maurice? Is that you? You better not be eating me out of house and home."

"Not at all" came back his voice. "Come up quickly. I have something to show you." The excitement in his voice was enough to get Emilia and me up the spiral staircase that had never seemed more of an effort. We crossed the landing straight past the bathroom and bedroom and into the living room. "Come, sit," he ushered us over to my own sofa, and the brown leather hugged me with comfort, making me fight to stay interested in what Maurice had to say. "OK, Maurice, what's the rush?" I asked, stifling a yawn, and then noticed that the two of them were staring at each other. "Sorry, I should have formally introduced you to each other . . . You knew it was Maurice from outside though, how?"

"We've been watching you for a while, and I know Maurice by reputation," she answered back as if it were a normal reply.

"I have a reputation?" Maurice asked with a smile.

"Yes, you do. And it is a pleasure to make your acquaintance."

"Likewise . . ." He waited for her name.

"Emilia," she offered her name.

"Likewise, Emilia," Maurice finished, and they seemed happy in each other's company, even comfortable.

"I'm so happy you two could be friends. I was beginning to think no one in the magical community even liked each other and just attacked on sight." I threw my backhanded comment into the conversation.

Maurice sat on one of the stools opposite, looking us up and down and noticing our dirty and worn clothing, then asked, "Would it be fair to surmise that you encountered some resistance in obtaining Kelley's tarot cards?"

I replied, "Yes. That would be a fair summation."

"I encountered my own opposition in retrieving this for you." He revealed a tarot card from nowhere as if by magic, funny that. He held it up in the air, showing it off. "I met with Isobel and had a jolly good chat."

"And by chat, you mean you had to convince her?" I asked.

"You could say that. She did owe me a couple of favours, and I did have to make a trade of sorts."

"What kind of trade?"

"Just to keep her company . . ." he trailed off.

"Company?" asked Emilia.

"She has been in this world for a long time, and she said that she gets lonely, so I kept her company." His embarrassment at having to explain himself to us was amusing as his face turned redder and his eyes refused to meet ours. "I only did what any of you would have done." His face flushed red, and he pulled out his pipe, packed it, and lit it to keep his mind busy from his clear embarrassment.

"Not me!" Emilia exclaimed with a laugh.

"And," he continued, "I have brought back one of our mysterious cards, have I not?" he asked, hoping that we would see the service he had performed.

"You have, Maurice. You truly have helped us in your own *special* way," I joked. "Which card is it?"

"The Lover's card," Maurice said as Emilia and I exchanged a look and a giggle.

"Did you keep Isobel Gowdie company through choice or through the magic of the card?" Emilia asked from behind her rare smile.

"Through choice, I can assure you. She did not have in her possession the rest of the cards. Therefore, this card had no power over me," he said quite matter-of-factly.

"You are full of surprises, Maurice," I said with a tired laugh, before returning to the level of maturity I was expected to have.

"Let us just say that working with you on the collection of these cards is reminiscent of a time when I would chase after some obscure artefact alongside your grandfather George, tremendously exciting times."

"George?" queried Emilia.

"My grandfather. He owned the shop before me, raised me, befriended Maurice here, and recently passed away."

"He wasn't a Grimoire though, was he?" Emilia asked.

'He chose to live on the edge of both worlds rather than choosing one or the other. He loaned the grimoire to the Museum of Unnatural History, knowing no one could use it except for his bloodline, when and if the day would come that the Waywards step back on to the playing field and choose to roll the dice once again," Maurice finished.

"Learn something new every day," I mumbled to myself.

"There is more to that tale," Emilia offered, and as we looked on encouraging her to continue, she did with what I detected to be a hint of reluctance. "The Wayward grimoire was stolen from the Museum of Unnatural History."

"Word of this never reached my ears," Maurice blurted protectively as he was George's confidant and friend, if not a little out of it, especially as he did miss his dear friend's death and funeral being *indisposed* for many years. Whatever that means.

"The theft was not made public, from my understanding. The Court was worried that someone other than a Wayward was trying to unlock the family magic," Emilia explained.

"Can that happen with the book?" I asked.

"The book of shadows is just a record. The magic is only alive when the Grimoire physically accepts the written word," she revealed. "There was an investigation, but not long after it ended up on the black market south of the river and the Servants of the Night bought it, and I was instructed to offer it to you along with our deal."

"Who instructed you?"

"I'm sorry, Wayward, I cannot start revealing the Servants' identities to an outsider." Emilia showed just how trustworthy she was with those few words. Tension filled the room, and Maurice saw an opportunity to break the building atmosphere and took it.

"There is one last thing," Maurice blurted out.

"Yes?" I asked, sensing the change in his voice.

"I told her she can have ten per cent off from any Smoke and Mirrors purchase when she comes to see the new Wayward."

"The new Wayward?"

"You're somewhat of an attraction," Maurice said with pride.

"Fine. Always happy to welcome a new customer. Now let me catch you up, and I guess Emilia can fill you in on the bits where I was hiding, indisposed or both." With that, we sat down together and recounted our chase and battle with Kelley on Burgh Island. Most importantly, we told Maurice all about the Seals and how determined Kelley was to make sure that we knew as much about them as possible.

We told him nearly everything that we could since we had parted ways and went after different cards. After all the exciting moments of action, bravery, and arguable cowardliness, he focused on exactly the same lesson I apparently needed to learn. Emilia had already spoken of this, and his sense of caution was infectious in the caring way he spoke. "You must listen to reason in your use of magic." Maurice nodded to Emilia as he spoke. "You say that this Sebastian Dove is your Alchemist, yet he does not tend to your education in the mystical arts. This is most peculiar."

"He has shown me things, like the elements, but hasn't really taught me anything or shown me how to control my use of magic. If anything, he encouraged me to use my magic and experiment, but I've told Emilia all this."

"Then we are duty bound to inform the Court," Maurice said with a clear sense of duty.

"Is that necessary, Maurice? Shouldn't we try to reach out to Sebastian and give him the chance to explain why he has been neglecting his alchemy duties?" Emilia asked as if that were what she wanted. Even though I have no doubt that Emilia was inquiring for my best interests, I wanted to know what else she had on her mind.

"Why are you so keen to speak to him when the Court will find the truth for us?" Maurice followed up.

"I have a few other questions I would like to ask him, once we have found out what we can for you," Emilia said.

"Like what? The Pillars thing?"

"Yes the Pillars of the Blackened Earth are no joke and should, not be overlooked, especially by a Servant of the Night like myself. We are duty bound. I must find out if he truly is affiliated with them and their abuse of magic. I need to know what he is up to by interfering with the Servants" business."

"You mean what Kelley told us? Do you trust him?" I asked.

"He has no reason to lie. He may have been disagreeable, but lying to us would have served no purpose," Emilia said before Maurice stood up and spoke directly to me with his hands clasped together as if he were begging me.

"Do you have a mirror, a large one that I may use?"

"We are called Smoke and *Mirrors*. In the bathroom around the corner just before the bedroom," I replied and raised an eyebrow at Emilia as he walked off down the corridor. "So you're serious about me not using my magic?" I asked.

"I am very serious," Emilia said in what I considered to be her stern yet normal voice.

"You said it was the easy path towards becoming a Pillar like Sebastian."

"The Pillars are known for their greed in their use of magic and what they do with it. They desire power and control through their magic and nothing more. Unless someone else has more power and more magic, then they will challenge them, and that never turns out well, as I'm sure you can imagine. There aren't that many of them around any more. Most of them were locked up, killed, or sent into exile during the Ignorance of the Masses. In fact, it was because of them that the magical community now has to go to huge lengths to keep itself hidden from the world of man," she explained. "If Sebastian is a Pillar of the Blackened Earth, then he has become so under the guise of an Alchemist, an honoured role seeking magical knowledge for the betterment of our kind and helping Grimoires and youth Mages master their skill set *over time*. To do this under the Court's nose and that there could be others who are working with the Pillars that we don't know about is worrying, to say the least. Possibly a threat to all magical and non-magical beings alike," she emphasised the words 'over time' to make her point once again.

Just as she had finished explaining to me a little more about the Pillars and some more history of this magical world I had found thrust upon me, Maurice came back into the room and explained what he had been up to. "We have about an hour before we have to go. I've made an appointment to see one of the Archmages, and we will need to explain everything as clearly as we can."

"Where are we going?" I asked in my consistent state of perpetual ignorance. "Did you say Archmage?"

"Is this really necessary, Maurice? They could call in C.O.V.E.N., and that's the last thing we need," Emilia asked in a respectful tone.

"I believe it is. I also believe that we would be prudent to alert the Archmages and the Court of the Primoris Dedúcet in case anything happens to the three of us. You said it yourself, Emilia, that The Pillars of the Blackened Earth are no joke."

"The Court of what and who?" I asked.

"The Court of the Primoris Dedúcet. They are the watchful eye that keeps the magical people of the world in line and behaving in a manner befitting who we are and what we strive to be. They are the Court of the First Conduct. And they have expressed their interest in meeting the new Wayward as much as they have their interest in understanding your absent Alchemist," Maurice explained.

"When?"

"When I spoke to them a moment ago."

"Where?"

"In your bathroom mirror."

"You just spoke to the magical Court of peacekeepers about our merry band? Explaining what? That we will *pop* in to see them? And you did all this through my bathroom mirror?" I asked in astonishment.

"Yes," he said.

"You could have let me clean the mirror."

"It was sufficient."

I had to take a moment to process what was happening; it seemed that every couple of hours, I was finding out some new inconceivable truth and seeing people do things that strictly wasn't possible outside the world of comic books and films. Now Maurice was talking to an Archmage and making appointments through my bathroom mirror. My mind had made as much sense as it could of what it had just learnt, and an acceptance washed over me. "Can you teach me to talk to people in the mirror?"

"Only yourself," Emilia said with a cheeky smile creeping across her face. Magic humour; it was only a matter of time before I fell victim to its power and my mastery of sarcasm found a whole new depth.

CHAPTER TWENTY

N88

We left Smoke and Mirrors together and made our way to the bus stop down at the end of the road near Tesco and its illuminating glow that allowed us to see through some of the threatening shadows of the night. None of us wanted to drive, and the tube was going to close soon, so we had three choices: one was to walk the whole way, but with tiredness nearly consuming us all, that was out; two was a taxi that would no doubt cost me so much money I would have to remortgage the shop, and three was to get the night bus, then tube, then night bus again and walk a few streets over to our final destination when we were in Central London. The night bus option won out, hands down.

It was dry outside, but the night sky was creeping in fast. The stars were out, and it was nice to get the London air back in my lungs, or at least whatever small percentage of the air in London was actually air. We had taken the first night bus and gotten the tube in zombie mode. We weren't waiting long before the second night bus turned up; it was the N88 that never failed to have one member of the public that either looked suicidal or homicidal. We were willing to take our chances, as we needed to get to the Museum of Unnatural History over by South Kensington Tube station, which would have been easier if we weren't travelling by night and didn't fancy bumping into the drunken public. At first, I heard Maurice say we were going to the Museum of Unnatural History and just accepted it, but now it had finally caught up with me. As the three of us made our way up the steps to the top deck and down the aisle to the back seats like naughty hooded school kids with blaring offensive Walkmans and some horrendous need to spit everywhere to mark territory, I decided to get some clarification.

"So we're going to the Natural History Museum?"

"Nope, we are going to the Museum of Unnatural History. It's a completely different place," replied Maurice with an undeniable excitement in his voice.

"The Museum of *Unnatural* History?" I questioned and then answered myself. "So is this like the normal museum but for magic and stuff?"

"You're not as dumb as you look, Wayward," Emilia chimed in with that smile still sitting pretty.

Maurice blurted out what the museum was because he was just so excited. "When the Court of the Primoris Dedúcet was first formed to exact their *conduct* on the Mages, Alchemists, and Grimoires of the world, it was decided that they would have a place to centre their efforts within each populace or city. There is another museum, almost twice the size, underneath the Natural History Museum, which houses the Archmages and the Court of the Primoris Dedúcet along with all our collected histories of magic and sorcery. This is why the Alchemists study here and liaise to all within the magical communities on the training and development of any new Mages or Grimoires, which doesn't happen as often as you'd think."

"So the Museum of Unnatural History is built under the Natural History Museum?" I asked.

"Nope, the Natural History Museum was built on top of the Museum of Unnatural History, which is built into the ground. Essentially, the Natural History Museum was a cover, literally, for the Museum of Unnatural History. But over time, it has appeared to be popular and has flourished, making it the perfect cover for our own needs." Maurice was racing onwards with his explanation as his excitement exuded from every fibre of his being.

"OK," I accepted. "So I'm going to just nod and pretend that everything you just said to me seemed normal, yet mildly absurd, but still within the realms of normality."

Emilia let out a giggle much unlike her nature that I had seen up until then; perhaps I had misjudged her, and now I was seeing her real side as her guard came down a little. She snapped me out of my mini daydream and brought me back into the conversation by asking Maurice a question I should have been asking myself. "How shall we present Wayward to the Archmage?"

"Present me?" I smoothed my waistcoat down, suddenly aware of my imminent presentation.

"You will be standing before an Archmage, and you will be questioned on your lineage and reason for taking on your ancestors' Grimoire," Maurice stated.

"It was an accident!"

"I wouldn't start with that," Emilia advised. "He'll want to know more about the tarot cards and why I hired you."

"Why did you hire me? I'm sure there were others who you could have coerced into finding the cards?" I asked, remembering I had never really put Emilia on the spot about why I was hunting down these cards for her and who gave her instructions. Yes, it was a job, and yes, I had been quite distracted by all the magic and family history that had gotten in the way, but that shouldn't have blinded me to the fact that before Emilia walked in through my door, all soaked in rain and looking more beautiful than a goddess at a health spa, I was just meandering unaware through my life in a harmless enough way.

"I told you when I met you that this would not be a clear-cut case. That you were either in or out, and you didn't seem to have a problem with it then," Emilia said almost defensively as the night bus wheeled around a corner and the glare from the street lamps oozed in through the windows of the top deck.

"Why do you want the cards so badly, Emilia?" I asked.

"I can't tell you." She looked at me and then at Maurice and could see that she was putting a clear wedge between the three of us by not offering what she knew. "I'm sorry. I would tell you if I could, but . . ." We sat there for what seemed like a long time as the street lamps zipped by illuminating the bus in their false promise of light and warmth, then Emilia spoke up again. "You need to know how the cards work, don't you? Before going in front of the Archmage, you will need to know what they can do." A smile crept on her face. "Try one on me. I'll show you I can still be trusted." I exchanged a look with Maurice, which could have said any number of things, then I went for it.

"OK. But I get to choose the card, and you have to play along," I said.

"Fine."

"And if you think I'm going to stop asking why you want these cards, you are very much mistaken."

"Fine."

"Well, OK then." I turned to Maurice and pulled out the A.K.T. box, opening it carefully and lifting out the cards that we had. For the first time, I could see that we had gathered nearly all the cards. I lifted them out and thumbed through them to search the pack, looking for the one I wanted to *test* on Emilia.

It was a no-brainer. I had to choose a card that would make Emilia act in a way that she wouldn't normally, and I would need to see her take it to an extreme to prove they work, and her loyalty to us. I slipped the card from the deck without letting Emilia see it and held it out. I could sense Maurice looking at me with a disapproving eye, but he wanted to see just how far Emilia was willing to go to prove herself an ally. I was assuming that lone Mages and Grimoires didn't often start forming teams, especially when one of them had sworn loyalties to her own cult or club or whatever the Servants of the Night were. She slid the card from my fingers and placed it in her pocket without even looking at it. That was very much Emilia's behaviour, trying to show that she was brave enough to face whatever challenge stood in front of her, without flinching. The deck of cards in my other hand pulsed with a warmth for a few seconds and then reverted back to just being a pack of tarot cards. Nothing happened.

"Should we be doing something? Should I say something?" I asked Maurice as we were just sitting on the back seat of the bus. I turned to Emilia to see if she felt like she was in control and met her eyes staring right back into mine. Seeing her that close was a spectacle as the emerald spiral flecks of her eyes were limitless. I could have searched for days and still not have seen all the beauty there was on offer. "How are you feeling?" I asked in the split second before I felt something on my leg. Looking down, I saw Emilia's hand sitting on my knee, and I swallowed one large gulp, realising I was well in over my head.

"Jon?" Emilia asked to get my attention back to her eyes.

"Yes?"

"I never did thank you for saving my life earlier." She sounded completely in control, except for the fact that she was clearly flirting with me and that meant I knew she was not in control.

"Did I?"

"Oh yes," she said, sliding ever so slightly further up to me on the seat. "Without you I would be nothing, less than nothing." And with that, she leaned in and kissed me. I would like to tell you that I held her back, took the card from her, and explained everything that had happened whilst she was in possession of the tarot card, but I would be lying. Her lips met mine, and I was nowhere near stopping her. Her hand lifted to the back of my neck as she continued to kiss me with those incredibly soft lips, and I could swear that I heard someone telling me off in the back of mind, maybe it was my subconscious. The voices were shouting about *being responsible* and *spells wearing off*, but at that moment, I was in a very happy place, finally allowing myself to admit that I had wanted to do this since the first moment

I had seen her walk through my shop door soaked to the bone and needing my help.

Something hit the roof of the night bus with an almighty thud, breaking me away from my stolen kiss. I turned and could see that Maurice was standing in the aisle, where he had been telling me off, looking up at the roof which had been indented by whatever had landed on it. I stood up instinctually to face whatever had hit the metal and was pulled back down by Emilia. "Where are you going?" she asked as she was still pursing her lips to try to kiss me. As tempting as it was, I knew we had other matters to deal with. I reached down into Emilia's pocket and snatched out the lover's tarot card, placing it back into the deck in my other hand and sealing them away in the A.K.T. box. As I'm sure you can imagine, Emilia wasn't best pleased with me, but luckily, she was taken aback by our kiss and sat dumbfounded for a moment, no doubt planning how to make me pay for kissing her under the influence of magic or some such thing.

Another thud and crumple of metal hit above our heads, and all three of us were now trained in on the dented metal canopy above our heads, my momentary lack of self-control forgotten for a few minutes.

"What in the name of Merlin was that?" asked Maurice with all the seriousness of a man about to be attacked.

As a contrast, I dropped my guard, turned to Maurice, and asked him a question that I knew could not wait a single moment longer. "Did you really just say "in the name of Merlin?""

"Yes," Maurice replied without taking his eyes from the roof of the bus. "Merlin is a Grimoire of the first order, and if anyone could protect you, then it would be him." Instead of a thud and crunch of metal, we heard the piercing tear of thin metal, leaving three lines of darkness in the metallic cover above our heads. Whatever it was, it had claws, and it wanted to say hello.

CHAPTER TWENTY-ONE

Ride of Your Life

"We have to get to the Museum!" Emilia shouted at us, making sure we had our priorities in order. "You two stay alive! I'll be back in a second!" she added, not giving us a choice. She darted down the aisle to the stairs at the front of the bus, leading to the seating level below the driver and the way out.

"Where are you going?" I shouted after Emilia as she disappeared down the stairs from the top deck. I took a step to follow, but above my head, a complete panel of the metal roof tore open with a scream of twisting steel and sparks that not only tore open the night bus's roof but also found its way into my nerves. Eyes peered in from the darkness – eyes I had seen before that had wanted to do me harm, the eyes of a monster, the eyes of a Lamiac. "Maurice? What do we do?" I asked, wanting to use my magic, but then remembered the warning that both of my would-be accomplices had given me and ignoring the brief teachings of my supposed sometime Alchemist. I knew that I should show restraint unless I fell victim to my own magical greed and desire. *But is my restriction of magic worth my life?*

"We stand our ground," Maurice said, stepping out into the aisle and placing himself on the other side of the hole ripped into the roof.

"Hello?" I called up to the monster-made hole. "Lizard creature? Are you out there? I just wanted to apologise for your friend. Just so you know, he tried to kill me. So what happened, happened in self-defence." There was no reply unless you count the guttural snarling of the Lamiac on the roof. I was about to try to keep talking in my incredible scared and nervous state, which is what I do best, but the Lamiac lowered its head through the hole with its yellow eyes flickering around the upper deck until they found me. They stopped and bore two slits through my soul, and any hint of confidence I may once have had against the Lamiac trickled away.

Just at that moment, the N88 night bus swung around a corner, and I had to grab on to one of the seats in front of me. Maurice had to steady himself with one of the seats next to him. With everything that was happening, I hadn't noticed that the bus was speeding up, and I couldn't help but think, *Why has Emilia abandoned us now?* The night bus swung around another corner at its increased speed, and we both had to grab on to the seating on the other side of the aisle. The Lamiac dangled, and as the night bus straightened out, it dropped to the floor. Its feet spread and knees bent as it sat on its haunches, waiting to pounce, with its eyes still glued to my own. "Do you understand me? Your friend seemed to be able to talk?" I asked the monster, wondering if reasoning with the creature may be more effective than last time. I caught a glimpse of Maurice who stared at the back of the Lamiac's head, ready to release whatever magic he could to save my life should it attack, hopefully.

"Brother," It hissed through bile and saliva.

"I'm sorry?" I asked, hoping to open the lines of communication further.

"Not friend . . . brother," It spat out, still without blinking.

"The other one was your brother?" I asked with incredible feelings of guilt swooping over me and my face turning red and warm. I was trying to fight the urge to feel guilty as I had only acted in self-defence, and yes, maybe I could have found another outcome, but it was actively trying to kill me. My stomach hollowed within a second and then twisted in on itself. "I am sorry that it happened that way, but he left me no choice." I decided that I could use this to my advantage. "But that's what happens when you threaten a Wayward." I raised my voice to sound in control and show that I knew what I was doing. I gave Maurice a wink to try to let him in on my plan. "Are you going to make the same mistake as your brother? Because he came at me all on his own, and look what happened to him." By this point, I almost believed my own hype, until I looked to see Maurice looking at me in astonishment, and not the good kind. His look asked a simple question: *How could anyone be so stupid and still be alive?*

"What makes you . . ." It coughed and spluttered its vile saliva on to the floor that instantly became discoloured and strained.

"Come on, handsome, spit it out," I said now I had it tripping over its own words.

". . . think I am alone?" Those last four words came out as perfectly as I had ever heard one of these creatures speak.

Both Maurice and I turned to look at the windows on either side of the bus. As we did, the Lamiac in front of us let out a scream that only a nightmarish reptile monster creature could, scurrying claws on metal and black scaled arms and legs with red flecks padded on the windows and roof, overcoming all my senses building in speed and sound, then they all stopped as if the night was taking in a breath of calm before the chaos started.

The night whipped past in flashes of street lamps and buildings gliding by the windows at an increasingly fast speed. Emilia crept back up from the stairs leading down to the lower level of the bus, and her silent movements meant that neither the Lamiac in front of me nor Maurice knew she was there. Sensing that a potentially horrendous battle was about to begin, I tried to buy some more time before allowing any biting to ruin my day. "Why are you doing this?" I asked.

"Murdering my brother is not reason enough?" It hissed and cracked.

"There must be more to it. You could have jumped me at any time and torn me in two," I said, snatching a quick glance over the monster's shoulder to see Maurice and Emilia looking through the windows and up at the hole in the roof.

"My master wills it," It said, forcing my attention back to its shards of broken teeth and haunting yellow eyes. I wasn't sure if I was reading its expression right, as I found it hard to look at its face directly, but I thought I could see it smiling. "He wants you." Its face tightened, and its eyes grew wider with the mouth resembling a maw of shards offering a horrible and painful death. I knew that now it was definitely smiling. "He wants you alive.'

"Alive?"

Typically as I was about to get an answer and find a piece of the puzzle that I desperately needed, a louder thud than before hit the canopy of the night bus followed by the multiple Lamiac on the roof, scuttling around the metal shell above. We all looked up, including the Lamiac in front of me, surprised at the sound and the movement of the other monsters who were poised and ready to attack us. There was a shimmer of metal being drawn cleanly, unlike the tearing of the roof above us, and then a war cry that sounded human, much like I imagine my own would if I was in a position to try it. This was then drowned out by multiple screams of the Lamiac taking its place as the new most terrifying sound in history.

The screaming kept decreasing and the heroic war cry kept increasing. It finished in an almighty crash with metal screeching through metal and the point of what I could only guess to be a huge blade now piercing the panel above Maurice's head. Our eyes darted to the tip of the sword which stayed momentarily still for a moment as we saw the black gloopy blood of the Lamiac drip from the fuller groove of its point. After a moment of staring at the protruding blade, it whipped back up through the roof, leaving us all to look at each other in confusion. I was hoping someone was about to take credit for the new player in this merry little game, but everyone had the same expression on their face, an expression that said, *Who the hell is attacking the night bus?*

The Lamiac looked at me and then I looked at it. I could see Emilia and Maurice refocusing on the monster about to make its move. Another set of street lights whipped past, illuminating the top floor of the night bus and showing us that the windows were now streaked with the glutinous black blood of the Lamiacs who were waiting to attack. The remaining Lamiac in front of me realised that it was now alone and had to make a move. Its eyes widened, and its muscles tensed as it lowered itself to pounce from its crouched position; time itself seemed to slow as I turned and aimed to throw myself into the corner of the back seat where it would be harder to bite, rip, or tear at my delicate and well-kept flesh. Maurice and Emilia mirrored each other by coincidence and called upon an elemental flame, much like Kelley's weapon of choice, expanding in their hands to increase the diameter of the fiery death they were to unleash on the monster to save my life.

They were beaten to it. The rear window behind my head exploded and threw shattered glass in every direction. A shadow flew over me as I hit the side panel of the bus to take cover. I shrugged off the pain as best as I could and rounded myself to see what insanely destructive magic one of my compatriots was using to explode the night bus around us, but it wasn't them. A stranger stood before me with a sword raised, covered in black blood. He had shoulder-length blond hair stuck to his face and neck, and what was most striking about this man was that he wore a dark blue suit and a white shirt with a thin black tie, and both the suit and shirtsleeves were rolled up above his elbows along with random tattoos and an unkempt beard. A bizarre look, but I had a feeling he could pull off just about any look. An untimely jealous thought, as I could be killed at any moment by either the hissing Lamiac or the sword-wielding stranger.

"Wayward?" the stranger asked in the direction of the Lamiac, Maurice, and Emilia. They all just continued to look in surprise.

"Here I am," I called, pulling myself up from the back seats and peering over. The stranger turned only his head and kept his body poised and ready, facing the Lamiac. He had the eyes of a . . . a . . . I don't know what, they seemed to be golden like a burst sun tinged with red. I didn't even know that was an eye colour that humans could have. Well, *he* did, and all I can say is they made an impression. He flashed a cocksure smile and whirled back to the others. He spoke clearly and demanded answers. "Which of you fight on the side of Wayward?" he asked, his eyes passing over all three who were before him.

"I do," Maurice said, still holding his fireball.

"Me too," said Emilia, still holding hers. The stranger looked to the Lamiac and began to speak. "You dare attack a Grimoire? You beast of darkness. You filth, you monster. You shall pay with your life!" the Lamiac shrieked as it jumped back, pushing its hand out in front of it to block the stranger's upstroke of his sword. The monster screamed so loudly the rest of the windows in the top deck of the night bus shattered, and I opened my eyes. Once the noise had dissipated, I saw it holding its clawed hand in the air, minus its forefinger and middle finger, accompanied by an open gash across its face from its right eye to its left cheek.

It used all its force to push itself from where it sat, through the hole in the roof it had created earlier, to land back on the night bus's roof. It peered down to the stranger and spoke in a voice that carried more pain and suffering than usual. "My master will not forgive such insults."

"Tell me his name, and I will apologise in person," the stranger said, and for the first time, I noticed he had a hint of Scandinavian to his accent.

The creature attempted a laugh but was in too much pain and, therefore, merely coughed up some more of its vile-smelling black ooze. "I won't give you his name." The bus rounded another corner, and I was reminded of the speed we were travelling at. "But he will have yours, Helsing!" the creature shouted as it threw itself from the roof of the bus and down into the shadows of the London streets.

Silence took over from the heat of the battle, and we all just stood for a moment. When someone did finally move, it was no surprise to me that it was the stranger. He turned to me and took out a white handkerchief from his pocket to wipe the black blood from his sword rather than his face. When he was done, he sheathed it in its scabbard by his hip. I couldn't help noticing the hilt, which was designed with a dragon swept from the cross guard to extend into the hilt. He held out his hand after letting the sword rest against his side and spoke to me directly. "Wayward, may I offer my assistance?" I nodded and took his hand. Standing next to him was a good feeling, especially since he had just saved all our lives. "May we sit and exchange tales of adventure until we reach our destination?"

"Our destination?" Emilia asked sharply.

"The Museum of Unnatural History. We are expected," he replied.

"We are expected? When did we become *we*?" Emilia asked, gesturing to all of us.

"Since I was sent to make sure you arrived safely to the Archmage."

"And who exactly are you? You could be anybody. Why should we trust you?" Emilia accused.

It was Maurice who answered her, but by addressing all of us. "This is Ludolf Van Helsing, the great-great-great-grandson of Abraham Van Helsing and the current Grimoire of the Helsing bloodline." We all sat in silence for a moment, either taking in that small piece of information or stunned by it. Emilia looked a little embarrassed that she didn't know who he was and that she probably should have done.

Naturally, it was I who broke it. "Van Helsing?"

"Just Helsing, please."

"OK, Helsing," I confirmed. "Can I ask you a question?"

"Of course, I was excited to come and introduce myself to the new Wayward Grimoire and discuss all manner of intricacies," he said with a big smile parting his rugged beard.

"Was Dracula real?"

"Seriously?" he asked with his increasingly pronounced Dutch accent creeping through.

Chapter Twenty-Two

Museum of Unnatural History

We had all taken a seat on one or two of the back rows on the N88 night bus and introduced ourselves to Helsing as the night air whipped past us through the multiple gaping shadows now torn into the night bus's frame. As we talked, I don't think any of us was aware of how much damage and destruction was lying around us. We had more important issues to deal with, one of which was that Abraham Van Helsing's descendant was sitting right across from me after fighting for my life. Literally *for my life*, as I was face down behind a seat. Now, I was sitting on that seat and asking him questions. I don't think he noticed, but I was a little awestruck. I mean, I had loved Dracula movies ever since I was a kid. In fact, I can remember my grandfather reading Bram Stoker's *Dracula* to me, and I loved it. Except for the chapter about all the shipping manifests, that was a tiny bit boring, but it was just a book, wasn't it? "So the book?" I asked timidly.

"Yes." Helsing nodded.

"That wasn't . . ." I trailed off and looked at Maurice who had once again adapted that look of *Are you really this stupid and I'm* just *noticing?* Emilia's look wasn't much different, but luckily for me, I think they were too stunned by my line of questioning to stop me.

"Factual?" Helsing finished for me.

"Yeah. I mean, you know, did your great-great-great-granddaddy really face off with the prince of darkness?"

"He did," he answered as coolly as anyone could have.

"So the book—" I said before being cut off, which he did whilst still keeping his smile beaming out from beneath his beard.

"Is partly true. Leaked information and guesswork. Stoker was an Alchemist in Ireland. Not exactly very high up the ladder. He enjoyed his drink a little too much. Got ahead of himself with some information he wasn't supposed to be privy to and wrote a *fictional* novel based on fact. The Court found out what he had done, too late to stop it going to print, so they exiled him and took away his magical knowledge, banishing him to the world of man for the rest of his days." Helsing told the tale as though it was gossip about a co-worker back at the office.

"Vampires are real?" I asked.

"Of course. You find that so hard to believe after being attacked by a lounge of lizards?"

"We're on a bus."

"Yes."

"Don't you mean a bus of lizards? Or even a night bus of lizards?"

"No. A group or gathering of lizards is called a lounge of lizards," Helsing insisted.

"What about a group or gathering of Lamiacs?" I asked. Helsing took a moment to gauge me and check that I wasn't trying to make fun, and after making up his mind, he slapped his thigh and laughed out loud. Typically, he had one of those laughs that made you want to laugh with him, and within a few seconds, I found myself joining him. "You are funny, Wayward. I like that. I think we can be friends."

"I think so too," I said as I was a step away from being ecstatic, completely forgetting where we were going and what we were supposed to be discussing, something which Emilia had no trouble in reminding us all of.

"Helsing, how did you find us? And why are you here?" She put to him without any of the grace I knew she had.

"I think what Emilia is trying to say is *thank you* for saving our lives and how we can help," I added, which I knew would annoy her but bring a smile to my new friend.

"This is not a problem. I am here to serve and escort, so please let me explain my presence. I hunt a vampire nest in your Brixton, south of the river, and was relaying my findings and actions to your Halls of Knowledge when your Archmage asked if I could bring you back to them alive," Helsing offered with his friendly English second language.

"What are the Halls of Knowledge?" I asked.

"The Halls are a tuning fork for all magical happenings across all the Courts of the world. Your name has been in constant use since you took your family's magic," Maurice piped up.

"I have been in this land for sometime and was studying at your Court when the Wayward name was once again echoed in the Halls of Knowledge.

I wanted to introduce myself to the new Grimoire and share the war stories of our ancestors." Helsing seemed to constantly have that big smile stretched under his beard.

"How are we . . ." Maurice began to stand asking a question that we had taken for granted.

"Still moving?" Emilia finished with a hint of pride in her voice. Secretly, I thought that she had been waiting for someone to ask so she could explain how we were, in fact, still moving. "When the Lamiac first burst in through the ceiling, I ran downstairs."

"Escaped downstairs," I offered, half joking, half serious.

"Ran downstairs," she corrected. "I was making my way to the driver to make sure he wasn't going to stop when we started tearing the top deck into pieces, which we inevitably did."

"I didn't," Maurice objected, offended by the idea that he could possibly be a part of anything that would cause such destruction. Emilia put his mind at rest. "Fine. *We* inevitably did," she said, gesturing to Helsing, herself, and me.

"Will your driver keep driving?" Helsing asked.

"He will take us directly to the Museum of Unnatural History, which is only a few streets away from what I can tell," Emilia informed us, and she peered into the streets below.

Helsing stood to meet the half-standing Maurice, who had become a little self-conscious and nervous around him. "Then we must prepare to vacate this transport, send it on its way, get into the Museum of Unnatural History and then we can discuss matters further when you are safer," he said the last part to me, which was just another reminder that I was a giant target.

We began making our way across the top deck and down the stairs to wait by the night bus's door. I held Helsing's arm to slow him so I could ask him a question quietly that I had been trying to answer myself. "Helsing, what is a Grimoire? To you, I mean. What does being a Grimoire mean to you?"

"A Grimoire is . . ." he paused for a moment's thought to find the right words, rather than the right answer. I had no doubt he knew deep down to the core of his existence what being a Grimoire meant to him. "It is a birthright that so few are even aware of." The others disappeared into the seats below, and his voice lowered as we stopped by the driver, and he spoke directly to me. The others were listening but knew that their role in this topic was and would always be second to another Grimoire. "An honour, which I am duty bound to uphold and maintain, so that when my time comes to pass on the title and knowledge that comes with it, I know I will have left my family name in a better place than when I found it. Not just for the Helsings but also for those in the magical community that we help and protect. Our power may restrict us from being a member of the Courts, but that doesn't mean we have been cast out. It means that the Courts are allowed to govern over us all, over the world because we protect them and act for them when called upon." The pride in his voice told me more than the words he spoke.

"We can't be members of the Court?" I asked.

"You really know nothing, do you, Wayward?"

"Not really, but I'm a fast learner," I said as the night bus slowed to a stop. The bus's doors opened with a crunch, and as I stepped out, I looked back to make sure that everyone was coming. Emilia stopped and pulled her hand down over the bus driver's eyes as she whispered a few words in his ear. The closeness of her lips to his ear as she whispered gave me a flash of guilt. My mind was bombarded with images and sensations from the stolen kiss I had taken from Emilia. I knew we were going to have to talk about that, but I was hoping it wouldn't be for a while. Snapping me from my train of shameful thoughts was Helsing answering my question.

"Grimoires are not allowed in a position of influence or political power within any of the Courts of this world, due to their amassed knowledge and use of magical power." Then in a hushed voice, more for dramatic effect than anything else, he continued. "It is feared that they would be able to assume control over the entire Court and rule without anyone able to stand against them should they use their position for personal gain." We stepped from the night bus and heard it drive off.

"Has any Grimoire had a place in the Court before?" I asked.

"There have occasionally been those who have risen to the role of council to the Archmage's, but most Grimoires choose to work out in the field." He turned to look up at the columns and the stonewalls with the words 'Museum of Natural History' carved into the stone block above the door. "We have arrived, lady and gentlemen. Shall we?" he said, gesturing with his hand out to guide us to the huge wooden doors that stood before us.

"Is it open?" I asked.

"The Court of the Primoris Dedúcet never sleeps," Emilia offered as a comfort to anyone who was listening, but it sounded more like a threat. She took the first step, and we moved to the doors and stood next to them. I followed Emilia's lead and stood with my face no more than two inches away from the door. It was a little close, but I had learned by now to follow their lead in times like these. Emilia spoke to me without turning her head and in hushed tones, with the goal of not trying to embarrass me. "We will say the words together. '*Scientiam doce me si virtus*'. It means 'If knowledge is power, then teach me.'"

"OK," I said, running the Latin phrase over in my head as much as I possibly could. Within a few seconds of Maurice admiring the architecture of the building, he and Helsing were standing by us, and there was a momentary pause. I took in a breath to calm myself and found that the others had also taken in a breath and that we were breathing in simpatico. Before I had even made a conscious decision to do anything, I realised I was saying the words with the others. "*Scientiam doce me si virtus.*"

Now that I was aware I was chanting these words with my companions, I knew I couldn't stop, not that I wanted to, but even if I did, I would have had to fight the connection or bond or whatever you would call it, and I didn't want to, as it felt good. Our breathing had fallen into a synchronised pattern, and from nowhere, the left foot of all of us were up in the air, toes pointing at the large wooden door before us. Now leaning forward, we began to drop towards the door, potentially about to break our faces into the solid oak, but once again, something amazing happened. Our bodies, starting with our pointed feet, slid through the door with no more effort than pushing through water. The sensation left a tingle, depending on which body part was passing through the door, but once we were on the other side, I felt amazing, fresh, and alert as if I had passed through a body of water. Helsing was the first to let go of each of our hands and moved a few steps in front. I went to move next to him, but Maurice placed his hand on my shoulder and nodded for me to look at what Helsing was doing.

After drawing out a piece of chalk from his pocket, he knelt in front of a statue that was enclosed in what looked like a glass cage. The statue was of a woman who held her hands out to either side of her as claws helping her to scream her cry of fury further than the stone allowed. Her face was contorted with hatred and rage; even as a statue, she embodied everything about magic. I wanted to stay away from her because she scared me. For some reason, everything about her made me feel uncomfortable, almost as if I were standing on a cliff edge, looking over into an abyss I knew I could not survive. Maurice leant in over my shoulder, after seeing my gaze drawn to the glass-enclosed statue and whispered her name to me. "She's known as The Talon." But before he could say anything further, we were distracted by Helsing at the marble floor, who drew a circle, whilst rolling up his sleeves to keep them out of the way once again, adding symbols that I looked at and could see some similarities between those and the ones tattooed across my flesh. Somewhere Demotic, meaning that this was as old as the Egyptians, others were the criss-crossing lines of Druidic Ogham. As I looked at them, I could feel an ache in my mind, like a headache, but somehow sharper and with the effect of piercing needles being placed right in-between my eyes. I struck my gaze in a different direction, and instantly, the pain in my mind subsided. Emilia and Maurice were both looking at me with concern, which was new; usually, they took it in turns, and whilst one had the look of concern, the other usually had a look of desperation and disbelief.

"Wayward, your nose," Emilia said.

I couldn't feel anything, but out of reflex, I raised my fingers to my nostrils and felt her concern running to my lips. Pulling them away, they were dripping with red, which ran down the inside of my palm. I looked up to both of them and spoke. "I'm fine, honestly. It was just a headache."

"You're not fine, Wayward, you need to give your magic a rest," Emilia told me with a nodding agreement from Maurice.

"Helsing is finishing up. The sooner we speak to the Archmages the better, in my opinion," Maurice added.

"It's impressive how your opinion never changes," Emilia whipped back as was her way.

My tiredness was wearing me down, and I turned, seeing Helsing standing up from his detailed chalk pentagram with the Alchemist symbols for each of the elements drawn into their respective points of the symbols with all the wavy lines in the right place. Around each rune was even further sharp-edged little letters and words in Latin with symbolic shapes to deliver magical meanings of all sorts, a lot beyond my current knowledge. As my eyes floated over them, my mind fought back, and it felt as though a hot knife was being thrust into my forehead and slowly twisted. I dropped to my knees and not by choice. This time I could feel my nose run with a line of blood. The room blurred in my vision, and I could hear myself screaming and the others around me all shouting and crying my name. It sounded as if they were calling to me from the other end of a tunnel, long and stretched out into the distant. I wanted to talk to them, ask them for help. The common phrase '*head splitting in two*' came to whatever part of my mind I had left, and weakness flooded every cell within my body. Then the world started to black out around me, and I fell on to the hard marble floor, regardless of Emilia's arms holding on to me.

My face was at the tip of the water rune of the chalk pentagram, and that was when I could see the floor cracking in the shape of the giant five-pointed star. It split and began to grind down into the ground with dust dancing in the air in front of my eyes. Each rune glowed with a white light as the floor descended and left in its place a staircase leading down below. Before I lost consciousness through the pain that was tearing my mind in two, I thought of the staircase back home, leading up to my bedroom and, most importantly, my bed, which I missed so very, very much. And with a turn of my head, I saw the statue once again; it was in so much pain. This Talon's image found its way into my mind, and somehow it knew exactly where to find my fear and panic centres. I passed into the world of nightmares and premonitions, a place I was not exactly fond of but was becoming uncomfortably familiar with, and I knew I was about to see the man in the hood who had stalked me through my dreams.

CHAPTER TWENTY-THREE

I Had a Dream

Standing on the top of a mountainous peak offered jagged rocks as far as the edge and then nothing. A drop into the abyss, beyond the natural order of the world where sheer chaos lives in wait. Standing there surrounded by the night sky, I could feel the chill in the air slide over my clothes, trying to find a way in past my waistcoat and around the collar of my shirt flapping my trouser legs back and forth. The moon strode across the sky, and the clouds tailed it as if the night's canvas were playing in fast-forward. Within a few moments, I had seen the night sky turn into day with the sun tearing into the darkness and illuminating the entire mountaintop. Then the dirty snow began falling through the light again.

Beneath my feet, a rumbling turned into a full-fledged earthquake, and the rocks beneath me broke and broke and broke, creating a million smaller fragments of rock all fighting to get to the bottom of the pile. I jumped into the air and whispered, "werna-IHduth-nihn-gohrd-SOLyeh" as I was pulled up by my invisible wings of magic holding me as they beat the wind to keep me above the gaping maw burrowing into the mountain down from where I stood to who knows where. With each beat of my wings, the dirty snow raced around and over me. From within the mountain, I could hear clapping coming from the bottom, echoing up and spilling out over the top. An isolated noise bouncing from the sides of the tunnel and out through the top, just one clap, but after it had reached the top and echoed from my ears, a hundred more were seconds behind, bouncing faster and ricocheting off each other, fighting to climb out of the top of the tunnel and be the first to make it into the light.

I stared down deep into the bottom of the abyss, squinting my eyes to try to help me to see what was coming up. The thousands of clapping sounds merged to make a wave, and within that, something was coming, something was climbing its way out from within that mountain and coming for me.

Silence fell over the entire mountain, and the clapping froze. A shape appeared in the darkness that I had seen time and time again and always ran ice water into my veins. It was the hooded man who seemed to be floating up to me through the darkness, and his hand slowly stretched out to reach for me even though he was a long way off. The silence rippled as he spoke for the first time, and I replayed his whispered words in my mind, unbelieving that he had spoken at all. He said, "Ελα μαζί μου για να βρείτε τον εαυτό σας" in Greek, which was babble to me at first, then the cogs fell into synchronisation with each other in my mind, and I knew exactly what he meant. His foreign words meant, "Join me to find yourself". The snow kept falling, and as it covered my face again, I tasted its gritted texture and realised that it wasn't snow at all; it was ash.

A white flash. A dove flew out of the cave as pristine as a dinner napkin at a high society ball. Its wings clapping into each other above and below its body, it flew up to me above the cave and circled for the moment it took for the wave of sound to become a physical push. A hundred, thousand doves shot from the hollow mouth of the abyss, and all came at me within a heartbeat, surrounding me, engulfing me, consuming me, and leaving no light to shine in-between their wings. There were so many that they blocked the living world out; they had devoured me, and there was no way out, so I did all I could and screamed as loud as my lungs would let me. No words or names, just a scream filled with complete terror in the face of absolute death. Nothing but white wings and the shadow of a face from within a hood.

I peeled my eyes open and blinked slowly a few times to allow my eyes to adjust to the low light in the room I was in. People were talking, and I could hear Emilia and Maurice speaking to one another; they seemed to be having a heated debate. I had no idea what they were talking about, but I could hear my name being bandied about as though they had plans for me. I'm sure I would have been a bit more interested in these plans once I had full control over my body and was capable of standing, listening, and talking all at the same time. But I'll be the first to admit I've never been good with hangovers, especially ones that are fuelled by magic and fighting monster lizard people employed by a secret evil genius.

I saw the blurs of people moving towards me now saying my name in what sounded like a sympathetic tone. This I assumed was Maurice, mainly because we had company, and Emilia didn't do well at showing emotions, especially sympathy, in front of more than one person at a time. That included people who had spelled her into a kiss to prove her loyalty to the team. "What's happening?" I asked groggily.

"You overwhelmed yourself with exorbitant demonstrations of magic. With your lack of training, physically and mentally, you are fortunate not to be a Void." This stranger's voice sounded full of authority and reminded me of my English teacher that I had at school, straight to the point with minimum nonsense, condescending enough to know I had been an idiot and not to argue back. He held out a glass with some light blue liquid in, smoke pouring over the top, and he lifted it in front of my face. "Drink this, m'boy, and you'll be up and causing more mischief and mayhem in no time." I would say that I *let* him put the glass to my mouth before he started to tip it into my mouth, but then I would be lying. I had no way of stopping him from doing anything to me in the state I was in, so I just followed his lead. Maurice and Emilia were there, and I was hoping that they wouldn't let anything horrible happen to me. The liquid felt smooth and velvety as it passed my tongue and hit the back of my throat. It was creamy with a taste that I couldn't pin down, and I could feel the coldness of its texture coating wherever it touched. By the time it had found its way to my stomach, it had left a path of its cool nectar, like I had just downed a pint of Sambuca and the cold air was hitting the wakeful path. I was already starting to open my eyes fully, and the blurred vision that had limited my ability to see who was with me was fading. 'How does that do ya?' he said, taking the glass away from my lips with only a dribble left in the bottom of the glass. 'Good?'

'Better,' I said before I realised that I was able to speak now as well as see the man before me. He smiled at my progress as I fell back into the world of the living, showing small gaps between his teeth, surrounded by a neatly trimmed ginger beard, small dark eyes, and a side parting. Not only did he sound like a teacher but also dressed like one. He was wearing a well-fitted tweed suit with brown moccasins and looked like he could be incredibly devious or incredibly charming. I was hoping the latter would prove to be more accurate.

"Glad to see you coming back to us, Mr Wayward," he said in his clear and direct tone.

"Thank you," I said, not quite being able to believe that as the cool glow in my throat and stomach faded, my energy and constitution returned.

"How are you feeling, Mr Wayward?" he asked as he pulled out a brown pipe from his suit jacket pocket, only adding to the image of him being an old school master. He pinched some tobacco from his other suit jacket pocket and dropped it into the pipe's bulb, which he then lit with a click of his thumb and finger above the bulb. Within seconds, he was puffing away, looking like he was a couple of hundred years too late to be in fashion. He held his pipe to me and looked inquisitive. "Smoke?"

"No, thank you," I said, looking from this healer to Maurice and back; it was as if they could've been family. Maurice was not helping my evil twin or clone theory as he also brought his pipe to life, taking the lead from the good English professor.

"Well?"

"I feel fine. Better than fine. I feel great," I answered. "Rejuvenated."

"Any side effects?" he asked.

"Side effects? Like what?"

"Apart from feeling *rejuvenated*, do you feel anything else? Any sensations? Some who have volunteered feel a freezing sensation."

"Yes, I had a cold sensation, but as I began to feel more awake, that faded."

"I see," he said, looking at me inquisitively.

With this, the metallic door at the back of the room clicked and swung open, and for the first time, I was aware of the room we were in. It was very clinical and mostly coloured in white. It felt like we were in a medical bay or an interrogation room, but at this stage, I didn't know which. It wasn't just the room that took me by surprise; from behind the opening door, another strange man came strolling into the room. He was tall and wearing a grey suit, matching tie, and a white shirt, all secondary to his eye-catching bushy goatee beard and pulled-back curly grey hair. His pointed nose added to his long face and the speed at which he crossed the room barking at the three standing in front of him. "Move back. Let me see him." His voice was sharp and direct, not one to conceal any hidden meaning or agenda. He stood in the gap that the three of them had made and looked at me from top to bottom. I wasn't sure what to do apart from sit there and wait for him to finish his visual examination. I felt like one of those dogs in Crufts who are graded and eventually get a pat on the head for being a good boy. I didn't get a pat on the head, but I did get a nod. Same difference. "This is him?" he asked to no one in particular.

"Yes, sir," said the pipe-smoking man in tweed.

"And he is compos mentis?" he asked everyone and no one again.

"Yes, sir," the pipe-smoking man answered once again.

"Well done, Faust. You never cease to amaze us. I believe this is another one for your journals?" he asked with a hint of pride in his subordinate's work.

"I shall record its success immediately." He turned to me, held out his hand, which I took, shook it, and said his farewell. "Mr Wayward, it has been an absolute pleasure to make your acquaintance, and I hope it will not be long before we meet again."

"I hope I will be in better health next time our paths cross," I said in reaction to Faust's polite departure.

"Meeting healthy Grimoires isn't exactly a vocation I indulge in regularly," he explained with a hidden smile creeping from behind his straight face. "Still I hope to offer you my services when you may need them, for whatever reason."

"Thank you, Mr Faust," I said, aware that Maurice, Emilia, and Mr Faust's boss was waiting for me to finish this conversation. Faust left the room, leaving his pipe's smell lingering in the air, reminding me that he had saved me from a fate worse than a Void, whatever it was. "So?" I offered openly to any of the three in the room standing in front of me. Maurice's eyes were wider than usual, and Emilia had yet to make any kind of eye contact with Faust's boss. I saw Maurice sneakily empty his pipe, trying not to let the grey beardy man see him.

"So?" Faust's boss threw back at me, waiting for me to fill the silence I had inadvertently created.

"Archmage of the Court of the Primoris Dedúcet, it is an honour to meet you." I found the words and hoped they would find the reception I wanted them to have, being as polite as I could.

"Manners and insight! You have already become my favourite, Wayward. But before you let that go to your head, let me tell you I have never really been a fan of your reckless bloodline and the sides that they have *chosen* in the past." He finished his small scolding and stared at me, waiting to see if I had something to say back like a petulant child. I did; I had a hundred insults and quips I would have loved to have thrown in this pompous ass' face, but Maurice's eyes were almost bulging with sheer panic, and the fact that Emilia still refused to engage in the conversation told me that humility would be the right card to play. So I waited to be spoken to.

"You have attracted some attention and managed to find your way into the *bad books* of The Servants of the Night." He let a moment stagnate between us and then turned his attention elsewhere. "Isn't that so, Emilia?" he asked without turning his eyes, which seemed never to blink.

"We encountered some—" she tried to explain herself but was interrupted by the big man himself.

". . . A simple yes or no, Emilia. I will get the truth from him," he fired at her whilst still maintaining eye contact with me. Slightly unnerving.

"Yes," she said, lifting her head up to answer, then dropping it back to avoid further questioning.

"You two will leave young Wayward and me to *converse*," he said this as a command rather than a suggestion as Maurice and Emilia skulked from the room. "Now," he said, taking a step towards me and slowly raising his hands, fingers stretched, closing towards my head. "Let me find out what you have been up to." His hands closed in, and his fingers came to rest on the sides of my face. In that split second, a wave of power tingled from his fingers and forced its way into my facial muscle culture and deep into my skull, finding its home in my mind. I could feel it swimming through my head; it did not hurt, but I felt as if I was almost drunk. My mind and body knew that what I was experiencing was something that wasn't normal or anywhere near me being in control of this interaction.

When this man put his hands on my flesh, I felt the same second sight coming over me as I had when my hand brushed Emilia's. There was no shadowy monster in the darkness or subconscious feelings I could pick up on this time. There were just thin black stripes in the shape of tall iron gates surrounded by fog with ivy that had grown around the bars, showing me that no one had been through this mental or psychic defence for a long time, if ever. I literally couldn't glean anything from him, but then, again, he was an Archmage of the Court, and if anyone should be able to protect themselves from my quite unintentional Jedi mind trick, then I hoped it would be one of the guys who are supposedly in charge of the magical world.

The gates went dark as did the rest of the world around me, and that was the end of that. The man in front of me pulled his hands from the side of my head after he had found what he was looking for. It was like a magnet being pulled from my head in ten different spots, which did snap me out of my mini mind swirl and the vision of the iron gates. Then he spoke to me for the first time, now that we were alone and he had what he wanted. "Well, this is interesting. You have been a busy young Grimoire, haven't you?" he asked as a rhetorical question and showed me a hint of a smile.

"Archmage?" I asked for his attention, using the title Faust had offered. "May I know your name? And what you were just doing to me?" I asked calmly as I shook the cobwebs from my mind. I wanted to get answers, and I knew that this was a man to stay on the right side of if I wanted to find out what was going on. I knew Maurice had brought us here to get answers. To share with the Court what had been going on and why we had a *lounge* of lizards trying to rip us to pieces. I still felt like I needed to be kept in the loop, who wouldn't? "Please?"

"My name is Archmage Bloyse. I was accessing your memories to see what your intentions are and what you wanted to discuss with the Court from your personal perspective, to allow you to have someone understand your specific situation before you are questioned and have the chance to be untruthful," he said very matter-of-factly.

"You read my mind?" I felt extremely vulnerable.

"Yes. I also wanted to see what our new Wayward had to offer." He gave a smug curl to his smile.

"And?" I tested him.

"I can see the Wayward need for disturbing the peace has been inherited, and I am sure you will not let your ancestors down – if that were even possible," he threw at me.

"My ancestors?"

"Unfortunately, we don't have time for you to fumble blindly down memory lane, as you will need to sit before the Court with your chosen confederates to decide what is to be done with you."

"To be done with us? We came here for advice," I snapped and straightaway wished I hadn't.

'You will get your advice, Wayward,' he said slowly and hit each word like he was punching it. 'Now follow me.' He finished as he turned his back, and I got up, feeling completely recharged but also full with a sense of dread. I couldn't imagine that anything helpful would come from a man who so clearly had already taken a dislike to me. To be fair though, I have always had a marmite effect, and it seemed to me that involving myself in magic had only amplified my love or hate abilities.

CHAPTER TWENTY-FOUR

Point of View

Following Bloyse into a round room with familiar white walls that didn't show how the different tiles joined together, I found their light was slightly too bright to look at for any period of time and couldn't distinguish how they were put together. I saw Maurice and Emilia sitting at one half of a circular white table and two strangers flanking what I could only imagine was Bloyse's larger and more regal chair. White, of course. A woman with blonde hair sat at one side with an unnaturally straight back and a smiling man sat at the other, clean-shaven with short cropped hair. Both of them had their eyes locked into mine, following as I moved over to sit next to my *chosen confederates*. I sat at the same time as Bloyse, not wanting to show him I was ignorant of his title, but also not so beneath him that he would get used to treating me like a second-class citizen, allowing him to sit first like the lord of the manor. I don't think he noticed my attempt at equal opportunities as he started talking to *his* confederates in arms as if we were not in the same room. The three of us watched the three of them, listening to their understanding of events. "Wayward has found himself in some bother and has come for *advice* as to what he should be doing and not doing," Bloyse explained with a self-important smile.

"You have seen this?" the blonde woman asked without emotion, and I noticed just how striking she was. She carried an air of grace, exuding it as she sat upright and held herself. She wore a dark blue gown as if she were at the Hilton for dinner rather than this interrogation chamber.

"I have," Bloyse answered. "I have seen his memories at first hand and know of his actions and the actions of those involved."

I could feel Maurice's eyes flickering to look at Emilia and then at me who sat as still as a statue, whispering quietly enough for me to hear from the side of her mouth. "You let him read your mind?" she accused.

"I didn't let him do anything," I whispered back defensively.

"So he forced you?"

"I didn't know what he was doing until afterwards."

"Convenient." She didn't sound happy.

"It wasn't my idea to come here and let some Archmage dip his fingers into my brain and stir around my memories, just so he could insult my family name and the ancestors I know nothing about!" I said, not realising that I had raised my voice and the three across the table were watching and waiting for me to finish.

"I will introduce my peers so that you are aware of the informed advice you will receive." With this, he gestured to the man next to him who pulled a white crystal from a small velvet pouch at his waist and placed it in the centre of the table. With the tips of his fingers and thumb, he twisted it like a toy spinning top. It picked up speed and began emanating a yellow glow, lightly reflecting on the table and on to everyone's faces. When it was at the speed it needed to maintain its balance, it continued with no sign of wavering.

Bloyse could see me staring at it. "This is a chronicle, which, I am sure even you could deduce, is used to chronicle what is said within this room. Moving on, this . . ." he gestured to the lady sitting to his left, ". . . is the Lady Morgause, who acts as an Archmage within the Court of the Primoris Dedúcet. And this . . ." he gestured to the clean-shaven man to his right, ". . . is Roger Bacon, who also acts as an Archmage within the Court of the Primoris Dedúcet. We three are representatives of the magical order within this land and speak on behalf of the Grandmage. Our purpose today is to ascertain the reasons for the actions taken by you, Jon Wayward, and by those involved in your recent turbulent acts of magical abuse during your induction into the magical community."

"Who was the other Archmage? The one who healed me?" I asked, wanting to know as much about them as they now knew about me.

"He was no Archmage. He was our resident Arch Alchemist. Faust. You will have heard of his tales no doubt in poetry, novels, and upon the stage," Morgause explained, assuming the answer was yes rather than asking the question. Her voice was direct and unwavering like Bloyse's, but her eyes had more of an inquisitive nature to them. "Archmage Bloyse, will you relay the actions taken by the Grimoire Jon Wayward and the suggested action he will take to atone for these behaviours?"

"Atone? For what? I've been dragged into all kinds of craziness since being dropped into this puddle of madness, and this is the first time I've had to catch my breath, and you're accusing me of magical abuse! Everything I've done, I've done to protect myself or those in this room," I finished with what I thought was the most honourable part of my survival instinct whilst being spilled into the paths of others.

"Have you quite finished bellowing like a self-important teenager with authority issues? We are all intelligent adults capable of examining the evidence before us," Bacon said happily as he gestured to Bloyse and the evidence he meant for us to examine.

"Before we present the evidence, are there any words that any in attendance would like to have spoken for the record?" Morgause asked to the room, never focusing her attention on anyone for more than a few seconds. Her quick movements were reminiscent of a cat looking for a weakness in the obvious prey that had been set before her.

The room was silent, not because we had nothing to say, but because we were intimidated by the three most influential magic users in the land, and we were being asked to add our voices to what felt like my judgement, jury, and potential execution. I am not afraid to say I was nervous, mostly because I could see that my companions were also unsure of what was happening or that they knew better. I promised myself that when we got out of here, *if* we got out of here, I was going to ask Maurice why in the name of all that is magical he insisted on taking us to the Court of the Primoris Dedúcet and what he was going to do to atone for *his* actions. Then to break the silence, Emilia spoke quietly and respectfully; both Maurice and myself looked at her in surprise. "In regards to our encounter with Kelley, Wayward's actions were in self-defence, as he said, or in defence of me and my safety to procure certain objects I had employed him to recover."

"Thank you for your cooperation, Emilia Nótt. If there are no more statements, we must now hear from Archmage Bloyse and his observation of the Grimoire Wayward's improper use of magic." Morgause looked to Bloyse for his words, as did everyone else, except for me who looked at Emilia and mouthed the word *Nótt*, letting her know I wanted to know more on this name and, by proxy, more about her. Typically, she just nodded towards Bloyse like a teacher to a distracted schoolboy who needed refocusing on the lesson to learn.

With our collected attention all on Bloyse, he stood to make sure that he would be able to address those he needed to in the manner he desired. He then began speaking in his direct and authoritative voice. "The Wayward grimoire was rejoined to its rightful bloodline by Emilia Nótt in exchange for services agreed upon, namely the collection of the tarot cards first created by Jean-Baptiste Alliette, also known as Etteilla, which was his professional title and reversed surname during the late 1700s. If the cards are, in fact, one of the Seals of Ascendance, then they cannot be from Etteilla origin and must predate or directly influence tarot cards and how they came to popular use within certain magical circles. Wayward then absorbed his grimoire and book of shadows, allowing it to join with his spirit, releasing his ancestor's power into his person and over his flesh. Upon receiving his power and alerting the Halls of Knowledge to the Wayward's return to magic, one of our most accomplished Alchemists was sent to attend and train him in his first steps to realising his power and place within the world of magic." Bloyse paused for a moment before carrying on, and he allowed himself a side glance at Bacon and Morgause as if he were preparing them for what he would say next. "Sebastian Dove *encouraged* Wayward to use elemental magic in its baser states, opening up wider branches to further magics without understanding or mastery of elemental essence. It was known to Dove that Wayward's abuse of magic could have been damaging to his own person, but he gave no warning or reason for the control of said elemental magic, ignoring the Court's rules. The reasons for Dove's irresponsible teachings of magic are at this point unknown. After leaving Wayward playing with magics he was not yet ready to encounter, he was approached and attacked by a rogue Lamiac in his home and place of business. Having no magical defences as he had not been taught simple boundary wards by Alchemist Dove, the Lamiac was able to enter and go after the tarot cards without revealing what Its motives were and whom It was working for.

"Wayward was then accompanied to The Charmed Pot by Maurice Talpidae to question a Mr Pryce on his knowledge of the tarot cards but was intervened by two Mages, The Poet and The Bard." He paused for a second as the three Archmages passed a knowing look among them. "After another unrestricted and unauthorised use of magics, which luckily fell in their favour, Wayward and Talpidae were able to walk away with more cards and continue their search. Talpidae went north, and Wayward went south, where he coincidentally met Emilia Nótt and the Servants of the Night communing with their Gods." He finished his unemotional itemising of my memories with a mocking half smile aimed at Emilia, and this was my first hint that he wasn't a fan of her Gods of the Night, or anyone who didn't prescribe to the Court as the first and last line of government and rule.

"Who is this Poet and this Bard?" Bacon asked, excited by the story and wanting more details on the nefarious characters that had made an attempt on my life.

"They seemed like . . ." I wanted to say that they were working for whoever was sending the lizard folk to try to kill me, but before I managed another word, Maurice's hand was on my arm, literally as well as metaphorically, holding me back. I noticed that everyone in the room was staring at me as if I had insulted each one individually with a horrendous swear word.

Maurice followed Emilia's example and whispered gently in my ear as not to further interrupt the Archmage's self-importance. "Our input is not welcome right now. All we can do is listen to the Archmage's understanding of events and accept their ruling on the matters.'

"Seriously?" I floundered.

"Seriously," Maurice said with a concerned look that confirmed his seriousness.

"Finished, have we?" Bloyse asked, so I nodded, smiled, and gestured with my open palm for him to continue, which I think he saw as an insult he didn't have time to deal with. These Archmages were so hard to please. After swallowing his distaste, he continued. "This Poet and Bard appear to be Mages. Their real names at this moment have yet to be revealed, as I could not identify them from the memory spatters. They were both trained in the use of elemental magic as well as Latin verse and bastardised Demotic spell craft."

"How exciting." Bacon clapped his hands together and smiled his full set of pearly whites, until seeing Bloyse who bored into him with his penetrating dark eyes and his goatee beard aimed like a spear for him to look down at his intended victim. Bacon reined his excitement back under control, and once again, Bloyse began to deliver his version of my memories. "Intruding on the Servants of the Night, Wayward ran away and was eventually taken hostage by Emilia Nótt, in an unconscious state, to a hotel where he was to recover. Discussing each other's motives, Emilia Nótt had discovered that Edward Kelley was in possession of one of the tarot cards she had employed Wayward to find and was enraged and encouraged to obtain it from her fellow Servant of the Night. They summoned him upon Burgh Island, and once again, an excessive magical dispute led to a gross misuse of magics on behalf of a neoteric Grimoire Wayward. After achieving their goal and obtaining the tarot card, along with Kelley's superstitious ramblings of *Seals* and children's stories on the Reformation of the Mages, Wayward and Emilia Nótt returned to Wayward's place of business."

"Nonsense and insulting," Morgause blurted out unashamedly. "Kelley has always been fond of spreading foul heresy among the magical communities. He is an embarrassment to us all and will no doubt continue to be so," she continued.

"After this, Maurice Talpidae contacted the Court of the Primoris Dedúcet, asking for an audience in our presence to take our advice on the events that have occurred. This is where I will knowingly interject my own actions to aid Wayward's memories. Firstly, I asked Grimoire Ludolf Van Helsing to contact Wayward en route to the Museum of Unnatural History to stop any more unnecessary and excessive use of magics. Wayward's memories of the event are as follows. He demonstrated the use of a *specific* tarot card to prove the packs' authenticity." With this, Emilia blushed like I had never seen before. Bloyse only hinted at a smile and carried on with his words. "Then there was an attack from multiple Lamiac, which Helsing dealt with, effectively bringing Wayward, Talpidae, and Nótt directly to the Court once the threat had been removed.

"Once here, Wayward was still fortunate enough to be in control of himself only then to finally succumb to his complete and indulgent abuse of his magics, leading to Faust's treatment and Wayward's recovery."

"Busy chap, eh, Wayward?" Bacon asked me with a wink. This surprised me as up until this point, they had acted like we didn't exist.

The three Archmages rose from their clinical white seats at the same time, and Bacon leant forward, picking up the chronicle that was still spinning. As soon as he did, he held it up and examined it in the light of the room, and with a whispered word, the yellow glow faded from it, and he replaced it into his velvet pouch sitting at his waist. Bloyse gestured to the door with his hand and held a practised smile on his face. 'If you would be so kind as to wait outside, we will discuss what, if any, action should be taken in these matters.' Emilia could sense I was about to retort with some comment that I thought was witty, and everyone else thought provocative, so she placed her hand at the base of my back and ushered me out of the room with Maurice a step behind.

The door closed silently behind us, and I could see them both exhale as if they could finally take a breath and gather themselves. Neither of them said anything, so I thought they were most likely waiting for my nervous disposition to begin the conversation. I didn't disappoint. "Well, that was a waste of time!" Both Emilia and Maurice looked at me with their all-too familiar expression of *Are you serious?*

CHAPTER TWENTY-FIVE

Advice with a Price

Sitting on another identical white piece of furniture, in the form of a bench this time, all three of us waited outside the *interrogation* room we had been in with the Archmages. Emilia and Maurice were not in the mood for talking, but I think it was more accurate to say that they were so paranoid that someone was listening to every word they said that they chose not to voice their thoughts.

When I saw Helsing step around the corner, I was delighted to have someone to take my mind from the self-appointed masters of the magical universe deciding my fate with their Draconian concept of right and wrong without listening to me explain my own memories. "Helsing!" I called, even though he was walking over to us.

"Grimoire Wayward. How did your time with the Archmages pass?" he said with his light accent through his mane-like beard.

"Slowly. I don't think they liked me," I answered.

"I wouldn't worry too much. They don't like anyone." He laughed at his own joke, if it was a joke. Either way, I couldn't help but smile along with him. 'They may act like they do not care for you, Grimoire Wayward, but they take a keen interest in all their Grimoires, especially the new ones who are under attack from ancient monsters. Exciting times, isn't it?"

"Well, that does make me feel better, a bit," I offered a kind word in return for his. "So what are you up to now, Helsing? You're not gonna stick around and work for these clowns, are you?" I said and then laughed at my own quip. Helsing didn't laugh, and I wondered if I had overstepped the mark in his loyalty to the Court, even though this was a foreign Court to him. Then I wondered if his Court was different. A moment passed, and after noticing that he was no longer looking at me but past me, I turned to follow his gaze, expecting to see Emilia or Maurice getting up to tell me off or slap me for bad-mouthing the Court where someone could hear. But no, it was the almighty Archmages themselves, standing in a line, all looking as though I had let my dog take a crap on their front lawn and not bought a poop scoop baggie.

"Wayward," Bloyse said through gritted teeth, "may I have a word?" I guessed it was a rhetorical question and kept my mouth shut. *And they say you can't teach an old dog new tricks. What do they know?*

He was clearly waiting for a moment to pass even though I was offering no resistance. As soon as he was happy with his silent passage of time, Bloyse spoke on behalf of the Archmages once again. "For a Grimoire new to the world of magic, we advise that you refrain from interacting with such groups as the Servants of the Night. We would also suggest that you do not disassociate yourself with your non-magical life. We are restraining your use of magic to allow you to develop in a timely and healthy fashion and stopping you from becoming an abuser of your magic and fallen victim to your own power becoming one of the Void." Bloyse waved a finger at Morgause who pulled a dull metal ring from some hidden pocket on her elegant gown and held it up for all to see.

"Yes, I will marry you!" I exclaimed, to all their amazement and confusion.

"Stop" was all Morgause needed to say to bring me back into the conversation and away from my distractive comments. "Here." She offered the ring to me in order for me to see it on the palm of her soft hand.

"You're giving me a ring?" I asked.

"This ring," Morgause stepped forward and took my right hand in hers, "will restrain you from putting yourself in danger. It will allow you to master certain aspects of your magic." Her hand was as soft and cold as marble, and the way her words slipped from her mouth, I couldn't help but listen. I was enchanted to find out what my new limitations were. "This iron ring bears the runes of baser magics." She waved her hand over the ring, and as she did, deep blue runes were shining from it, showing different forms of magical disciplines. "Each time you master one of the disciplines of magical law, the rune will fade from your ring. Your relationship with magic thus far has been through your intellectual association and why you have used your childish knowledge of Latin to conjure up until now. You will become familiar with your ancestors' use of Druidic Ogham magic, which is where your true power really lies. It is the safest way for a Grimoire of your years to develop their skills as quickly and thoroughly as possible." She slid the ring over my thumb, and all the engraved runes shone brightly, reaching, what I imagined, to be their brightest. I had to turn my eyes away; they then faded to a light glow like a mobile phone on standby.

"Do I get to use *any* magic to protect myself?" I asked.

"You do," Bloyse continued for her. "You are allowed to manipulate your speed for defensive matters – *"Chronus Perceptio"* in the Latin tongue. You may also be inclined to use your native Druid tongue, *"TINgyuh-IHduth-mwin-EHduth"*. It matters not to us."

"Well, I guess that's something," I said more to myself than to Bloyse.

"You will be assigned a new Alchemist to develop your magic and train you in the Court's ways," Bloyse said.

"What about Sebastian? Is he trying to kill me or what?"

"Mr Dove will be sequestered for questioning for his lack of mentoring and instruction as your given Alchemist. The matter will be thoroughly investigated," Bloyse explained.

"Is that all? OK then, what about the Poet and Bard fellas?" I was losing my cool and my patience. It seemed like we had come for help and now I was the one in trouble.

"Their role in the proceedings are still unknown, as are their real identities and intentions."

"So what happens now?" I asked.

"You go home and begin your training as a Grimoire in the safest possible way. Your new Alchemist will make himself known to you, and you will follow his instructions in your training. You will stay out of this magical conspiracy you have been involved in, and you will forget about these tarot cards and superstitious children's stories, understand?" Bloyse fired at me, getting angrier with each new thought.

"Yeah, I understand." I kept my words to a minimum, not wanting to show how angry I was with their complete lack of action. Sure I could use help developing my magic safely, but couldn't Maurice or Emilia do that?

"Your new Alchemist will report to us on your progress. Hopefully, we will not be seeing you until your training nears completion." Bloyse leant forward and took my right forearm in his hands, holding my wrist with one and pushing up my sleeve with his other past my elbow. He then turned my arm so that my wrist was showing its vulnerable self to the all-powerful and quite intimidating Archmages. He began talking to me in his usual fashion of not making eye contact and focusing instead on what his hands were doing. He considered this to be the important part of the exchange. He found a spot on the inside of my tattoo-covered forearm an inch down from my elbow and placed the tip of his finger there. Immediately, all the tattoos shimmered as if they were on the surface of a lake. They slithered their way to finding a new resting place upon my flesh, and I could feel the tattoos, or magic, or both, flowing across my skin as if someone were stroking me from the inside of my epidermis, allowing a tingle to swim down my spine, forcing a whole body shimmer.

Bloyse tickling me was not the purpose of this exercise, unless I had wildly misjudged his character. After my tattoos had left a circular white fleshy gap on the inside of my forearm, he closed his eyes and tapped the space three times. Then he let my arm go without as much as a thank you. As he did, I thought I saw something reaching between the spot on my arm and the tip of his finger. It looked to be a brown wisp or mist with green flecked throughout. I looked at him in confusion, hoping he would explain why he was reordering my body art. He kept his gaze on the blank circular space of flesh he had tapped. I hadn't noticed what he had. I saw for the first time a small black mark in the middle of that supposed blank space that he had left behind when tapping it. "What's that?" I asked.

"Your family's coat of arms. It is your ancestors" symbol of magic and how they were recognised within the magical world. It is associated with the Wayward bloodline alone and can help us observe your magical actions," Bloyse said completely unaffected by his true meaning, which was that he had essentially just placed a magical tracker on my magic. "All Grimoires have their coat of arms present upon the person and magic, even some Mages. It is a point of pride to show the world you are unashamed of your magical use and that you do not fear the Court's judgement of misguided magical behaviour, as you are a Grimoire and above such behaviour."

"Not a tracking device or spell?"

"Perhaps a little of both. We call it your magical signature," he said as his eyes grew, still watching my arm.

Once again, I turned to follow Bloyse's gaze and found that there were little squiggly lines poking out of the black dot, slowly squirming their way across my flesh. "Great!" I said. "My ancestors were represented by a . . . baby octopus?"

"The seed of an oak tree," Morgause offered, her eyes glued to the seed growing upon my arm. The roots were clawing their way from the seed with that familiar tickling sensation, then they went into overdrive, and at once, the desire to scratch the skin from inside my muscle was hard to fight. I resisted, knowing that if I made a move to scratch, one of the Archmages would scold me for the attempt. *Strong willpower, you see?* Over the last five seconds of its growth, the seed had stretched, grown, and tickled to finding its way into a fully grown oak tree, filling the blank flesh with roots pointing to my wrist at one end and tree branches at the other, showing a leafless, strong, thick, black-shaded tree that had taken its exquisitely detailed home upon my inner arm.

"I've seen that before," I said as much to myself as to anyone else.

"The Druidic tree of life," Bloyse stated.

"Balance of body, mind, and magic," Morgause built upon.

"We are done," Bloyse said and then he turned on his heel and began walking away, with Bacon quickly turning and following. Morgause took a slower turn and left a lingering gaze that haunted me as she slunk down the corridor, making me want to chase her down just so she could hold my hand again and put as many rings on my fingers as she wanted. I realised once again that I was being a sucker for the ladies.

I turned to find Emilia and Maurice. "I guess you're off the hook," I said.

"We all got off lightly," Maurice offered.

"After I get a good night's sleep and I've put these muppets in the back of mind, you are going to explain to me why you thought it was a good idea to come here, Maurice," I said, still looking at the mighty Druid oak tattoo.

"It was for your safety, Wayward. If anything happens to you, there will be an official inquiry," Maurice justified.

"Not now. Later," I said matter-of-factly.

"If we are to discuss our next steps tomorrow, I shall take my leave today and reconvene with the Servants of the Night," Emilia said, then walked off down the corridor in the opposite direction to the Archmages.

"Quite." Maurice followed her a few steps behind. I think he was licking his wounds after I attacked his decision to come here, especially since he thought it was in my best interests.

I stood in front of Helsing in the corridor, waiting for him to make his exit, but he just stood there waiting for me to say something, so I did. "Looks like I'm in for a quite night then." I laughed a hollow laugh.

"Maybe, Grimoire Wayward. But just in case you are not, I have a present for you," Helsing said to my surprise.

"A present?" I was genuinely shocked. I had only known Helsing for half a night and that wasn't much time to earn a present, not a good one anyway.

"Here." He held out a cotton sheet that had runes sewn into the top. It was covering something large beneath that he held out with one hand. I leaned in and began unwrapping the present. I let the rune-covered cotton drop to the sides of his hands and reveal the present that sat within.

"Knives?" I asked in a way that said I was concerned but definitely impressed. There was a large brown leather belt that had three small knives tucked into the width of the belt and one large dagger that had a sheath in the back of the belt. Each blade had words inscribed along the edge which I couldn't translate, and there was the symbol of a dragon embedded into the cross guard of each blade.

"They are my family's combat knives, three throwing blades, and a dagger in the form of a *releasing* stake. I can't think you will be encountering vampires on your travels home, but you may need to stake a Lamiac or two," Helsing finished with one of his big smiles.

"Helsing, I don't know what to say," I said. He dropped the cloth and reached around me to tie on the belt with the dagger at my back on a diagonal slant and the throwing knives by my hip. "I've never thrown a knife in my life."

"You will practise, along with your magic. Yes?" Helsing asked.

"Yes."

With that, he patted me on the back, walked me out on to the street in front of the Museum of Unnatural History, and told me he had a pack of vampires to track in Ireland. He pushed his suit sleeves up over his elbows, threw his hands into his pockets, and walked off, whistling some tune to himself I had never heard. I waved a taxi down and hoped that my ride home would be a little less eventful than my ride in. Making sure I tucked my new weapons of slicing destruction under my waistcoat, I sat slouched into the back seat and could feel myself falling asleep. I asked the cabbie if he wouldn't mind waking me up when we got back to the shop in Amersham. I knew this was going to cost me a lot, but with a day like I'd just had, I was willing to pay for a few hours where I could just sit back and check my eyelids for holes.

Chapter Twenty-Six

Down Time

I must have been in need of a good sleep as I don't remember much about getting out of the taxi and getting into bed apart from vaguely checking to make sure there weren't any lizard monsters or attacking poets or bards hiding in my shop. I then climbed up the spiral stairs to my sanctuary above. I unbuckled my new belt full of deadly blades and dropped it on to the rocking chair by the window of the living room. I love to sit in the rocking chair and watch people down in the street to satisfy my extremely nosey tendencies. I made my way back to the bedroom and indelicately pulled off my waistcoat, shirt, and trousers and literally fell into bed. I lay there absorbing the clean softness of my bed and started thinking about what and how the last couple of days had unfolded and how quickly it was all becoming the norm. That scared me a little bit. I raised my hand to look at the iron ring on my thumb with its dimly lit runes, reminding me that I needed to take things a little slower, and I turned my arm to examine my oak tree coat of arms tattooed across my flesh. I guess it was a reminder of my family, my *real* family. That wasn't such a bad thought to fall asleep to. *I'll wake up in the morning and takes things as they come, one step at a time. I will find out who Jon Wayward really is. And who he can be.*

Falling asleep with the blinds up was something I was adept at. It was my failsafe alarm clock to allow the morning light to blind me into embracing the waking world. I slowly pulled myself out of bed and dragged my body down the corridor to the bathroom. Before getting in the shower, I looked into the mirror and wondered whether anyone was looking back other than my handsome tattooed self. When Maurice had somehow called the Court through my mirror, I hadn't seen him do it and had no idea whether he had ended the call. I grabbed my towel from the rail and threw it over the full-length mirror to stop whatever could be looking in from doing so and to also hide the spare tyre that seemed to be gaining tread around my love handles and making me consider that gym membership I knew I would never invest in. *Maybe there is some form of magic that could keep my weight in check?* I thought before looking back at the iron ring on my thumb. It reminded me that almost all magic was out of my league for the time being, that is until I got a new Alchemist. *Hooray!*

There was one type of magic I could play with, but I couldn't remember what they called it. I racked my brains trying to find the name, and I was muttering to myself as I took off my boxers and stepped into the shower. The water flowed freely, and I was thankful for one of the few things in my life that never changed: my power shower with super-high temperatures and super-high pressure. No matter what happened, I could always come back to my flat to wash off the craziness of the day, and that was exactly what I was doing. I was still mumbling to myself, trying to remember the words that Morgause had used, but I was getting distracted just by thinking of her. She was beautiful but also scary, and that brought a whole lot of distracting thoughts to play with. Then my blood rushed, and I could see her full lips saying the words to me, and I mouthed them as I saw her in my mind's eye – '*Chronus Perceptio*' in the Latin tongue. You may also be inclined to use your native Druid tongue. "*TINgyuh-IHduth-mwin-EHduth.*"

I had known and seen a few types of magic over the last week, and every single one of them had redefined my understanding of the world and how incredible it could be, but as soon as I had said those words, the first of the runes on my iron ring glowed brighter than the rest and reminded me of my tattoos flaring from my flesh, and the same wisp of brown jagged lines I had seen before formed around my hand like a glove. I could see now that they were not a random formation of brown markings flowing within its own mist, but they were moving roots, reaching around my hand as I had inadvertently worked my magic. This was my magical signature. *It's beautiful,* I thought as everything else in the room slowed down to a tenth of the speed it was moving before. The water pouring from the shower head was falling in streams and droplets, making the most beautiful shapes and colours as the light reflected and refracted, showing a thousand colours spiralling within the water at its mesmerisingly slow trajectory. I moved my hand which seemed to move at an incredibly fast speed through the slow motion water droplets, as if I were breaking the laws of physics, and it was no effort at all, but I guess that's what magic really is . . . A break in the laws of physics. I turned the shower off, slid the door open, and stepped out on to the shower mat where I whipped my towel from the mirror and held it in my hand as I looked at my reflection. I stood perfectly still with a hundred droplets falling like reluctant snowflakes exploding into the mat and tiled floor. It was a hypnotic performance that left me speechless. Out of nowhere, the droplets picked up momentum and began to fall to the floor at an increasing rate before catching up to reality. The spell had worn off, and my shower mat was soaked through; I was left once again in awe of what the magical realm had to offer, although for the foreseeable future that time, manipulation spell was all I had to be in awe of.

I shook myself out of my morning's entertainment and threw on another suit, which was another variation of the three-piece get-ups I owned. I wasn't planning on leaving the shop that day, and with my opening hours being the erratic type at best, I thought it would be a smart move to open up and let the world know that I was still taking their money, especially with the consideration that my clients were rare and unpredictable in their own hours of commerce. I climbed down the spiral staircase, poured myself a coffee, and headed straight for the shop door where I flipped over my welcome sign and showed the happy pedestrians of Amersham Old Town that I was open for business. Honestly, I didn't expect to see many customers, but if any turned up, they would be a welcome break from the hefty research I was predicting that would consume most of my day.

I trotted off to the back of the shop where I had a huge collection of old bound rare books that my grandfather had acquired over the years, although I was now suspecting that his collection had started much earlier with his grandfather, or his grandfather's grandfather. I let my fingers glide over the bindings and the spines of the books. They were always my grandfather's most favoured possessions, and he treasured them a lot more than some of the relics and antiques he had coveted over the years that had a far superior financial value. I was looking for something specific, something I knew I had seen on these shelves many times before but had never had the need or desire to take down and look at. Why would a child want to read through any of these books? For one thing, they're half written in Latin and are full of pictures drawn by some eleventh-century Alchemist who chronicled the magical events of the time and obviously hadn't been introduced to Manga's epic work. *I should probably suggest that to Archmage Bloyse.*

I found it sitting in-between two other volumes that no doubt recorded other events and times of Mages and Grimoires doing wonderful and terrible deeds within the world. I pulled the dark hardback book from the shelf and took it over to the counter so I could peruse it, while drinking my coffee, and be ready to offer my winning charm should a customer come calling. The book's title was *How the Pillar's Fell, and* the image on the cover of the book portrayed nine men standing straight, holding up a falling roof. They acted as the pillars that were falling into the black mud and earth beneath them. I was pretty sure that I was looking in the right place.

After what felt like a good hour of running through the various chapters, three cups of coffee, and endless descriptions of Mages and Grimoire who had used magic in a selfish and open manner, I managed to find what I was looking for: the Wayward family name. It was, to my surprise, listed among those who had abused their magic for their own gain. I couldn't believe what was written in those old and delicate pages, so I read and reread what was there to make sure that I understood my family's part in all this craziness.

> *Several of the prestigious Grimoire houses had fallen in battle during the War of Influence. Their family's knowledge was either lost or stolen by the victor as it returned to their grimoire and was inherited by another family or lost in time. The skirmishes of the Pillars of the Blackened Earth were sudden, ruthless, and open; there was no attempt to hide their actions from the world of man. As the courts of Europe sent their own Mages and Grimoires to intercept the Pillars, the battles spilled on to streets, towns, cities, and the battle for power became a nest of backstabbing and turncoats all fighting for survival as much as they were vying for power.*
>
> *During the battle of Silverwood, so named due to the werewolves paid to fight by the side of the Pillars, many Mages lost their lives, and many magics were exposed to the world that should not have been. Silverwood is known as the confrontation that brought the Pillars and the Court to stand-off. Many new and unpredictable magics had been practised and exploited, but what had been learned could not be unlearned, and the evils that had been brought into the world in the name of magic could not be forgotten, only hidden.*
>
> *Neither side was willing to step down, allowing the other to gain ground within the War of Influence. Both sides resorted to guerrilla tactics, assassinating key members from each command. The biggest loss during the stalemate to the Pillars was one of the most influential generals, a woman known as The Talon. She was a furious battle Grimoire and used blade-tipped gloves to tear into her victims after her magic had allowed her to get close. Her family name was Sanngriðr, and her ancestors dated back to the invading Vikings against the Saxons. It is said her clan stayed behind to continue to reap the glory and that her family passed down the mantle of The Talon in honour of the Valkyries that watched over them in battle.*

*Throughout her campaign of terror and aggression, it is said that
she would take advice from her most trusted lieutenant and councillor,
Godric Wayward.*

Bugger. A tingle ran down my spine as I read the name written on the
page. I read that line over and over to make sure I had understood what it
said and, more importantly, what it had meant. It meant that my ancestor,
Godric Wayward, was not only the right-hand man to one of the most
terrifying battle Grimoires in the history of magic but also fought on the
side of the Pillars, meaning the bad guys. It's no wonder that the Archmages
were wary of me and wouldn't take my word for granted. My bloodline is
famous for fighting against the Court! A thousand thoughts ran through
my mind, but one in particular took hold and wouldn't let go. *If my ancestors
fought with the Pillars, and my grandfather worked with the Court, does that
make me a traitor or a loyalist?* That thought then took another form entirely.
Do I even need to declare a side to fight for? I knew as soon as I had thought
this that it would stay with me for a long time. I thought of my friends, or at
least those I perceived to be my friends, and questioned who they fought for.
Helsing was obviously loyal to the Courts of the world, protecting people
from what the Court considered to be magic abuse and danger. Maurice
believed this as well; otherwise, he wouldn't have contacted them when
he thought I was in danger. Sebastian was an Alchemist for the Court,
but Kelley said he was in league with the Pillars, and to be fair, he hadn't
exactly been around to prove either theory right or wrong, so he got a big
question mark. Emilia was completely loyal to the Servants of the Night,
but whether that meant she would fight for the Court, I didn't know. She
had also claimed that she was loyal to me, but that was before I had used
the lover's tarot card and kissed her. *Only half regret that one.*

I asked myself the same question from a different point of view and
without judgement. *Who am I loyal to?* I stopped for a moment and thought
about it before I continued reading to find out how far my ancestor's devious
nature travelled. *My loyalty is to my friends and my family. As far as choosing a
side . . . That will have to wait until I know more about what is at stake.* I looked
down at the book in front of me, and as I looked back over the passage I
had just read, I remembered the statue in the doorway of the Museum of
Unnatural History. The screaming battle Grimoire was The Talon; she was
Godric Wayward's superior, Sanngriðr. I rolled her name around my mouth
and remembered how she had made me feel – 'Sanngriðr'. As soon as that
hollow feeling in my stomach reprised its grip, I knew I had to read on and
find out what my ancestor had been responsible for and why the Court had

been wary and disapproving of me. I picked up where I had left off, finding out that my family name isn't as honourable as I thought it was.

Her most trusted lieutenant and councillor, Godric Wayward, was charged with locating the Grandmage of the Courts, and he had left the battlefield for some months, trying to locate the leader of the opposition, during which time he tasked himself with finding any and all magically imbued items or relics that may sway the War of Influence in the Pillar's favour. Travelling through Knossos on the island of Crete, belonging to Greece, Wayward heard rumours of a God relic, and in his desire to obtain it, he disappeared from the War and his campaign completely.

It is rumoured that The Talon was furious with Wayward's disappearance and considered it to be a sign of his defection to the Court. She continued in her attacks, making no effort to keep the world of man out of the magical war, becoming even more reckless and aggressive. Her last skirmish, and some say the reason Wayward acted as he did, was in Pudding Lane, London. She had taken three Mages with her to advance a stealth attack that would focus on the Court itself. The Court had prior knowledge of the attack from anonymous sources and lay in wait for her, knowing that this may be their only chance to engage and defeat The Talon. In time, this would prove to be the Pillar's most damaging and defining moment in the war. Waiting with eight Grimoires, the Court had the advantage, and when The Talon was in sight, the ambush began. The battle lasted no longer than a few minutes, and within that time, some of the most deadly and destructive magic that has ever been cast was spelled as if they were everyday commonplace magic.

The Talon had lost her Mages, and the Court still had four of their eight Grimoires standing. The Talon had single-handedly devoured the other four, leaving her own Mages as bait to take some of the Grimoires' force from her. She was surrounded by the Grimoires and by the fire that had been caused by the destructive magics. By this time, all the surrounding dwellings and businesses were blazing fiercely, spreading from building to building for at least half a mile. They started the fire of London? I knew it wasn't a bloody baker living in Pudding Lane. Way too obvious! *Knowing that she had no way out of the ambush alive, the Talon made two promises to the Grimoires who maintained a deadline around her, allowing no escape. "The Court will fall under my right Talon," she promised. "Under the left, the turncoat Wayward who betrayed his brothers and sisters."*

Personal accounts from the surviving Grimoires claim that she crouched into a protective ball and removed a small marble from her person, holding it high into the air. The Grimoires were preparing for another attack and braced themselves into defensive positions.

She didn't attack. She stood slowly and then swallowed the marble. Stretching her claws out, she screamed the name she had learned to hate – "Wayward!" She turned to stone where she stood, allowing neither the Grimoires nor the fire nor time itself to harm her.

I wasn't sure how to feel about any of this. All I knew was that I was now *even* more scared of a statue than I had been before. But it was no good; I knew I had to find out what happened to Godric Wayward. So, obviously, I kept reading.

Finding that his superior had fossilised herself against her enemies and the ravages of time, he knew he would never see her again. He also saw that in her absence, the tide of the War had turned, and high-ranking officers in the Pillars were starting to fall or go into hiding. Wayward made a different choice. He found a way to get word to the Grandmage of the Court to broker a face-to-face meeting. Wayward agreed to all the Grandmage's security measures and Grimoire personal guard, the strongest of which was the great and powerful Merlin who had personally seen to the Court's protection within his jurisdiction.

Upon meeting in the protective circle of Stone Henge, Wayward openly made his way into the middle to talk with Grandmage Prideaux surrounded as much by the stones of the Henge as he was by the Grimoires ready to attack at the first sign of aggression or deception. None of them realised that Wayward was there with an offer. He knew that the war was coming to an end, and he knew that if he didn't make the first move, his family name and magic would suffer. So he presented the Grandmage with an offer he knew he would not be able to refuse, and it would allow him to safely live out his days as a soldier for the winning side.

Wayward offered the Grandmage his deal. He wanted complete immunity from the Court and any punishment to his family name and magic if he were to deliver the one thing that could end the war in a matter of days. The Grandmage thought on Wayward's offer, and after much deliberation, he conceded to accept Wayward's offer, if what he was offering could end the war. With a handshake that allowed each of the parties to cast on the other, which neither of them did, etiquette and manners of magical deals, Wayward stepped back and slowly pulled from his satchel a two-pronged pipe; he then spoke to the Grandmage with instructions. "Grandmage, please place your fingers deep into your ears to block the noise from my pipe. If your Grimoires will indulge me, I will demonstrate my offer of power." The Grandmage nodded, and Wayward played his pipe. There is no recording of what sound the pipe created, but it was enough to drop all the Grimoires to the ground within a few seconds. They screamed in agony and begged for him to stop, including the great and powerful Merlin that everyone feared so much. The Grandmage watched in horror as his entire personal guard had been incapacitated. When Wayward stopped and showed he had the Grimoires writhing on the floor, unable to stand and protect their master, the Grandmage looked on to Wayward with the knowledge that he was about to be slain by the trickster Godric Wayward and knew in that moment that everything he had heard about the Waywards was true. Then the strangest thing happened. Wayward approached the Grandmage and looked deep into his eyes, but before the Grandmage could manage to beg for his life, Wayward dropped to one knee and offered up the two-pronged flute with outstretched arms and spoke to the Grandmage, full of reverence and humility. "I present to you Pan's flute, the God of the wild, flocks, and hunting. May you use this to bring peace and order to the magical world once again."

The Grandmage had no choice but to publicly present Wayward with his pardon and immunity as the tide of the Court flooded and drowned the Pillars into defeat after defeat. The Court forced the remaining soldiers to die in God-fuelled agony as the flute was played and the enemies' minds were set on fire, listening to the song of the hunter. No prisoners were taken, but a few had fled the war before Pan's flute reached their ears.

What followed was what became commonly known as the 'Ignorance of the Masses'. The remainder of the Court and the supporting magical communities joined their power to cast the largest spell the world had ever seen. They created a spell to be cast on each land, forcing the world of man to slumber, forget, and become ignorant of all magic, allowing the magical communities of the world to heal and repair what damage the Pillars had left in their wake, without being persecuted and reviled by their fellow man.

I stopped reading to find that my breathing was a lot faster than usual. My heart was pounding in my chest, and my jaw had likely dropped a long time ago. I know some people have skeletons in their closet, but it's always a shock to find that you have an entire bloody magical war locked up, waiting for you to find.

I'm not sure about the sins of the father, but how about the sins of the great-great-great-great-great-great-great-great-great-great-grandfather? Because his were pretty damn impressive.

CHAPTER TWENTY-SEVEN

Th' Inconstant Moon

A long time had passed before I was holding an empty cup of coffee and staring at the page of a book with pupils that had long ago relaxed. That could no longer see any definition of the italic words on the worn and fragile pages depicting my ancestor's self-preservation and turncoat nature within one of the biggest magical campaigns that had ever been recorded in any world's history.

When I did snap out of my blurry distraction and looked at the empty mug in my hand, I made my way into the kitchen to sort myself another drink and tried to put what new information I had into some form of helpful knowledge. It was that rather than seeing it as a worrying glimpse at what my bloodline was capable of. What I could take from the book was some knowledge of the Pillars and what they had wanted. Apparently, what they wanted was to replace the Courts of the world and allow a legal system that encouraged an eye for an eye and displays of power and threats as a means to right and privilege. How very Old Testament of them in their Draconian mindset! Must be the privilege of the very powerful Mages and Grimoires. *I'm sure these already forceful characters looked forward to their fighting for the biggest seat at the table*. On the other hand, the books I had read hinted strongly that the Courts were known for supporting all magical users and collecting magical findings through their Alchemists and allowing all access to the powers of the world and what it had to offer.

After my coffee was suitably strong, I headed straight to the bookshelves at the back of the shop once again. I knew there was more research that I had to get my teeth into. *What had Kelley called it? Reformation of magic?* I searched through my grandfather's books and read, then reread the titles on the bound spines that sat waiting to be examined. Luckily, I had a time manipulation spell to hand. For a few hours, nothing showed itself to have any link to a reformation, magical or otherwise. I thought back to that conversation I had had with Kelley and Emilia up on the top of that island, and it was her words that came to me rather than his: *"You're telling us a children's tale to buy time!"* That was it. I was looking in the wrong place. I didn't have any children's books in my grandfather's collection, but I needed to get one.

I ran into the office and turned my grandfather's Rolodex around to search through the names of people he knew who owned magical items that may have a copy of the book. It wasn't going to be an easy search as I didn't even know the name of the book, but I was sure that once I started explaining what I was after, it couldn't be that hard to find. *Could it?*

An hour went past that felt like an eternity, without any time manipulation, and I had only proved that my patience was in need of some practice. I had called a lot of numbers that didn't have answer machines, and no one was picking up. I called a lot of numbers where people picked up and had no idea what I was talking about, but I wasn't too bothered as it allowed me to get into a pattern of asking for the children's book directly and without sounding like one crazy son of a gun. Although I was pretty good at sounding like a crazy son of a gun. Sometimes I got through and had a potential lead that seemed to fizzle at the last minute. For example, I called an antique bookseller from my grandfather's list, and he had explained that there was this little old lady who had always requested that they hold on to anything to do with 'real' magic as she called it. They gave me her number after I had convinced them that I was a collector looking to buy a specific book. The conversation I had with her resembled the kind of quick chat you would have with a criminally insane patient who had escaped from a psychiatric ward and standing in the street as she looked at the nearest estate agent's listings, asking, "How much is that doggy in the window?" Bizarre, to say the least.

Another call I made was to a chap in Camden, who ran a shop that didn't sound to dissimilar from my own. To be fair, I assume he was busy because I called and he knew what to say before I had even asked. "Hello there, I'm . . ."

". . . Looking for a children's book?" he said with an unimpressed voice.

"Yeah," I admitted with confusion. "How did you . . ."

". . . Know? Trust me, pal, I just do. And before you ask, no, I don't have your book. I have heard of the reformation but can't really talk openly on the phone at the moment. I suggest you try . . ." He paused for a moment as though he was thinking and then, with a sudden breath, began talking again. "OK, there's a guy who deals out of a place in Ally Pally called Moon."

"Alexandra Palace?"

"The very same."

"Do you have his number?" I asked this oracle-like being on the other end of the phone.

"Seriously? C'mon, mate, you have to do some of the legwork. Otherwise, there's no fun in it," he quipped at me before hanging up. Interesting fella; I decided to make a point of dropping in some day and thanking him if his lead turned out to be something I could use.

I flicked through the Rolodex to see if there was a 'Moon', and lo and behold, there was. He was down as the proprietor of *Th'inconstant Moon*, a rare book dealer who traded out of the back of a pub next to the train station. Perfect! If he had the book, I could jump on the overground, throw in a bit of train, tube, and pedestrian action, and be there in an hour and a half. I dialled his number quickly with excitement and caffeine pumping through me, and when the call connected, my excitement for the chase grew, allowing each ring to feel like a desperate minute of anticipation. Finally, he picked up. "*Th'inconstant Moon* at your service. How may we 'elp on this glorious day?" A fast thick south London accent greeted me.

"Hello, is that . . ." I paused for a second, realising that I didn't know his first name, and thought how silly what I was about to say actually was, but then, again, he must hear it every day. ". . . Mr Moon?"

"Speaking," he affirmed my question.

"I was hoping you have a book I am looking for."

"I'm sure we do. Any book, any subject, any time for anyone." He gave me his business' tag line, which I actually thought was quite effective. Let's just say he had me at 'any book'.

"I am looking for a specific book," I warned him.

"Not a problem, sir, ya just tell me the title or author and I can put my finger on it."

"Well, the trouble is, I don't exactly know the title of the book, but I do know it's rare and what it's about. It is a subject-specific book. I can't imagine many folks have in their "to read" pile at home."

"Sir, I'm sure whateva information ya 'ave to give me will be sufficient in detail for my research team to place and locate the volume ya looking for. So, please, do tell," he invited me, so I decided now wasn't the time for caution. If he had the book or could get the book, I wanted it, and I had to show my hand and, possibly, face the questions and consequences later.

"It's a children's story." I paused to see if he would react. He didn't. "It's a book about magic and wizards, supposedly a prophecy and the end of the Mages who abuse magic or something. I think it's a pretty old children's book, and I'm not sure if it's still in print."

"My research team 'as already located two potentials, Mr . . . ?" He was fishing for my name in his South London accent that jumped in pitch when he was excited.

"Mr Bond." What could I say? I panicked.

"Mr Bond?"

"Yep, James Bond." Then I panicked some more.

"Like 007?" Moon's voice had a glimmer of disbelief.

"Exactly. Only my license to kill was revoked. Ha!" I laughed forcefully, trying to make light of my incredibly poor choice of aliases and hoped he wouldn't see through my false name. I'm not even too sure why I gave a false name; I was only looking for a children's book. But I guess after having been put on the naughty step by the Court and having everyone I know, with the exception of Maurice, show me some form of secrecy and mistrust, then I wasn't exactly sure who I wanted knowing my name and picking up the tasty breadcrumbs I was leaving behind in my investigation into children's magical literature. Unsurprisingly, Moon didn't laugh with me.

"Well then, *Mr Bond*, we 'ave *Paws of a Monkey's Prophecy* and *The Auguries of Sorcery*."

"I see."

"Can ya tell me any more about the volume ya looking for?" he asked. But I decided that since I was so paranoid about the use of my own name, I wasn't about to start blurting out alarm bells like *Reformation of the Mages* and ask if I could have the one that prophesied the end of all magic as we know it.

"I think I'll take both if that's OK?"

"That'll be fine, Mr Bond."

"I'll come right over to collect them."

"Now?" He sounded surprised.

"If that's OK." I didn't realise I had to play the game this much with a bookseller. It felt like I was on a first date and trying not to reveal too much about myself and try to just let the crazy come out one drip at a time. "I was hoping to have them for my nephew. It's his birthday, and he loves this kind of stuff."

"Lovely, Mr Bond. May I ask 'ow old he is?" Moon dug deeper.

"He's only smallish. He's probably about . . ." I panicked in true Wayward style. *What age do children start reading about magical prophecy?* ". . . About six, no! Ten!" *Yeah, ten is more believable.* "I always get that mixed up. Ha!" I brought out the false laugh again. And again, he didn't join in. "So where can I meet you?"

By the time I had gotten to the Alexandra Palace train station, it was way past lunchtime, and my stomach was growling at me to get something to eat. I knew it would have to wait. Moon told me he would meet me on the bridge leading from the North-bound train to the South-bound train above the tracks, and sure enough, there he was. He was a short man, probably only coming up to my shoulder, with sharp little eyes that darted all over the bridge. He wore a tattered black leather jacket that seemed to have more worn areas than not and somehow reflected his short unkempt hair. His rapid eye movements matched his pace of speech as he made sure I was me. "Mr Bond?" His South London cockney spat out in its charming manner, and his whole persona made me think of a mangy city fox.

"That's right. Pleasure to meet you, Mr Moon," I replied.

"The pleasure is all mine, my friend."

"I was hoping to thank your research team for their quick work. They couldn't make it?" I was digging. It was becoming a habit.

"They take care of the research and I take care of the customers. It's a deal we've 'ad for donkey's years and it's worked pretty well so far." He smiled a big smile and his eyes widened as his thoughts moved on. "Speaking of deals Mr Bond, 'ere are the books you asked for." He produced a plastic bag and pulled out the volumes one at a time to show me the titles and their condition.

"They look like the right ones. How much do I owe you?" I said, reaching into the back pocket of my trousers for my wallet.

"Owe me?" He sounded as if I had just dumped him after dinner and a movie.

"Yeah, for the books?"

"No, Mr Bond." His hurtful look now changed into something with a bit more of a smile and warmth. "I was 'oping we could make more of an arrangement rather than a deal." His South London accent rolled the words of excitement in his mouth.

"An arrangement?"

"Firstly, I would never knowingly charge a Grimoire full price for any of my books. Secondly, I would never charge a Wayward *any* price at all," he said with his yellow smile in full beam. So he knew my name; I think it was fair to say that 'Mr James Bond' wasn't the best alias to use, and if he had connections into the magical world, my name was new juice on the grapevine. I couldn't be too annoyed, especially if I wanted to get my hands on those books.

"You never charge a Wayward? So what do you want from this *arrangement* of ours?" I asked.

"A business partner," he stated matter-of-factly.

"A business partner? To sell books? With you?" I was a little confused.

"No, no, no. A business partner, yes. To sell books, yes. With me, no. For me, yes!" He started to walk towards me, and as he got to my side, he gestured that I walk alongside him down the steps I had walked up and back to the pavement. "Ya see, Mr Wayward, I do a lot of specific business for specific clients looking for specific items, and over the years, I've tried to set myself up 'ere and there. Even opened my own shop in the early Sixties, but no one knows the family name as well as they should. So that got me thinking. Who 'as a well-known and trusted name in our special little community? *'A Grimoire.'* I fought to myself. "And which Grimoire do I know that already 'as an established business, selling rare items and mystic artefacts?"

"George Wayward," I said to myself.

"Then I pop around to your very lovely and classy shop and make my offer to your predecessor. A couple of days later and 'e pops 'is clogs."

"My grandfather passed away, yes," I said with a slightly more serious tone than Moon.

"Well, no one knew if you would follow in his footsteps, so I carried on scraping by, trying to earn enough to eat a little something and to try to sleep indoors. Then what do I 'ear when I was 'aving a drink in the Lonely Lantern – *"See, the Wayward line is back. 'e's even taken on Smoke and Mirrors."* I 'eard a small pointy little man say to the bartender, *"Looks like we are taking a turn for old times."* And with that, I knew I 'ad to get in touch and find ya."

"But I called you."

"Fate!" Moon exclaimed.

"Fate?" I questioned.

"Don't you see, Wayward, we are supposed to combine our businesses for the greater good of the magical communities."

"Hold on! Look, you've given me a lot to think about . . . and I'm not saying no," I said, then had to change direction as Moon's smile stretched so far across his face I thought it might tear. "I'm not saying yes either. What I'm saying is, I came here for the books, and I guess if you really wanted to discuss a business proposal, then you should come around for a cup of tea with a business plan." Moon stood still for a second with his eyes on mine, no rapid movement or uncontrollable flickering. He was obviously thinking hard about what I had said and what he would say next.

"OK then. I will."

"You will?" I nudged him to tell me more.

"I will, but for now, consider the books a sample of me fast and quality work. A gesture of good faith from me to your good self. Will ya accept?" He said with pride, holding the paper bag out with the books in.

"I will. Thank you, Mr Moon," I said, taking the bag from him.

"Just call me Moon," he said.

"Will do." I turned and walked back to the platform, needing to head home as a lot of thoughts crashed through my mind at the same time. *A business partner, really? I wonder what else he's heard about me? Why am I being discussed in pubs? Do people still associate my name with the War of Influence? Are these books going to help? Who are his research partners? Will they become my partners by proxy?* Before I walked out of sight, I turned back to Moon who was just starting to turn and lope back the way he had come. I shouted up to him on the bridge across the tracks. "Moon!" Moon stopped and looked over, so I carried on. "Bring your research team with your proposal!" I shouted. He watched me for a second, nodded, then moved off across the bridge, down the steps at the far end and off around a corner, and out of sight like a rat into the sewer. *A business partner? Stranger things have happened. Literally!*

CHAPTER TWENTY-EIGHT

Child's Play

After some pretty standard detective skills, mainly through Internet searches, allowing me to discover that Mages don't advertise online, I had my hands on two books, thanks to Moon. One was the book I needed to give me some more information on the Reformation malarkey that I've heard about, and the other was no doubt a damn good read for a ten-year-old fictional nephew. I got back to the shop and flipped over the sign on the shop door, just in case anyone wandered in and decided they wanted to contribute to my grocery bill by buying a once-in-a-lifetime antiquity of the absurd and occult.

No one did, at least for not as long as I tried to get my head around the two children's books I had to read. I propped myself up at the counter and threw a cup of coffee down my throat and looked at the first of the books. It had a picture on the front, of a hairy, long, and broken-nailed paw with three outstretched fingers and an opposable thumb. I opened it, and there was a warning laid out in gold cracked lettering, showing the age of the book. It read . . .

> *To my innocent and unfortunate reader,*
> *You are in possession of the monkey's paw, and I implore you to tell your loved ones that you care for them and you will miss them before leaving in order to keep them safe from the paw's grasp.*
> *The monkey's paw is not for child's play and must be considered a weapon of self-dest . . .*

The gold lettering flaked off from the front page, leaving the rest of the text unreadable on that page. I flicked through a few more pages written in a faded typeface just to feed my curiosity. Everyone had heard of the monkey's paw. I even remember the stories from my childhood. I think I saw a cartoon about it when I was sick with chicken pox and watched crap television for a week. *I guess there's a little truth in everything, except Bigfoot.* You could use the monkey's paw for making wishes, but the bottom line was that it would kill you for having the guts to try to make your life something better without earning it yourself, or some other such metaphor that makes you realise you have to work for what you get in the world we live in.

I pushed it to the side, knowing it wasn't what I was looking for. I gulped the dregs of coffee that had gone subzero on the counter and pulled the *Auguries of Sorcery* towards me. On the cover were five pentagrams circling a tree growing and blossoming upside down with blue leaves and white veins running down the trunk and the branches of the etched image. I had no idea what it was supposed to represent, but it looked important and would no doubt present itself to me at some point. I glanced at my arm and the Wayward oak tree tattoo, just to double-check that they didn't resemble each other; they didn't, and I breathed a sigh of relief. I'm not sure how much more coincidence I could take. I opened the book slowly pulling the cover back and found the author's name in a wild calligraphy moving diagonally across the page. *Numa Pompilius, second king of Rome and Haruspex of the magi.* I stopped and thought to myself that I had heard that word before, *Haruspex*.

I sat back and thought about it for a moment, picturing myself sitting at my grandfather's knee and listening to him tell me a story just like those Werther's sweet adverts. Except that my grandfather wasn't telling me about his fishing trip or that time he got up to some humorous mischief and only just got away with it by the skin of his teeth. He was telling me about the different types of monsters in the world and the different people in history who had strived to steer safely into today. As any child would, I loved it and lapped up everything he had to say about it. I assumed it was make-believe. How wrong was I?

He told me children's stories for a wildly imaginative mind, or real magical mind, as it turns out, but what he was telling me had happened throughout the history of his world. It was my world now, and one of the stories my grandfather told me was about a woman who divined the future, past, and present through animal entrails. She could literally see what she needed to through the shape and condition of the intestines and entrails of the bloodied animal she had dissected, and in the story, my grandfather told she ended up wearing the entrails as a part of her new outfit and role as diviner. An imaginative plot point I can only hope was from the recesses of my grandfather's ability to tell a dark and twisted tale.

Haruspex is what they called these diviners of the magical realms. Back when they were considered to be a vital member of the ruler's advisory council, Numa was a Haruspex who would read the auguries from bird's intestines as he ruled Rome in concordance with his divinations.

I looked back at the book and flicked to the contents page, and there was a scribe's note explaining that it had been translated from Latin in the 1930s by the Alchemists of Europa and then it was initialled SMB, with an elongated M in the middle. I turned over and began reading the first page.

> *The divinations of Haruspex Numa Pompilius were designed to allow him to rule as emperor of Rome and its provinces across the known world. Until the divinations of Numa Pompilius began to manifest the same fateful future every time, he read auguries of the birds' flight patterns and their innards. His dreams were haunted by a vision that could end magic as we know it, a reformation of the use of magic, who it chooses and how it can be used by its bearer. Below is the story of the Reformation of Mages foreseen to bring about the end of magical days known to the world of man.*

> *"Upon the eve of the mantle of the first Grimoires, where they would be able to imbue their families with the magical disciplines they had learnt, there was one who refused. He would not let his knowledge and power pass on to his offspring. This was a man who revelled in his own power and knew that if he allowed his magic to be recorded into a book, then others would be able to tap into his dominion and challenge him."*

I hadn't even realised until this moment that Grimoires were chosen from Mages or that it happened more than once. I was pretty sure that within the first few lines of the book, I was not only picking up a few home truths about where my lineage had come from, but most importantly, I had the right one, and I was getting into a little bit of magical history through the medium of a child's entertainment. You couldn't write this stuff, eh?

> *"He kept his immense learning and knowledge to himself, refusing to enter into the ritual of ascendance, creating a family bloodline to share his magic down through the ages as a Grimoire. Instead, he hid away from the world. But before he took to the shadows, he told the Courts across the world that by choosing a few privileged Mages to share their magic, they were creating a class system of the*

self-appointed who would take control of the world of magic and never let go, turning on their precious Court in the process.

The Court's Archmages reassured themselves that the Grimoires were created to protect the Courts and all those in the magical communities. The man refused to accept the Court's decisions and made them a promise. "With all my power, I will strike at the heart of the Courts and their oppression towards their own magical people and their own selfish lust for power and control. I will make each and every one of you pay for the assumption that you know what is best for the rest of us and how we should be controlled from up on high, like gods and their forced worshipping slaves. I will destroy each and every one of you, along with any who stand at your side, to free the people from your despotic grip and allow the harsh but fair reign of magical freedom to engulf the world as it once did."

The Courts were worried as the man had refused to share his knowledge and practice of magic with anyone as he was considered one of the most practised and powerful Mages the Court had ever seen. Before the man could take action against the Courts, a meeting of all the Archmages of the world was held to decide what should be done with the one who stood to oppose them and endanger everything they had worked so hard to create for nearly a thousand years. After days of squabbling and fighting, shouting and screaming, only two paths remained as a way to take care of their undeniable threat. The first was to attack the man who opposed them and not stop until he was defeated. If he were allowed to live, his ways of ignoring the laws and conventions of the magical world would spread and destroy the peaceful protection they fought to uphold. The second was to imprison the man and hold him captive as a message to anyone else who might attempt to attack the peoples of the magical world. The arguing of case against case went on for three days and three nights, allowing new voices to add new reasoning as to the question of his proposed death or imprisonment. Voices were heard asking, "If we kill him, we'll be just as bad, maybe even worse." And "We need to strike before he does. It is the only way to be sure!"

When the time came, and everyone had had his or her voice heard, the decision was put to a vote. A spell was cast to take away the sight of the Archmages, temporarily, to allow them to raise their hands and vote without being judged by one another. A voice was heard calling out the two paths they could take, and a swarm of hands was raised and lowered, deciding the fate of the man who would not bow.

Three moons passed, and the sentence was carried out. The seventeen Mages who had gone through the ritual of ascendance to become the first Grimoires were called to deliver the man's punishment. The man did not hide or run; he waited where he felt most comfortable at home with his magic, in the woodlands. The Grimoires found the man and addressed him. "Aktor Thoön!" The man simply nodded in acknowledgement, so the Grimoires continued. "You are ordered by the Courts to be imprisoned indefinitely so that you may harm no one but yourself and act as an example to all those who challenge the laws of magic and the protection of the Court."

"The laws of the Court?" Aktor Thoön spat back.

"Do you intend to oppose the Court's ruling?"

"I do not recognise the Court or its ruling. Therefore, you give me nothing to oppose."

"Then prepare to face the might of the Court!" And with that, an almighty battle ensued, changing the landscape of the woodlands and the surrounding area for miles. All that could be seen of the confrontation were flashes of light in a vast variety of colours, each brighter than the last and sounds so loud they could shame a thunder clap from the Viking God himself. At the end of the battle, the remaining nine Grimoires had Aktor Thoön trapped.

He had single-handedly killed eight Grimoires before falling to the onslaught of his former peers. They performed a ritual to magically imprison Aktor Thoön within the tree he had fallen against, allowing the very fabric of nature to trap him. Each Grimoire presented a possession they had upon their person to act as a Seal layered upon the prison, allowing no single Grimoire access. This made the cage extremely hard to open, as each Seal would need to be present at the prison before they could reverse the ritual.

As the last words to the ritual were being spoken, Aktor Thoön lifted his head against the magic of his prison and spoke to his captors one last time. "I will find my way back from this cage you keep me in and take my vengeance upon the Courts and those who stood by and did nothing. I will take my vengeance upon the Grimoires who bind me to this cage, and I will take the world of magic and free it from your oppression! This I promise you," he said without fear or panic. Then Aktor Thoön was drawn into the tree he lay against, the bark and moss growing over and under his skin with Aktor Thoön fighting not to show the excruciating pain he must have felt to the eyes of those who oppressed him. The magical world drew a breath of relief. His face pushed out from inside the bark, open mouth screaming from his living prison, but he no longer posed a threat.

Each Grimoire hid the items used by the Grimoires to Seal Aktor Thoön within his prison secretly. They were sworn to protect them and have their children and their children's children keep hidden the Seals so that none could release him from his bondage and invite him to take his vengeance on the world as he promised. The Grimoires were allowed back to their Courts and back to their homes, to protect their Courts from those who would attempt to attack them. The world found an uneasy peace with Aktor Thoön fading from memory. Mage kind ignored the occasional whisper in the wind that said there are those who believe he will help them take back what is rightfully theirs, a world of unrestricted and unrestrained magic.

"Children's tales of betrayals and heroes? If I knew that was your bag, I would have brought you Merlin's diary to have a nose through," said a voice from the other side of the shop. I couldn't quite see who it was as I pulled my eyes shut to find she was looking at something behind the hanging cloaks. I knew she was a woman because her voice was gentle and feminine, carrying her quirky comment over to me as a gentle nudge back to reality, no doubt waiting to see how I would return the jest. After reading what I had just read, I wasn't exactly in the mood for a jest; I was in the mood to talk to someone about what the hell it all meant to the now and, more importantly, to the me in the now.

"You're obviously some magic user, so I'm going to be pretty straight with you. If you can tell me anything about Thoön, the Reformation, or whether any of it is true, I will entertain your company." I paused to see if she would react, but she didn't, so I carried on for another few words. "If not, kindly purchase something. Leave a tip *and* me in peace." I forced myself to look down at the closing book in my hands, examining the cover once again, waiting to see what she would do.

She paused, no doubt trying to work out why I was being so rude. Then she finally moved from her hiding place and moved slowly through the aisle to where I could see her. I had to work really hard not to force myself to look up and engage in conversation with her. I wanted her to feel on the back foot. She appeared from nowhere and began to tease me. My natural reaction was to tease back. She stood in front of the counter. After allowing her to wait for a few seconds, I looked up to say something witty and charming, but when I laid eyes on her pixie-like face, I lost all power of speech and just gawped. *Classic Wayward.*

CHAPTER TWENTY-NINE

Alchemist's Rules

I had never seen someone smile so completely after being teased, and that was putting it lightly, as I was outright rude to this young lady, and here she was just standing in front of me and smiling her infectious smile. Her wide eyes and expression said, "*Try what you want, but I won't be losing this grin anytime soon.*" So I just smiled back up at her from my seat behind the counter. A substantial amount of time passed with both of us looking at the other, not really saying or even signalling for one of us to take the initiative to break the rather bizarre smile off.

"*The Auguries of Sorcery*? That's some heavy-duty lower school reading," the red-headed young lady before me taunted, showing that we were still playing this game of mocking wit she seemed so fond of.

"I'm reasonably new to the magic thing," I said in my defence and embarrassment.

"Maybe I can help?" she said, placing her elbows on the edge of the counter and her head in her hands. There was a hint of Cornish in her accent, but only a hint. "I'm not so new to the magic thing."

"Really?" I asked sceptically. "Then why don't you tell me something I don't already know?" I found challenging her was easy, almost natural.

"I can tell you that your man, Aktor Thoön, was supposed to be Greek of origin, a man travelling the world of magic, studying and learning whatever he could whenever he could. I can tell you that the prophecy of him returning has scared children of magic for centuries, as they are told of his promise to come back and destroy the world if they do not behave and use their magic responsibly, and I can tell you that it is a load of rubbish," she finished abruptly.

"What?"

"Nonsense."

"What do you mean?"

"I mean you are wasting your time or trying to waste mine." She now had a sense of authority about her, even through that smile, and I didn't like it.

"Wasting your time? You are free to leave. Don't let the door slap you on the ass on your way out," I said with a growl and instantly regretted my mention of her bottom. She was only young, probably about twenty. I mean I'm not old, or prudish . . . but, well, manners, y'know?

"My ass will stay un-slapped, thank you very much," she said as her smile turned more into a mischievous grin before carrying on, "as I will not be walking out of your door anytime soon. In fact, I was assuming you were going to let me stay."

"Stay? As in the night?" I was genuinely shocked, and that takes some doing after my recent social activities.

"I was thinking I'd stay for as long as it takes," she said, still grinning and throwing her hands into the pockets of her body warmer.

"As long as what takes?" I asked, still shocked.

"Your training."

"My training?"

"Has anyone ever told you that you are a bit like a giant parrot? Only with less feathers."

"What?" I was falling further down the rabbit hole with each new half-asked or half-answered question.

"I am your assigned Alchemist from the Court of the Primoris Dedúcet. Welcome to your training through the magical arts."

"You're my Alchemist, trainer, partner, buddy? Like Mickey from Rocky?" I joked as a reaction.

"More like a kung fu film."

"Karate kid?" I guessed.

"Kill Bill," she corrected. But I liked her. *IT! I liked that she joked, that was what I liked . . . I'm in over my head.*

Once again, we found a moment of awkward silence, with her grin and my confused face, daring each other to be the first one to break the frozen image. I knew I would have to say something since she seemed so well practised at not making the first move, and I had a feeling that this was going to become a regular thing. *Regular? Does that mean she's staying?*

"How would you like a cup of tea?" I asked, glad to find an excuse to stand up and do something other than think of something to say to the girl who had just told me she was hoping she could sleep under my roof. "Tea would be lovely. Milk, no sugar, thank you," she replied.

"Stay here, look around, entertain yourself and I'll be back in a mo," I said as I trotted into the kitchen. I filled the kettle, prepared the mugs with tea bags of high calibre, and found that I was intently focused on the correct method of tea making. In my eyes, this consisted of a tea bag, then water, then remove bag and add milk; anyone who left the tea bag in and added milk was considered to be a barbaric animal and unwelcome under my roof. *I wonder how she makes a cup of tea? She? What's her bloody name?* I thought in a panic. I knew I had to bite the bullet and ask her name; yes, it would be embarrassing, as the moment for names had passed, but I had been in a situation before where I had played along calling an unnamed acquaintance pal, guy, friendo, and mate for far too long, making any conversation or further introduction almost impossible. I knew I had to end that other friendship there, but if she was going to be my Alchemist, I had to get her name, and fast.

As I got to the kitchen door with two full mugs in my hands – mine was the Batman mug, and being the gentleman I am, I made sure she had the Catwoman mug – I called, "Tea's ready", and she came over; that's when I made my move. "My name's Jon, Jon Wayward."

"I know," she said after a slurp of tea.

"Right . . ."

"You want my name," she stated rather than asked.

"It would help," I said honestly. It earned me a smile, which I can imagine wasn't hard to muster from the girl who never stopped smiling.

"My name is Tamsin Blight, and I've been an Alchemist for a long time, so you have nothing to worry about," she said reassuringly and then continued. "Why is your kitchen downstairs but your flat upstairs?"

"I inherited the place, I didn't design it," I said defensively.

"Good. Where can I put my things?" She nodded at the suitcase and worn brown leather handbag that sat at the side of the counter.

"You can, erm, take the, er, room in the, huh." I didn't know what to say. I lived upstairs, and I wasn't about to start sharing my room with this girl I had only just met. For one, I'm not the type to take advantage, even when they turn up on my doorstep and *tell me* that they are moving in. Second, I've got some personal space issues, and I don't like people going through my things, good intentions or not. There was one place that came to mind, but I hadn't been down there since I was a child or more recently to get rid of the Lamiac corpse in the furnace, and I'd felt *It* both times, a presence that was watching and waiting; when I was young, I ran so fast back up the stairs and straight into the street outside the shop to get away from whatever it was that my grandfather had to come out to find me and ask what was wrong. After I told him, he didn't laugh or make fun but just promised me that I would never have to go down there ever again unless I wanted to.

But I was a child at the time, and Tamsin was more than capable of looking after herself, I guess. To be honest, there was nowhere else; as long as she was OK with it, then she could stay. *Am I really going to offer this strange young lady a bed in my haunted cellar?* "Tamsin, there is really only one room you can have, if you're staying longer than a night."

"Sounds good to me. Where do I sign?" she asked excitedly.

"Hang on a mo. There is something I need to tell you about the cellar." I was building up to it.

"You're putting me in the cellar?" she asked a little surprised.

"It's the only space I have, and it's quite spacious. But seriously, I don't really go down to the cellar that often. It has a weird feeling to it." I was clearly avoiding what I wanted to tell Tamsin about.

"Weird feeling to it? Like what?" she asked, and I knew I had to tell her the truth.

"Like there is something watching you." I tried to sound casual but failed.

"A ghost?" She sounded sceptical as if I was tricking her.

"Yeah, a ghost."

"Seriously."

"Dead serious." Maybe not the best choice of words I could have chosen.

"Cool," she said with her familiar smile growing into an impressively larger one. "I've always wanted to study ghosts, but it's so time-consuming. Living with one is ideal!" She whipped her bags into her arms and stood ready to be taken to her new room.

"OK then . . . follow me." I turned and started walking over to the back of the shop where we took the spiral stairs down instead of up. The stairs down didn't see much action, but I had a feeling that that would change.

Looking back at it now, I'm glad that someone moved into the cellar, as there were a few secrets down there that needed to see the light of day, and it might be best for someone else to uncover those, but that story is for another time.

Taking Tamsin down to the cellar was a quick and nerve-racking experience. As soon as we had stepped from the last metal-clanging stair, I had that old familiar feeling. Tamsin giggled to herself, and I could tell that she could feel it as well; just that she was enjoying it. I took the last step and could feel a bead of cold sweat forming on my forehead and hear my pulse thumping in my eardrums; blood was racing around my body like a scooter in a cul-de-sac. I was trying to hide my uneasiness from Tamsin, as she seemed to be in her element. I started up a conversation to take my mind off whatever I could feel getting closer and watching me. "So how long do you think you'll be staying?"

"However long it takes." She looked around with wide eyes. "This place is amazing! Help me move this." She jumped at the biggest box in the cellar, so I leant over and helped shift one of the many dust-covered boxes to reveal a fair amount of space hidden behind. "This is going to be perfect, but there are a few things I'm going to need you to get." She pulled out a small notebook and pen from her back jeans pocket and scribbled a list on to a sheet of paper before tearing it off and handing it to me. "If you sort the list out, I'll tidy up down here."

"You're serious about this?"

"I'm serious about teaching you to use your magic in a safe way."

"How did you get into this? You can only be about . . ." I paused as I saw the look on her face turn with low light, showing her bright eyes like candles in the dark. I changed my failing approach. ". . . How old are you? Roughly?"

"Roughly? About 200 years older than you," she said in a tone that told me not to second-guess her.

"Two hundred. Wow! You look so . . ." – thinking on my feet was becoming an instinct – ". . . young and lovely." I smiled what I hoped was my least creepy smile. She was standing and staring with her usual smile, waiting for me to make another classic mistake, which I imagine is how she looks when she is not impressed. I had to stop digging a hole for myself and get out of the cellar where I was being watched by more than one pair of eyes. "Right! Well, I'll jump straight on to this list to make sure you feel at home. I'll be back in an hour or so." By the time I had finished speaking, I was halfway up the stairs clanging over her head and back into the light and fresh air of my ghost-free antiquarian dealership.

Getting to the top of the stairs and taking a step back into the shop, I leaned up against a display case for a moment. It held a variety of some showy and some real divination products. I heard the crystal balls rattle and cleromancy bowls full of bones slide with my weight on the frame, but I didn't care if they had moved. They could predict what they wanted whenever they wanted; I never really checked. What I was checking was my sanity. So much had happened in the last week, and as the feeling of dead eyes looking into the depths of my soul was beginning to fade, I thought back and couldn't believe where I had ended up, especially after thinking that I had been dealt a quiet life looking after a shop just outside of North

London that not many people visit; I mean, I live in zone 9 on the tube map! Not many Londoners even know that there is a zone 9. A week ago, my main concern was finding a way to develop customer traffic through my door; that was still a fairly big concern, but now I was thinking how I could become a Grimoire and engage my new magical acquaintances into business with Smoke and Mirrors whilst staying alive and stopping the reformation, if it's even real. That and making suitable living conditions for my new tenant, if that is what I could have called her.

I still had the list in my hand and knew that if I wanted any peace and a good start to my training, I was going to have to make my new teacher comfortable. As I walked to the shop door, I looked down at the ring on my thumb and felt its magic keeping mine in check. The thought of being trained up as a powerful Grimoire was exciting. *I could be like Helsing!* I would also have to find the time to learn how to properly use that dagger and throwing knives; otherwise, he might think I'd just leave it in my rocking chair, which I thought I had. *They weren't there this morning, were they?* I knew I must have put them away somewhere safer in my morning daze, in what I refer to as B.C. Meaning before coffee, and I would look for them later.

I turned the OPEN sign over in the shop door and showed the world we were closed for the rest of the day as I stepped out on to the street. It was then that a brick-sized fist crashed into my nose with an almighty crack. That was my nose breaking, and a thump as I hit the pavement floor. I was scooped off the street as a van screeched by the mini roundabout and then to a stop next to me. The van doors were thrown open and then I was hurled, literally hurled, into the back; the doors were slammed shut and locked, and I found myself rolling around the metal floor, trying to get my head above my knees and shift around from the heap I was in. I knew screaming wasn't going to do me any good, so I conserved my energy and tried to calm myself down with the thought, *If they wanted me dead, then they would have done it at the side of the road.* Not the most comforting thought, but it was all I had. Small mercy.

CHAPTER THIRTY

Question Time

My nose had stopped bleeding, and the pain in my face had become bearable for the moment. I was still being rolled around the back of the van as it took sharp corners and whipped down the roads leading out of Amersham. I'm not sure which way we were leaving the town because it felt like we were constantly swinging around corners, but we had definitely done a couple of miles before we pulled over at the side of the road.

It was only when we had stopped that I saw the runes layering the entirety of the inside cabin of the van drawn in what I guessed was a permanent marker pen. Whether it was the water in my eyes, from my throbbing bleeding nose, or my lack of rune knowledge, I couldn't tell what the purpose of them were, but I could make a guess that they wanted to stop me from using any magic. They didn't have to worry about that too much as the Court had taken care of that for them, with their ring and their threats as to what will happen if I abuse my power. Just when I had calmed myself and tried to work out what was happening to me, I heard the front doors of the driver's cabin open and then close. Two different footfalls walked either side of the van up to the back doors. I prepared myself and knew that the only magic I was capable of using, without breaking the Court's laws, was that of time manipulation. Otherwise, I would have the Archmage trinity of law and boring breathing down my neck, which could put me in a worse position than I was in now.

The van's doors swung open, and as the light flooded the cabin, I tried to dart out into the street using my time manipulation spell but found that I only stumbled to the end of the cabin and fell over the bumper and out on to the floor at my captors' feet. They stood above me and looked down in surprise. One of them who was coming into focus spoke to the other, saying, "*Chronus Perceptio*? Magic, against us?" He looked down to my hanging body. "You're obviously a slow learner, Wayward. It must be hereditary." His voice was familiarly annoying, and I knew who it was before his face blurred into focus. Poet continued to talk. "Unfortunately for you, *we* learn quickly. Dampening runes disarm you of your magic. Looks like you'll have to rely on your smarts for a while." He laughed his high-pitched laugh as if he were some kind of jackal, and his big lumbering moustached friend laughed with no sound like a silent movie in colour and on steroids, lots and lots of steroids. "Good luck with that."

Bard's hands clamped on to my face, with one of them covering my eyes and the other grabbing me under my chin and lifting me from the floor. I had to hold on to his arms to lift my weight from my neck and stop Bard from pulling my head from my shoulders. His arms were like steel pistons with knotted rope twisting beneath the taut skin, and I had no idea where he was carrying me to as I was dangling like a rag doll in an overgrown child's hand. I could see the light change through a small gap in his fingers as we moved inside a building, and the pain of his hand resting just on the bridge of my nose was like a metal rod being pushed through my brain. He threw me down on to a concrete floor, and I bounced before I found some stability and rested my bruised back up against a metal barrel. It was nice to be sitting up and have a few seconds to check whether my nose was still pointing forward. It was, if I tilted my head to the left.

"Wayward, old buddy, old pal! It's bloody good to see you in one piece. I'll be honest I had my money on the Lamiac tearing you and your pals to pieces, but you've got more lives than a litter of kittens." He laughed to himself as he stepped out from Bard's shadow and stood shoulder to shoulder with him as best as he could for someone who was at least a foot and a half shorter.

"You sent the lizards?" I managed to ask as I wiped blood from my nose with the sleeve of my shirt.

"I'll be asking the questions around here, me old mucker. Otherwise, Bard here will break your nose," Poet said with a lyrical beat to his sentences.

"But it's already broken!" I exclaimed.

"Bard," Poet said as an instruction. In a flash, the hulking Bard took a giant step and once again used my nose to crack his knuckles with. I let out a scream followed by some words my mother would have been ashamed to hear me say. "Well, listen to you sweary Mary. If I were you, I'd cut the rudeness and tell us what we want to know. Otherwise, my friend here gets to play with his new toy until he breaks it." He nodded up to Bard who was now standing next to him again.

So I was crying in front of two grown men, and I wasn't afraid to say that shame was far from my mind. I did manage to squeeze a few words out between the feeling of that metal rod being rammed back into my brain through my nose and the blood and tears running down my face and on to my shirt collar. "Fine." I sounded bunged up and half-choking. "I'll tell you what you want to know," I admitted even though I wasn't sure what I was and what I wasn't going to say; my plan was to say just enough to keep me alive.

"We want the cards, Wayward, the tarot cards you've been collecting from all over the country. We want them – now," Poet said without much humour in his voice.

"Well, I don't have them on me," I said.

"Where are they?"

"Hidden from you, so you can't kill me and take them for free."

"OK, let's try something else," Poet said, now pacing across the room and back to help him think of what he wanted to ask. "We know you have been working with the Court and the Servants of the Night. Who else is helping you and why?"

"I haven't been working with anyone!" I assured him.

"Maurice Talpidae, Emilia Nótt, Sebastian Dove, and the Archmages of the Court! We know who you have been working with. We're not stupid," Poet almost spat his point at me. I had nothing else to offer but a delirious laugh as I sat on the floor, feeling the concrete's cold grip soak up into my legs and begin to numb my body.

"Dove?" I said, then took a deep breath to stop myself from talking in-between laughs. "You think I'm working with Dove?"

"He has been teaching you magic, and he works for the Court as an Alchemist. Why wouldn't you be working with him? He's your assigned Alchemist."

"Until just now I thought he was the one hiring you two chuckle brothers."

"Hiring us?" Poet stopped pacing and looked to his gigantic friend. I took a second to look at the room we were in, and all I could glean was that it was dark, cold, and hidden from any source of natural light. To be fair, I'm not exactly a Columbo in the making, and I don't know if I could've found any clues to help me even if the lights were on.

"I think we both know you've been hired to get the cards, same as me, except you're slightly more aggressive and a lot less intellectual. So come on, tell me who the boss man is if it isn't Dove." Poet looked from me to

Bard and then back to me, wondering what he should do. I don't think he was counting on the interrogation being a two-way exercise in information exchange. "Kelley? Is he pulling the strings?"

"Let's just say that when all this is over and the Wayward clan is back in the ground with the tarot cards in our possession, we'll be protected from up on high, by the Prince of Darkness himself." Poet's smarmy smile returned with his false sense of security. His smile soon fell from his face when he saw mine stretch from one side to the other. "Why are you so bloody happy?"

"Because the cavalry has arrived." With that, Sebastian Dove coughed from behind Poet and Bard loud enough for them to hear and turn around. What they hadn't seen was Sebastian marking the floor with his own runes in chalk as Poet was telling me how he would like to see me in the ground. I saw Sebastian creep in and start to make his markings, but they didn't know I played Clarence in Richard the Third at school and was quite the amateur performer. I got myself into character to allow Poet to walk straight into the trap. Hidden talent number one. Speaking of traps, when Poet and Bard saw Sebastian, they charged at him, not thinking that an Alchemist would give them as much trouble as they could dish out, and they hit one of the runic wards he had drawn on to the concrete just behind them. This was where the fun began. As they hit the ward, an orange light flashed at them as if they were hit by a small star going supernova, and they were flung across the room, landing in a pile of metallic barrels like the one I was leaning against, Bard on top of Poet. "Where the hell have you been?" I sighed and took a badly needed deep breath that allowed me to feel the cold seeping into my bruised body once again.

"I think you meant to say *thank you for saving me and being my hero*," Sebastian joked as he pulled me to my feet.

"But seriously, where the hell have you been?" I said as he was leading me up a ramp in the opposite direction to where I had been brought in by the terrible twosome. We got to the end of the ramp, and he kicked open a door, which led us into an alley. "Hold on to your questions for now, Wayward. Let's get you fixed up and safe before we care and share. I know a place not far that will take us in," he said as I began to move on my own, and we half jogged, half stumbled down the alley and out into the street. I followed him without asking where we were going; I was just glad to be away from those two psychopaths and their one-sided double act.

It felt like we had been running for quite a long time, but since I wasn't really built for running, there's no telling how long it had been before my body began to reject the idea of physical exercise when not in immediate danger of death. To the relief of my lungs, as I was having a hard time breathing with all the blood pouring and half drying around my nose, we hit a solid wooden door off the street and burst through into a large and dim-lit room, landing very ungracefully on to a spit-and-sawdust-covered floor. Immediately, I knew that we weren't the only ones in there, and I scanned the room whilst wiping the sweat from my brow. "Where are we?" I asked from the side of my mouth, noticing that only one or two of the people inside had given us a glance.

"Somewhere safe," Sebastian said. He rose from the spot at which we fell in through the door, and I followed, trying to keep my calm and not be as noticeable as a man covered in blood lying on the floor could be. "We're OK. We won't have any trouble here." He moved forward, and as I followed like some nervous younger brother trotting along to keep up with the older kid, I saw that we were in a pub.

I had to ask, "What is this place?"

"This is one of the few refuges left to us normal magic users in the city limits," he said with pride. "The Middle of the Road."

"What do you mean *normal* magic users?" My attention was drawn momentarily to the man standing at the jukebox as one of my favourite songs came on dimly over the speakers, just enough to obscure the words of the other patrons in the pub. The guitar riff was instantly recognisable, and I knew every word of "Carry On, My Wayward Son", almost claiming it as my name's sake. But I didn't sing along; it was grown-up time around the table, and I could still taste my own gritty iron blood in the back of my mouth.

"Some would say that the Court and their Grimoires of high society are too good for our kind and don't like to mix with the likes of us." Sebastian looked at me to see how I had digested his comment. "Not you, of course. You're one of us. You're going to help me change all that."

"I am?"

"Drink?" he asked as we were standing at the bar by this point.

"Yeah, whatever he's having," I said to the barman.

"And you?" asked the uninterested and balding barman.

"Dry martini with twist," he said as I jumped in and changed my order.

"On second thoughts, I'll have a pale ale, please." The barman wiped his hands on his white apron, which was stained with some interesting shade of yellow, standing out against his *actual* white T-shirt beneath as he leant over and began pouring my pint.

"What happened to your face, lad?" the barman asked without looking up at me.

"It's the altitude," I said almost as a reaction.

"The altitude?"

"Stood up too quickly, dizzy spell and all that." I waited for him to dig deeper, but he didn't care that much, and Sebastian just smirked at my flippant comment. With the drinks in Sebastian's hands, he paid, and we found ourselves a table in the furthest and darkest corner of the room. He slid my drink across the table to me as we sat opposite each other. It all reminded me of some film where the main characters sit down to plot what their next move is, and I thought, *All I need now is for Sebastian to say some Eighties' action movie line, and I'll be living the dream!* I took a sip of my drink, and Sebastian mumbled to himself, "Hasta la vista, Baby!" Then he threw his drink down his throat and let out a sigh of relief. Quoting Arnie put Sebastian back into my good books immediately. In fact, I was tempted to start quoting the big man myself, but I knew we had slightly more urgent things to discuss.

"What's happening, Sebastian?" I asked.

"I've come back from the future to warn you," he said as he sat back into his chair.

"Really?!" I asked in shock.

"Nope. Just making sure I had your full attention." He smiled at his own little joke before draining the dregs of his dry martini.

Chapter Thirty-One

Flip a Coin?

He began to tell me where he had been and what he had been up to, and I was lost in his story, wanting to understand every last detail. I knew that asking questions I wanted the answers to would just slow down the whole thing down, so I just listened. He told me that after he had exposed me to *real* magic and its *real* power, the Courts had asked him to come in for questioning, which he would have gone to if he hadn't come across the two Mages for hire, Poet and Bard. They had been hired to get their hands on the same tarot cards I had been sent after by Emilia's employer, whoever that was. He said that he couldn't give me a name, as I was *too involved* and that it could put me in more danger than I already was, but the one who had hired Poet and Bard was one within the Court. I couldn't believe it. The faces of the Archmages flashed before my eyes, each one looking guilty with malicious smiles and daggers in the eyes as they stared back.

He stopped for a moment, finished his second drink, and nodded for me to take a sip of mine as I was mesmerised by his story and who was involved. He had only given me a taster, and I had to ask the obvious. "Why does everyone want these cards?" Even though I had done my own research and knew the answer for myself, I wanted to see what he would tell me and to see if I could really trust him. *He's popped back from nowhere in the nick of time to save me, which I'm grateful for, and now he's asking me to join him in his quest against the Court.* If he was about to spin me some nonsense heartbreak, I was about to walk out. "What is so special about them?" I thought back to Kelley's words and waited for Sebastian, hoping his story would hit the mark. "Well?" I pushed for him to spill the beans.

"The cards" – he put his drink down – "are a source of power, a key if you will, to allow a great Mage back into the world of magic along with spells and incantations long forgotten and lost by the Court's heavy-handed approach to control. It is one of many Seals we must find in order to release this falsely imprisoned man and bring justice back to the world." He sounded confident in his own words.

"Innocent man? From what I have read, Aktor Thoön is not innocent."

"You know of Aktor Thoön? Well, what you have read is Court propaganda that has been forced down the world's throat for far too long," he shot back, looking at his empty glass.

"Some would say he doesn't even exist," I offered, playing the devil's advocate.

"He. Does. Exist." He slowly looked up to me from across the table. "The Reformation of the Mages is a way to share the power of the Court fairly and not keep it a secret for themselves. Aktor Thoön is the instigator to allow us to begin this shift of power, a shift to all magic users to share the power the Court keeps for itself, taking away their need to define and control each of us. Some without even knowing it."

"Do you mean the Grimoires?" I jumped the gun to what he was really hinting at.

"Yes. I mean the Grimoires. The Court has allowed the Grimoires to control the rest of us for generations, keeping the rest of our families at the bottom of the food chain, having to learn everything anew with each new magic-born generation." He waited for my reaction, but I gave none. I held my near-empty pint glass in my hand and kept my gaze on the half-faded logo printed on the outside to hide my uncertainty with these new accusations I was hearing. "You are different, Wayward. You are the Grimoire who has the power and the knowledge to help me help the world," he said with a genuine tone. "I need you, Wayward. The world needs you. These Mages and Archmages do not trust you. They think you are the same as those who have gone before you who hold your family name, those who have betrayed everyone they know to survive and succeed. I can see that you're not one of them. I can see that you are a better Grimoire than any who has carried your family's crest before you, and I can see that you are a better man than most in this world. I will not tell you what you have to do. I will only *ask* you to do what is right."

We sat there for a while as he gave me time to allow his words to sink in and take hold in my mind. I genuinely didn't know what to say or do. I had believed for sometime that Sebastian was the bad guy, trying to get me killed. Now I learned that Poet and Bard were working for one of the Archmages, and if I could have put some money on it, I would have said

Bloyse. He hated me from the moment he saw me, and I had a feeling he hated a few others who carried my name before me, and I bet no one had seen behind that closed iron gate in his subconscious where he kept all his secrets. I finally found some words to let Sebastian know I had not given up completely and taken a vow of silence. "If I did believe you, which is still up for debate, then what *right* would you have me do?"

"Bring me the tarot cards and help me find the rest of the Seals. Then together, we can challenge the Courts of this world with Aktor Thoön by our sides to bring equality and fairness to all magic users. The Court's tyranny *must* come to an end," Sebastian pleaded.

"Is the Court really that bad? Yeah, OK. They're pretty up their own arses and self-important, but are they really tyrants?"

"You have no idea what I have seen them do. I was placed as an Alchemist with the Court, doing their research and due diligence for centuries."

"Centuries?" I asked sceptically.

"The Mages and other magic users you've met are a lot older than you think. The use of magic allows a symbiotic relationship, keeping you biologically healthy in order to allow the use of magic to last longer and to prolong its own life cycle. The Mage and the magic have a coexistence, one allowing the other to keep the magic alive and in the world. As such, a few men and women are naturally attuned to the ways of magic." Something else that all my *so-called* friends had neglected to tell me, I thought about how long I would live for, and if I did, did I want to fight with or against Sebastian?

"Listen, Sebastian, I may not like Bloyse, but I can't see them ruling with an iron fist," I said.

"Well, I *have* seen them, Wayward. I've seen what they do to those who disappoint them and the horrors that befall those who stand against them.' He held his hand out over the table between us and nodded at it. 'I can show you.' I felt a wave of heat and cautiously moved my hand across the table to meet his, and as I placed my palm in his, he brought his other hand on top and closed his eyes as he gave me his last word of warning. 'I am sorry for this, Wayward. But if you are to fight by my side for the good of all Mage kind, you must see the sins of those who we must oppose.' With that, a cold ripple poured from his hands and into mine, running up my palm, falling into my wrist and racing up my arm into my neck and straight to my eyes. This all reminded me of my tattoos when they claimed my flesh, but what I saw was one of those few rare visions that you are never able to un-see again, a sight that was burnt into my soul and changed me as a person.

What I saw was a nightmare come to life. What I saw had to be stopped. I'm not going to go into details right now, but let me tell you that Bloyse, Morgause, and even Bacon have been torturing Mages who wouldn't follow their plans for the Court's dominance for thousands of years, even those who worked for them at the Court who failed to produce the answers they wanted. I saw Sebastian working by their side, terrified of the Court's right hand, the Grimoire Merlin, and what he would do if he found out that Sebastian was working against the Court. He had been put on the Seals project, where he was ordered to research and locate the Seals in which a Grimoire was prophesied to acquire them and then they could be hidden from the world, locking Thoön away indefinitely. To keep his name separate from the project, he spoke to a Grimoire with discreet vassals to act on his behalf. This allowed him to work in the shadows and hide his true purpose of finding the Seals, bringing them together, releasing the one person who has defied the Courts of the world and could again. Sebastian employed Doctor John Dee to use a messenger from his order to bring the Wayward line back to the path of magic, as a Grimoire rather than as an unaware observer.

The images that Sebastian had shown me began to run back from my eyes and down my arms and into the palm of my hand where the cool feeling they brought rescinded into Sebastian's hands and left me empty. I was stuck with the image of Sebastian's contact, a man with curly dark hair giving an order to a purple-robed figure. I had seen that man before, in a dream, in a vision, when I was in a hotel in Devon, waking up in a strange room with a strange woman. He was giving the robed figure a leather-bound book, a book with an extravagant *W* engraved into the front. It was my family grimoire. The robed figure took the book and spoke. "By the night's black mantle." And as the robed figure turned to leave, I saw Emilia leaving the man behind, and I knew that Dee was in charge of the Servants of the Night, helping Sebastian from the shadows with his plot against the Court. Dee was Emilia's boss . . . *Wow!*

"You need time to think, Wayward," Sebastian said with an understanding smile and bowing head. "If you do decide to stand with me, break this." He handed me a small glass ball that was cloudy inside with flickering lights flashing wherever he touched it. As I took it, I felt a tingle and examined it up close. It was beautiful to look at and reminded me of one of those Eighties' electrical balls that you would touch and they would create a static charge, but much, much smaller. "Keep it somewhere safe, and when the time is right and you have all the tarot cards, completing the first Seal, break it, and it will transport you to wherever I am. But be careful." He gave me a serious look as he got up from the table and stood to look down at me. "They could be watching you, Wayward. They could be listening to everything you say. Just because your *friends* follow the Court's whims, it doesn't mean you should. Or that you can trust them." With those words of caution, he walked away from our table and out of the front door, leaving me in this strange pub with my traitorous thoughts and a choice that lay before me. I did what any sane Grimoire in my position would do. I pulled out a coin and thought to myself *heads for Court and tails for Dove*. I flipped the coin high into the air to see what my fate would be, but before it had even reached the tabletop, I was on my way out of the pub following in Sebastian's footsteps, knowing what I needed to do.

CHAPTER THIRTY-TWO

The Last Card

By the time I got back to Smoke and Mirrors, my nose and brain had started to hurt a little less, and I had come up with my reasons as to why my face and clothes had a fair amount of my own blood smeared across them. I stood outside the shop door for a second, gathering my thoughts and trying to push down the horrible feeling that was holding fast in my gut, letting me know that hiding things from the people I'm supposed to trust felt wrong. In fact, just having to pretend that everything was fine and lie through my teeth had an adverse effect on my conscience and, therefore, my stomach. *But I had seen it with my own eyes!* I thought. *Well, Sebastian's eyes at least.*

I opened the door and quietly said "Hello", only as loud as my courage permitted but quiet enough to show the cowardliness of my conviction. Obviously, I was heard, although I'm not quite sure how, and a soft and gentle voice came twittering up from my haunted cellar. "Hi, Wayward! I'm down here tidying up a last few things. Come and have a look!" she called up to me. I slowly moved further into the shop, taking my time to get to the spiral stairs leading down to the cellar. I noticed that everything in the shop seemed a little brighter. The various antiques on the shelves all had a certain glow about them that they hadn't had before. I finally made my way down the stairs, trying to shrug off the feeling, that as soon as I had started down them, that horrible watching feeling gripped me, and I was sure there was something following me. I started talking to try to take my mind off it. "Hi, Tamsin. Are you managing to find some space in . . . this . . . dusty . . . old . . ." My words trailed into surprise and a loss of words as I looked upon the creepy old dirty haunted cellar of my childhood. It now resembled more of a high-end apartment/bedroom with all the mod cons. It was spotless; everything had been stacked to the side and organised into alphabetical order, except for the items Tamsin had decided to use for her new living space. She had taken an ottoman that had belonged to the first prefect of Constantinople called Honoratus, and let me tell you, he had a little preternatural help to become the first prefect. She had pulled over the Marie Antoinette's chopping block as a coffee table and Aleister Crowley's red leather sofa. It all took on a bizarre collection of styles and colours but somehow seemed to work. I guess it must be the bright yellow-painted walls and high ceilings that pulled it all together.

"When did you paint the walls?"

"Earlier. What do you think?" Her smile seemed to want me to be impressed, and I was.

"I think you're amazing! *It's* amazing," I corrected and repeated myself. "*It's* amazing."

"Well, I am kind of a big deal," she said with a giggle as she danced into the space to show me what she looked like in it. Then she looked at me properly for the first time since I had been back. "What in the name of the Divines has happened to you?"

"I was mugged."

"In Amersham?"

"Yeah, in Amersham."

"Why?" she exclaimed.

"They said they wanted my wallet and phone."

"So what happened?" she asked, wanting my side of the story. I knew it was time to deliver my brilliantly prepared version of events. So I told the story of how Poet and Bard had grabbed me, whilst leaving out their names, and how they broke my nose and went for my wallet and phone, just as I sprang into action and gave them a few slaps, sending them off into the underworld of Amersham, nursing their wounds. Surprisingly, she had questions. "Underworld of Amersham?"

"Oh yeah, horrible, nasty underworld. Don't worry though, I'll keep you safe," I said, not realising how creepy it sounded out loud compared to the smooth Han Solo voice in my head.

"Well, OK then. Why don't you let me clean you up?" she said as she moved off to what I had remembered as a half-rotted, half-misshapen set of drawers, which now appeared to be something George Clarke could use in one of his amazing spaces. She had worked wonders in the cellar, and I was beginning to think that as long as she was willing to stay in the cellar and help out with the shop, she could be a welcomed tenant rather than a mystical squatter. She rummaged around and pulled out a small tub that had the dark silhouette of a bird on the side with the word 'Caladrius' printed across the side with the D in the middle of the word as a capital letter. She dabbed her finger into the pot and then smoothed the cream over the cuts on my face and over my broken nose. "That should help kick-start the healing process."

"Thank you," I said nervously. Her touch was gentle and caring without a hint of maliciousness or deception. I couldn't understand how the Court had sucked in Tamsin, Maurice, and Emilia and how they were forcing their will upon the world unchecked. *Who watches the watchmen?* I thought to myself and felt a pang of guilt and pity at the same time. I was feeling for Tamsin who was so obviously under the Court's thumb, being sent here to watch me and make sure I did as they commanded and also for what I was going to do. I had made up my mind before I had even known it. I was going to get the last card and get them to Sebastian. *"Between us we can stop the Court's dominion over all Mage kind."* I played his words over in my mind. It was the right thing to do.

"Did you forget to buy the bits and bobs I asked for? Or were they stolen by the army of muggers you were fending off?" she asked with that smile I now knew was a near-permanent fixture.

"Yeah, erm." Just as I was grabbing at nothing and lost for words, the shop door opened, and the bell rang to let us know that someone had come in. "Customer!" I exclaimed. "Why don't you come up and I'll show you how to earn your keep around here?" I asked, turning to the stairs and finding that the feeling of being watched was still there, but it had changed its intention. It felt like it wasn't angry any more; it felt like it was protective, but not of me, of Tamsin.

We came out on to the shop floor to be greeted by Moon standing in his worn leather jacket with what looked like a pair of unwashed jeans and a casually stained T-shirt. He had a wooden board under his arm that looked like a chess set and a flask of coffee in his other hand. After taking a few steps into the shop, the door closed behind, and the bell tinkled again to let us know he had ventured past the threshold. He was looking up at the tall shelves with antiquities of magical descent from across the country and, in some cases, from across the world. He moved closer to a small statue sitting just above his eye level; it was an ancient Egyptian statue of a man holding a stele of "Horus on the crocodiles", which was rumoured to let someone pour water over the hundreds of magical inscriptions and then drink the liquid, healing them of any poison. I watched him for a moment as he studied the markings from some of the first magic users in the world, but before I could welcome him to the shop with any kind of formal and proper business-like introduction, Tamsin shouted from over my shoulder.

"Hello there! Welcome to Smoke and Mirrors! How can I help you?!" Both Moon and I jumped with the volume of her greeting.

"Little quieter next time," I said to Tamsin before turning to Moon. "Mr Moon, good to see you." I scrunched my nose quickly to see how bad it was, and it ached a bit, but Tamsin's special cream had worked wonders. I moved over to Moon with a newfound confidence that I hadn't had since my supposed mugging. "What have you brought for me?"

"I'm gonna show ya rather than tell ya," Moon said with his South London accent wrapping around his vowels and tripping over his consonants.

"Please," I gestured for him to come further in the shop. "Do you need anything?"

"I could do wiv a table and a glass o'water," he said as he walked to the back of the shop.

"There's one just behind the curse boxes," I said, pointing over to the far wall. We made our way over, and I cleared up some curse boxes, making sure that I didn't drop any of them and release some horrific plague loose in the shop. Moon laid out his chessboard, which turned out not to be a chessboard at all but an Ouija board. He then pulled out a Tippex pen and started drawing symbols around the board on the surface of the table. I was about to say something along the lines of "*Do you really need to draw all over my antique display table?*" But I kept my mouth closed and bit my lip. I guess I was learning to be a people person.

When I came back with the glass of water he wanted, I could see that the symbols he was drawing on to the table weren't familiar to me, and I watched as he worked to get his presentation ready. I had a thought of discomfort when I saw the Ouija board and had images of *The Exorcist* flashing before my eyes and prayed that projectile vomit and dead priests were not in my immediate future. Moon seemed to know what he was doing and didn't engage in conversation whilst he was setting his work area. I looked at Tamsin, and unsurprisingly, she was smiling back at me and nodded to Moon's Ouija board and raised her eyebrows to show her excitement at the chance to see it in action. Finally, he finished his Tippex runes, placed the lid back on the pen, sat back in his chair, and picked up his glass of water, which he drank in three long gulps. Afterwards, he let out a huge breath and slammed the glass down right in the centre of the Ouija board upside down. He placed the forefinger of both hands on the rim of the glass and began to breathe deeply through his nose and out through his mouth. His eyelids looked heavier with each breath, and he seemed to be mentally preparing himself to use the board.

"Moon?" I asked, quietly hoping I could get his attention and not break his concentration.

He half opened his right eye and spoke from the side of his mouth. "What?"

"What are you doing? I mean, what are you trying to do here?" I knew I had asked a dumb question, and I was pleased that Moon didn't quip some smart arse answer back at me.

Still speaking from the side of his mouth, but with both his eyes closed, he explained. "I am trying to show ya 'ow my business works. I'm getting in touch with my research assistants, and when I do, I want ya to ask them to find something for ya," Moon said and seemed to be working quite hard to talk to me and commune with whomever he was trying to find. "Don't make it easy for 'em," he said before he let out a quick sharp breath and dropped his head, letting his chin rest on his chest.

"Is he OK?" Tamsin asked me.

"I think this is supposed to happen." I moved closer to him and reached out to put a hand on his shoulder. "Moon? Are you OK?" He flinched before I could nudge him to see if he would respond and began sliding the glass at an incredible speed to the 'yes' written next to 'no' in the centre of the alphabet and number sequence that made up the Ouija board. As the glass sat over the 'yes', Moon spoke the word as well, but not in a voice that Tamsin or myself recognised as his. It was distant and deep, holding a growl back to allow human words to communicate rather than animalistic grunts and snarls.

"Shouldn't you ask him something?" Tamsin asked, obviously excited at the chance to see me communicate with the dead through Moon.

"I guess so," I said unconvincingly. I had no idea what to ask, so in the end, I just went with what seemed natural. I leaned over to the table and spoke loudly, slowly, and clearly to make sure I was heard. "What is your name?"

"You're not speaking to a foreigner. You're speaking to a spirit," Tamsin said as a joke at my expense. I didn't mind, and I was distracted by the voice and the answer that came out.

"*We are Legion, for we are many.*" This time it sounded like there were a hundred voices, all whispering at the same moment.

"Can you find something for me, Legion?" I asked.

"*There is nothing in your realm we cannot find,*" It said through Moon's dropped head.

"Can you find . . ?" I was thinking of a way to test the Legion, or whatever spirits or souls Moon had tapped into, and then it came to me. ". . . Horus on the crocodiles?"

"*Smoke and Mirrors, first display case, fifth shelf from the floor, three displays in.*" I hadn't noticed until now, but I could see that Moon's hands were sliding the glass around the board, spelling out what he was saying at an incredible speed. It was like watching a demonic *Rain Man* on acid. Not only that, but It was right about the Horus statue. Now I knew It had to be tested properly.

"Where is the Wayward Grimoire?" This I asked, knowing that Moon had no clue and that if It could tell me, I would begin to believe in Its authenticity.

"*Wrapped in a spelled cloth upon the bench in your laboratory,*" a hundred voices said as Moon's possessed hands whipped around the Ouija board, spelling it out, "*and standing before us,*" It finished as I stood still without speaking, trying to outthink the voices.

"OK," I said, readying myself to really test it, knowing now that I would ask it something only I had the answer to. "Where are the tarot cards I have been collecting?"

"*You leave their protective box upon your desk to fool your companions, but the cards lay upon your body, wrapped in a handkerchief, and placed in the inside pocket of your waistcoat,*" It said matter-of-factly.

"Bloody hell. You are good," I said, giving Moon's possessed body a nod of achievement and then looking at Tamsin who was also looking very impressed. "Which room are my Helsing daggers in?"

"*They are not in a room.*"

"What?!"

"Come on, Wayward, ask about something that will test it," Tamsin said.

That's when I had a thought that would only lead to this short-lived peace and quiet being cut even shorter. "Legion?" I asked. "Where is the last tarot card?"

"*On the street outside Smoke and Mirrors,*" It said coldly.

"What?" I managed to ask before hearing the door open and the bell ring, letting me know that someone or something had just entered the shop. "No rest for the wicked," I said under my breath as I stepped out from the display case to see who or what had just made its way into my day.

CHAPTER THIRTY-THREE

Subtle Pop

Standing before me next to the counter was Maurice and Emilia, and for a second, I forgot what I had just heard about the last of the tarot cards and trotted over, giving them both a big hug. I was sure this put them both well out of their comfort zones. They both looked at me with wide eyes, and I looked at them, and all of us were thinking about what we should say and how we should move on from the attack leading us into the hands of the Court and their rather aggressive *get to know you* policy. I chose to ignore all that and use my defensive witty charm to diffuse the awkward silence that was beginning to creep into the room. "I'm glad we cleared that up," I said, moving my eyes from Maurice to Emilia.

"We couldn't leave you on your own for more than a day or two. There's no telling what trouble you'd get yourself into," Maurice chirped.

"You don't know the half of it," I said with a huff of a laugh and turned to move back to Moon and Tamsin. "Come, I have some people for you to meet," I said, walking back down the aisle with them following close behind. I was very aware that Emilia hadn't spoken yet, but I knew the right move was to let her talk in her own time and not push her into saying something we'd both regret. "This is Tamsin Blight, my new Alchemist, who has moved into the basement to keep an eye on me and train me to use my magic *responsibly*." I said 'responsibly' in a high-pitched voice whilst pulling a scared face, and no one even cracked a smile. I carried on with the introductions without the further use of classic comedy voices. 'This is Legion *and* Moon. Legion, Moon, and Tamsin, this is Maurice and Emilia.'

'I believe we've met before,' Maurice said with a warm smile. Tamsin looked at Maurice and squinted slightly as people do when they are trying hard to remember something. Maurice tried to help her a little. "1888 Whitechapel?"

"Of course!" Tamsin blurted out with a flash of recognition. "An absolute pleasure."

"As in Jack the Ripper?" I asked, with my face losing all muscle control.

"We can't say—" Tamsin began.

"State secrets," Maurice finished.

"That sounds completely normal," I said in my most sarcastic voice.

"What is he doing?" Emilia asked, and I was happy that she was talking, whether or not it was to me. I explained why there was a very good-looking young girl living in my basement, which sounded creepier every time I mentioned it, but still hadn't had the chance to explain myself about the kiss on the bus and why I had done it. Apart from "I fancy you and wanted to kiss you", I'm not exactly sure what I was going to say, but I'm sure it would sort itself out as things do. Seriously, that's what I thought. I jumped at the chance to engage in a conversation with Emilia to show how calm and at ease I was with everything that had happened.

"He's communing with dead spirits to locate things."

"Why?" Emilia asked still not impressed.

"He's my new business partner. We can now advertise to customers that we can locate any item at their discretion, for a price we can even get it for them and sell it on. This is going to take Smoke and Mirrors into the twenty-first century and beyond!" I said a little too excited. I could feel my nerves pulsing through my body as I was trying to talk with everyone and somehow work out whether Maurice or Emilia had the last card. As soon as I knew who had the card, I was going to pull out the storm bolt little glass ball of magic teleportation thing and smash it, which apparently meant that I'd find myself next to Sebastian.

"*We are pleased to be business partners, Mr Wayward,*" Legion's many voices whispered, making us all turn to Moon swiping the glass around the board, spelling out each word at an inhuman speed.

"Would anyone like to give Legion a try?" I asked with my mind on the cards and not being able to carry on the conversation much further.

"Oh yes, please." Maurice jumped at the chance, then Tamsin, then Maurice again, then Emilia took a turn, and I hadn't heard a word of what they said. I had tuned everything out and was intently focused on who had the tarot card. Legion had said it was right outside the shop door just before Maurice and Emilia walked in, so one of them definitely had it on them.

Time was passing by, and all I could think of was that I needed to get my hands on the tarot card and get it to Sebastian quickly. Neither of us had any interest in hurting anyone; he just wanted to bring an equality to the magical world, and it was for the first time I properly questioned my motives. I was going to help Sebastian, but not for the reasons that he was fighting for. I wanted the chance as much as he did, but I wanted to clear my family name and prove to the Court, all my new friends, and myself that we Waywards were worthy of the Grimoire title and power. I knew there were those out there who didn't think I deserved to have this immense power passed down to me without earning it, and I wanted to show them and everyone else who wanted to listen that I would be a force of good in this world. I would be a man who stands up and is counted for what he believes in and for the betterment of Mage kind and mankind. Sebastian would help me in clearing my name; I could see something in him. Maybe something that I recognised in myself. Maybe it was just a need to find some common ground, but it felt right; it felt like I could trust him.

I had to act, and I knew it had to be now. If I allowed any more time to pass, or if I had tried to work out who had the last card, I knew I would have either talked myself out of using the magic electric teleporting ball or someone would have worked out something was wrong with my more-than-normal socially inept actions and taken it off me and made that decision for me. As the three of them giggled, I sprang into action as Tamsin was in the middle of asking Legion another question about where something was, which he always got exactly right, and took the magic electric teleportation glass ball from my pocket, dropped it on the floor, and threw a hand on Emilia's shoulder and a hand on Maurice's shoulder. When I had gripped them tight, and they turned to look at me as if to say *What the hell are you doing?* I stamped on the glass ball with my shoe and watched it explode. It grew into a huge sparkling sphere, throwing Tamsin and the possessed Moon into their respective walls. Around Maurice, Emilia, and me appeared a glowing ball of blue light and incredible amounts of static electricity firing between our fingers, strands of hair, and layers of clothing. There were a few seconds where we were able to look at the small amount of localised devastation around the glowing blue orb, but time and space seemed to slow before we felt the pull. Lightning had struck and taken us with it.

The pull started with our faces; it seemed to work like G-Force space shuttle pilots feel but in reverse. To begin with, I could feel the stretch in my lips and eyelids away from my face and then as it increased, I could feel all my skin and clothes being plucked forward along with Emilia and Maurice. I could feel it pulling from inside; my internal organs were being yanked on a shoestring towards the front of my body. It hurt, and judging by the sounds of immense screaming and shouting from Emilia and Maurice, I think it was safe to say that I wasn't alone in my pain. My eyes shut tight as my instincts screamed that I was about to be torn in half and then there was a subtle pop that left a clarity in my ears and I was lying on a cold, hard, and rough surface with the wind whipping up across my back, lifting the shirt up from beneath my waistcoat.

I had tried to say something and look around to find out where I was and where Sebastian was. He was supposed to be here waiting for me to bring the tarot cards to him. My words failed me as an instant wave of sickness hit me and I doubled over. For anyone who has been so ill that they are left with dry retching so consuming from within that all you can do is shudder, cry, and try to breathe, then you know what I am talking about. That is what your first teleportation feels like. Although they do get better the more you do it, which was clear from the state of Maurice and Emilia who were pulling themselves to their feet slowly but surely. They had also acquired the power of speech faster than I had after being pulled through time and space. "Wayward?" I heard Maurice sputter as he swallowed down his lunch. "Where are we?"

"I . . . don't . . ." I still couldn't quite manage a sentence in full and found myself still on the floor, ready to vomit or continue my graceful retching.

"Wayward, what have you done?" Emilia desperately asked. Those words echoed in my mind, and I heard her voice and mine asking *What did I do?* as if I was listening from far away. I had to constantly reassure myself that I was doing the right thing, and when I had the chance to explain myself when all this was over, hopefully, both Maurice and Emilia would understand. I couldn't allow myself to be second-guessed by my self-doubt, theirs, or anyone else's.

"You made it!" an excited and completely misplaced voice called out from somewhere against the whip of the wind. I saw that we were sitting in a low-lying fog or mist of some kind. I wasn't able to see anything past Maurice and Emilia standing either side of me. Greyness clung to everything around, and there was a bitter chill in the biting wind. If I hadn't known that it was late morning from being in my shop a few moments ago, I wouldn't have been able to tell you what time of day it was where we had appeared. The voice that spoke to us was one that I knew instantly, and he was half shouting to make sure we could hear him over the wind. I looked to find Sebastian amongst the grey blur of watercolours but could see him nowhere. He called loudly again without stepping into sight. "I see you have brought some companions."

"Sebastian?" I called, feeling Emilia and Maurice staring at me as I was just managing to pull myself up from the cold rock below me.

"Sebastian Dove?!" Emilia hissed at me.

"He wants the cards," I began to explain as calmly as I could before being interrupted and letting everything get out of hand.

"Where are they?" Sebastian called from what seemed like a different place as if he was moving from spot to spot to cause more disorientation.

"I have them," I called back, pulling out the pack from inside my waistcoat and holding them in the air. The fog was making everything so much harder, and I thought about using a spell to get rid of it so we could at least see Sebastian and talk with him face-to-face, but my ring restricted that type of magical behaviour for now. Maurice and Emilia may have even wanted to help after they found out what we were up to, but before I could say that Maurice or Emilia had the last card and that I would get it without any form of physical or magical violence, the cards I carried were whipped out of my hand and vanished into the fog behind me.

Silence fell over us, and all we could hear was the wind whistling between the holes in the rocks around us and beneath our feet. I could see Emilia and Maurice were ready for anything, and they looked at me with something between pity and disgust. They still stood by my side, which gave me some comfort in this whole mess. I turned to them to tell them that Sebastian was on our side and that we just needed to trust him. As I opened my mouth to speak, Emilia had other ideas and no doubt had enough of being kept blind by the fog. She closed her eyes, brought her palms together as if praying, and uttered the word "*Os*". As she pushed the fog away with her palms turning outwards and forcing it to part in the middle, I was stunned to see that we were standing on a mountaintop, and the further Emilia pushed the fog away, the further we could see. The fog rolled from the top of the mountain, revealing all the huge smooth stones we were standing on, with two stones plinths right in the middle, much taller than the rest framed by the blue sky.

Maurice spoke first. "*Where* are we?" I could only just hear him over the wind, and before any of us could reply, all three of us were pulled up into the air, held for a second, just long enough to see that the hard rock floor was about ten feet beneath us, and then we were dropped. Let me tell you that being dropped on to solid rock from a height isn't like it is in the movies where the hero just gets up and shakes it off. I was pretty sure that the crack I heard was at least one of my ribs breaking, and being the lucky guy I was, I managed to use my nose to stop the rest of my face from breaking. With two savage shooting pains throbbing through my body and into my being, I knew I was in a mess, and I hadn't even had a chance to see how Emilia and Maurice were doing.

Some days it's just not worth getting out of bed, and today was turning out to be a good contender for the top of the list.

CHAPTER THIRTY-FOUR

Truth Hurts

The taste of blood has always been described as a metallic taste, and as I lay on the rocks, staring up into the now clear sky, I couldn't help but wonder whether it was the iron in the blood that made it taste metallic or whether it was just a coincidence like all those foods that taste like chicken. By the time I was coming close to anything resembling an answer, I found myself being picked up and thrown into the air again. This time it was more of a straight up-and-down job as I hit the same huge rock that I had introduced to my fragile ribs. Unsurprisingly, the taste of blood, metal, or chicken or coincidence became overwhelming, and I rolled on to my side to spit out as much as I could and felt each one of my broken and chipped ribs grind against the rock and the jagged ends of each other. Pain was definitely not my friend.

I looked over to Emilia and Maurice to see if they were all right, but all I managed to see was Sebastian Dove standing on top of one of the two plinth-like rocks taller than the rest by a good six foot. "Sebastian? What's happening?" I managed to ask with blood running from the corner of my mouth.

"What's happening is fate. What's happening is justice. What's happening is the universe allowing me to set the world back on its right path," he said with a practised verse of words. Afterwards, he stepped from the edge of the plinth, dropped to the rock floor below, bringing him just a couple of metres in front of me. His white suit looked as pristine as ever, and the smile on his face matched the perfect creases in his shirt and trousers. I had never really noticed it until this moment, but looking back, I should have seen it from the first time I laid eyes on him. He looked false. He was a creation of minor, yet impeccably practised, routines and poses to allow the rest of us to think that Sebastian was the same as the rest of us, but really, he was no more than a mask, allowing him to hide his true wants and desires to blend in with the rest of us. "I bring you to one of the strongest magical focuses in the country, and you still can't get your act together. This is Tryfan, Jon, the seat of the summoning stones Adam and Eve." He gestured off to the two huge plinths behind him. "Jon Wayward, what a sorry excuse for a human, let alone the fabled Grimoire descended from legend."

"What are you talking about?" I asked.

"You can't even see it now. I pity you, Wayward, do you know that? I *pity* you," Sebastian said those last three words slowly to make sure that I really heard them, even if I didn't fully understand them.

"Dove! You better have a bloody good reason for bringing us here!" Emilia spat with her frightening ferocity flowing from her. Instead of answering, he lifted each one of his hands, one at Emilia and one at Maurice, and as he lifted them into the air, his magic lifted Emilia and Maurice, slamming them into the rocks beneath their feet. The crunching noise of muscle and bone was enough to turn my stomach, and I couldn't just watch Sebastian do this to the people I *should* have been loyal to. I pulled myself up to my feet, using the only magic the Court would let me have, moving at an incredible speed to tackle Sebastian to the ground and see how he liked a face full of rock.

As I got to his side, a weight hit me full in the chest and sent me spinning in the air and back down to the ground. The wind was knocked out of me, and as I dragged a breath back into my lungs in painful gasps, a figure appeared in front of me, blocking out the sun and covering his front in shade. It was Poet peering from behind Bard, the human colossus on steroids with an attitude. Bard loomed over me, his brow furrowed, and I could clearly see that if he could speak, he would quote the Hulk's extensive vocabulary with 'Puny Grimoire'. He leant over and grabbed my arm, pulling me off the floor to let me hang next to him. He pulled me close enough so that we were face-to-face, and he let out a snort of hot breath like a bull before it charges. "How're we doing, big fella? Did you miss me?" I asked through bloodied lips, knowing that the response I was about to get would be a physical one.

"Oh yes, we missed you. But don't worry, we never miss twice," said the smooth velvet voice of Poet who stepped out from behind Bard with his thumbs in his waistcoat pockets. He nodded and continued to speak. "A pleasure as always," he said as Sebastian still held Emilia and Maurice pinned to the rocks with some kind of unseen Alchemist power.

"I would offer to shake your hand . . ." I said through gritted teeth as I could feel my ribs separating with each breath. ". . . But the last time we crossed paths, you weren't so polite to me." Taking a second to digest what I had said, Poet began to laugh, which had at least bought me a few seconds to work out what the hell I was going to do, then I could see Bard's shoulders jumping up and down, and I looked at him in confusion as I could see that he was laughing with his mouth wide open and his eyes closed. I could see right into his mouth and count the fillings he had if I wanted to, three. But it wasn't the fillings that caught my attention; it was the stub of a tongue that should have continued up across the pallet of his mouth and poked out at the end, but there was nothing. No wonder he never said anything; he didn't have the ability to speak.

"Enough!" Sebastian shouted over his shoulder. "Put him down," he said sharply, which jolted Bard into action as he dropped me to the ground with another thump on to the solid rock beneath. I would say I was getting used to it, but I wasn't. What I was used to was saying things to upset people and that was the genius plan I had concocted with the few seconds I had. "So you two work for Sebastian, do you? I kind of figured neither of you were the brains of the operation." I made sure I was looking at Poet when I said it, before continuing to insult them to their faces. "And the incredible Sasquatch here is obviously the muscle," I said to Bard. I turned my eyes back to Poet and hoped I was about to force him to act, maybe allowing me the chance to distract Sebastian and get Emilia and Maurice back on their feet and fighting by my side. Hopefully. Three against three sounded like better odds than none against three. I had to make Poet lose it, and I thought questioning his usefulness was a good way to go. "So what exactly do you do around here, Poet? Oh, I get it, you're the tea boy! Well, that's great because I could really go for an Earl Grey right about now. Why don't you nip off and help a brother out. I like my tea like I like my Poets . . . Weak." Poet turned to me and raised his hands about to cast some horrific maiming or disembowelling spell, but luckily for me, Sebastian turned, letting his grip on Emilia and Maurice go to stop Poet from destroying me.

"STOP!" he shouted loud enough to make everyone on the mountaintop cover their ears to help stop the pain burrowing into their heads. "I need him alive!" he exclaimed.

Emilia pounced from her once-crumpled position in-between two rock edges, but Bard, who was now looking at Sebastian and saw her dive for him, swiped a blast of air that pulled her towards his hulking mass, straight into his arms, which locked around her in an impossibly tight grip, dropping me to the floor. Maurice followed her lead and jumped to his feet and darted in a series of directions all leading towards Sebastian through unpredictable sidestepping. I closed my eyes and inhaled through my nose, as best as I could, and willed time to slow down, repeating to myself, "*TINgyuh-IHduth-mwin-EHduth*". Before I opened my eyes, I could feel my magical signature swirling around my casting hand, and the wind around me took longer to whip past, making Emilia's struggling take on a sound of distorted growling. Sebastian was taking a step backwards as he realised that Maurice was closing in on him, but at this speed, it all looked so slow, and everyone appeared to be so vulnerable. I knew that this magic wouldn't last long and that I had to do something. I bounced from where I was and made a line for Sebastian as well. I could see that Sebastian was turning his arm under his waistcoat, and I couldn't believe what I was seeing. He was pulling out the dagger that Helsing had given me to protect myself. I could see the runes inscribed down the blade and the dragon looking up at me from the hilt. *How did he get my knives?* I asked myself, knowing that now was not the time to bring charges of theft to a lunatic with insane henchmen. *I knew they were missing!*

I could see that the dagger was coming around his side directed at Maurice and was sure that Maurice would counter the dagger and make Sebastian sorry for threatening him with a blade. Maurice didn't. He got to Sebastian, evading what he needed to, to be within an arm's breadth and then pulled himself on to the dagger, gripping Sebastian in what could only be described as a hug. What I saw was Maurice's eyes. They locked into my own and sent a clear message of shock. Then his eyes widened, and he drew in a small sudden breath, all as time played out at a fatefully slow pace. At first, I didn't believe and called his name. "M-a-u-r-i-c-e?" It came out slowly accentuating the vowels as all the other noises died into a stunned silence. Maurice's eyes flickered down and back up to mine and then they shot down in exactly the same way as if he were distracted by something. Sebastian stepped back, looking worried at what he had done. As he did, I saw him slide the dagger from Maurice's stomach uncomfortably and a little too quickly. Maurice grunted as he did and clasped a hand over the growing red stain on his shirt, and no one else moved. My time manipulation spell began to wear off, and I heard Emilia begin to scream. "Nooooo!" Her words quickened as she said it, and time found itself again.

It felt like I had been holding my breath for a long time, and when the world caught up with itself, I acted on instinct alone. Maurice lifted his hand from his stomach and looked at the blood dripping from his fingers, and as he did, a realisation of what he had done must have come over him, because he tipped forward weakly and began to fall. I crossed the distance and got to him this time. With tears welling in my eyes, my vision blurred as I caught him. He wasn't heavy, and I was able to drop to my knees and lean him back on to me to keep him from falling on to his wound. He turned his black eyes up to me and just stared at me for a moment as if he were trying to recall who I was, then he smiled and spoke, "You're a lot like your grandfather. He was gullible as well." He spattered a laugh filled with blood-lined spittle, and even in the savage wind, I could smell his familiar tobacco smell.

"I'm sorry" was all I could manage to say as the tears had begun to roll down my cheeks and the hollow in my soul stopped me from saying anything else.

Maurice used what strength he had to take my hand in his and to speak again. "Just because you are a Wayward doesn't mean . . ." – he drew in a sharp and what looked to be a painful breath, hiding his fear and weakening resilience before speaking his last words – ". . . that you are bound to *their* self-serving fate. You can make a difference . . . You just need to play the cards you have been dealt." He tried to force his smile for a moment longer, but he just seemed to be grimacing against the pain, sliding his hands from mine. I could feel his hand clasping for a grip to try to hold on until the black pits in his eyes froze and then slowly sank into lost pinholes, leaving my grandfather's friend, my friend, lying dead in my arms, on top of a mountain in the middle of nowhere. For all I knew, this was the hell I deserved for trusting Sebastian Dove.

CHAPTER THIRTY-FIVE

No Natural Storm

I sat with Maurice in my arms, speechless and only wanting to explain myself and tell him why I had done what I did. To say sorry for being wrong, for being a Wayward, for being me. He was gone, and it was my fault. Sebastian may have stabbed him, but it was my dagger, and I may as well have been holding it after I brought him to this place, this godforsaken mountain, where the wind howls at you as if it wants a piece of your mind and the sun that only allows for a grey gloom to slither over the mountaintop and show Maurice's blood like black oil. I could feel my shock-induced sorrow changing from its need to be accepted and its transformation into something much more primal and satisfying, a need to take revenge on Sebastian for what he had done to Emilia, Maurice, and me.

I sprang from Maurice's body, covering a few steps, before Sebastian pointed away from us whilst tutting and shaking his head. "One more step and the young lady loses her head," he said, enjoying himself, now that he could show me what he was pointing to. I turned to see that Poet and Bard stood side by side, but Bard had Emilia's head in his hands, which he could no doubt squeeze and pop at any given command from his boss, Sebastian. I stopped and stared, not knowing what to do next. Panic fell on me and churned together with my anger as my hands clenched and shook. "Well, it finally looks like you are ready to listen," Sebastian said with a flick of his wrist that sent me off my feet, but instead of hitting the rock beneath my feet, I hit one of the plinths with my back, which had already taken a beating. My arms were pulled up either side of me against my will, and he continued speaking. "You just don't get it, do you?"

"Whatever I do or don't know . . ." I spoke through gritted teeth, ". . . I know you will pay for what you have done." I kept my eyes focused on Sebastian. He laughed to himself and then pulled out a black marker pen with which he started drawing out runes on specific rocks around me as he continued to speak.

"You have to know that I had no intention of killing your friend and that if I were going to have anyone killed, it would have been your troublesome lady over there who has been sticking her nose where it doesn't belong for far too long."

"You're still going to pay," I said coldly.

"I'm sure I will, but not today and not by your hands. Did you really think you had any sort of chance? Seriously? I've been playing with you, all three of you. The best was when you walked right into Poet and Bard, taking a quick beating, just in time for your old friend and charming Alchemist Sebastian to swoop in and rescue you. You were so eager to find any kind of meaning in your little pathetic life that you drank up my story and potion about freedom for oppression as if you were the messiah himself. I do love a good *Believe me* serum." He laughed to himself. "And your lovely lady friend over there has no loyalty to you at all! She does what the Servants of the Night tell her to do, nothing more and nothing less. And guess what, buddy boy, I tell them what to do, when to do it, and how. Doctor Dee couldn't say no to a little blackmail, so he gave me her. If anything, Wayward, I should be thanking you. You activated your grimoire, check!

"You collected all the tarot cards I needed for the ritual, check!

"Then you brought everyone, who know nothing about this little game of mine, right here for me to deal with, check!

"Looks like we have a full house. And let's not forget, if I had wanted to, I could have set my Lamiac creatures upon you any time I desired." He tilted his head to the sky and forced three short bursts of air out whilst making a clicking noise, three at a time, louder than I thought possible for a human. From beneath the rocks and the unseen cracks and gaps came eyes, rotten yellow eyes that stared at its prey, void of any emotion I could relate with. They slithered out on to the rocks' surfaces, revealing themselves and keeping low to the ground. "I believe you have met my friends before," Sebastian said.

"You sent them?" I couldn't believe the extent to what Sebastian had done and tried to get his hands on the tarot cards.

"Who else?" He flicked his head and clicked only twice this time, and his lizard folk lowered themselves into a slightly more relaxed position, allowing him to show his control over them. Sebastian walked up to me and pulled out the Helsing dagger, holding the point up in front of my face; he held it there for a second and smiled at me from behind the blood-stained blade. "Think you misplaced this. And when I say misplaced, I mean that you left it lying out in your living room without any wards of protection. You know, many a night I have stood over you as you have slept, and I wanted to open your throat, just to watch your life flow from you, but they say patience is a virtue, and I guess they were right." He then dropped it out of my sight, as I was still locked in place against the plinth. I couldn't turn my head to see what he was doing, but I didn't need to, as he brought it up in a blur, and I heard the buttons on my waistcoat pop off and fall to the floor. He then did the same to my shirt with absolute precision. "Aren't you even going to ask me why?"

"I was assuming you were just going to tell me, since you went through the trouble of watching me sleep, you creepy freak," I shot back, armed only with my blunt wit and carelessness of whether I lived or died, just as long as *he* dies by my side.

"You know what they say about assumption?" he said.

"You'll always be a bigger ass than me."

"Petty insults. Could I have expected more from a Wayward? Probably not." He pulled out his marker pen and began drawing the symbols he had on the rocks on to my flesh wherever he could find a spare piece that didn't have my family's magic tattooed over it. "What you can expect, Wayward, is to die slowly and painfully as I rip all your family's magic from your body, leaving you as an empty husk. I could probably try to leave you alive, but I need to have a little fun after everything I've done to get here."

"You want my magic?" I was genuinely surprised.

"Did you really think that this was about fighting the good fight and bringing equality to the world of magic?" He laughed and looked over to Poet and Bard who were smiling along with him, Bard's hands still on either side of Emilia's head, ready to pop it like a ripe grape. "No, Wayward, this is about taking what is rightfully mine, and everybody knows that the Wayward grimoire of spells, whilst one of the most powerful, has not been earned by the family. Throughout history, every time that they have been called upon to make a difference, they have either failed, acted as a traitor to their own people or simply saved their own skin at the cost of others." His gaze was back on me, and for the first time, I could see that he was angry and that with each new rune he marked on my flesh, he pressed harder and harder. "The Doves weren't *good enough* to be chosen as a Grimoire lineage, so we have had to learn and relearn all our secrets from generation to generation, always losing a little something along the way as an Alchemist! There is no process as pure as the Grimoire inheritance and that is why I am going to take it from someone who doesn't deserve it." He leaned in close to my ear and whispered, "That's you." He moved back to finishing his runes in marker pen down my forearm. "And give it to someone who does, someone who is not afraid to make a difference, someone who won't shame their family name over and over." He stepped back to admire his handiwork of runic patterns across my body. "That's me," he said happily, grinning like an insane clown.

"All you want is my magic?"

"Only as a by-product, yes. What I want is your Grimoire inheritance. What I want is my family name to be held in high esteem as one of the greatest Grimoires the world has ever seen. I want my magic and knowledge to be passed on, and I want what we *should* have been given. I want to change the order of things and let someone who has the nerve to take charge and see if they can do better. Just a subtle little change here and there."

"You want power? Of course, you do," I asked and answered my own question without really speaking to Sebastian. Then a thought crossed my mind. "What about Aktor Thoön and his prison?" This was a question I snapped at Sebastian.

"Children's stories to keep them from abusing their magic at a young age. *Don't set your Alchemist on fire or Aktor Thoön will come for you,*" he said through his mockery and laughter as he put on an angry parent voice and found it funny that I thought that he really could be real. "Aktor Thoön is more mythology than history."

"But he's in the *Auguries of Sorcery*. I read it myself," I told him.

"The *name* Aktor Thoön is one of the few details that were changed when I had my hands on it at The Court, but no one really knows who he was. He probably died out when he wouldn't take the power of the Grimoire inheritance. Fool," Sebastian said in disgust. "No wonder the Wayward name has always been synonymous with failure. Look at you – gullible, weak, and an embarrassment. The Court will probably thank me for getting rid of you," he said as I turned away from him, not wanting to give him the satisfaction of seeing my self-doubt. He gripped my jaw with his thumb and fingers digging into the muscle and forced my face to his before repeating those words. "Look at you! You are a joke." He pushed my face away as he moved to the runes he had marked into the rocks and summoned a flame between his palms and spoke a few words he had mastered, that I now knew were the basic elemental magics that an Alchemist must spend decades mastering. He carefully chose his first point where he placed his flame, which seemed to burn without a fuel and blackened the rocks beneath. He then moved to his next pattern of runes and spat into his hand, and as he rubbed his palms together, his palms were being pushed out, and he opened them to show a ball of water that had expanded to the size of a golf ball hovering in the air above the runes as he placed it over a rock and moved on, letting it drip slowly. He moved to the next set of runes and picked up one of the smaller rocks, which he took in one hand. He turned his gaze to Emilia who was still being held by Bard's two mammoth-like hands; Sebastian then squeezed his hands tight, and I could hear the rock crumble. It was only when he opened his palm that the mound of dust fell into a ball-like shape, much like the water, hovering above the runes drawn on to the rock beneath. Sebastian brought his hand up to his mouth and released his breath, catching it as it poured into his cupped hand. He then placed it above the runes like he had done with the rest of the elements, and the air from his lungs had an unnatural violet tint, standing out with a shimmer.

With all four elements visible and in place, it was obvious where the fifth element was in the pentagram. It was me, to be technically right, it was *in* me. My spirit, soul, or magic. This allowed me a moment of panic but also a moment of peace. Sebastian's plans were coming to fruition, and a sense of calm came over me as I thought of everything that had happened since magic had come into my life. I hadn't even noticed that Sebastian had pulled the tarot cards out and was speaking words over each card before sliding it to the back of the oversized pack. Emilia tried to scream through the hand that held her face millimetres from being crushed into mush, and as soon as she felt the slightest pressure on her face, she stopped. She had seen that I had noticed her panic and the signal that I needed to do something, and giving up was not what she had in mind. Luckily for both of us, it was not what I had in mind either.

Reflex kicked in. "You don't have all the cards! You said it yourself, Sebastian. One of *them* had the last card!" I shouted, trying to stop his muttering.

"They're all here somewhere. I wouldn't be able to start the rites of transference without all the cards within my possession." He went straight back to his mumbled ritual words, and the moment of Maurice's death replayed itself in my mind at the slow speed that time was passing at when he died, but this time I saw what he wanted me to see. I saw not only why he died but also why he gave his life away so carelessly.

Sebastian was still speaking his words and sliding the cards he had spelled to the back of the pack as he moved towards me held at the fifth point of the pentagram. He spoke to the last three cards, slipping them to the back of the pack, and found himself smiling. "How apt," he said, looking from the card at the top of the pack to me and back. "The Fool for the fool." He slid the card from the top of the deck and pushed it into my trouser pocket and then turned his back on me as I was still held in place by

Sebastian's Alchemist's tricks, especially with the Court's limitations on my magic. Thing was, Sebastian hadn't seen Maurice pull the iron ring from my thumb when he was dying in my arms, and I had all my uncontrolled and dangerous power, according to the Court, literally at my fingertips. But I didn't know what to use and when. I could simply annoy Sebastian if I got my spell wrong or, in a worst-case scenario, I could kill us all and level the entire mountain.

He began chanting his words out loud, and I could finally hear his incantation. He spoke half of them in modern English and then repeated each line in Latin, which led me to believe that this was old magic we were playing with here.

"Allow me what the spirit holds,
Permitte mihi quid Spiritus habet,
This fate of his, mine to unfold,
Hic fata mea explicare,
Take what would be taken,
Tolle quod acciperentur,
Use what he has forsaken,
Uti quid dereliquisti,
Allow me my inheritance.
Permitte mihi haereditas mea."

He held the remaining cards high in the air, and his voice was growing in volume and confidence as the wind picked up, and there was an unmistakable feeling of growing magic in the air around us and the whole mountaintop. It felt like the calm before the storm, yet this was no natural storm; this was someone attempting to change what nature had decided long ago.

"Rewrite these Wayward wrongs,
Rescribo has iniurias devium,
With tales of heroes and songs,
Cum heroum fabulis et canticis,
This Dove's will is strong,
Columba voluntas est fortis,
And path is clear and long,
Et via longa et patet,
Allow me to take what is mine,
Capere quod meum est sine me,
See his weakness as your sign.
Vide ut vestri signum infirmitate sua."

The magic around us was building up, and I could see that Poet, Emilia, and Bard were all looking panicked, not knowing what was coming next.

I don't think that Poet and Bard had been privy to their boss's master plan, and stealing magic was enough to put any user on edge. Luckily for them, I had a secret plan. And by plan, I mean to talk my way into saving the day. It was a long shot, but hey, when you're faced with your own mortality by magic at the top of a mountain, you have to think outside the box.

CHAPTER THIRTY-SIX

Adam and Eve

The magic was almost crackling in the air, and I was expecting thunder and lightning to begin at any moment. What happened instead was the wind picked up around the top of Tryfan and was beginning to circle the pentagram with a slow but increasing speed. I could already feel it on my face and eyes, as I had to blink to allow myself to be able to keep watching Sebastian. He had finished his spell, but I was only just beginning to start mine; after all, words have power. "Sebastian, you want my power? You want what I have?" I had his attention and found that I had to shout over the wind just to be heard clearly. He was also squinting to try to listen to my words and see my intention. "You couldn't handle it! You're nothing! You never will be! The Court knows it! I know it, and deep down you know it too!" I could see anger rising in his face, and his focus was taken from the cards that he held high above his head with his spell concentrated upon them. "You were lucky to be taken in by the Court as it is, and now you want the power to defy them?! You must be joking?!" I forced myself to laugh hysterically, knowing that it would throw him as much as it could whilst holding two hostages on top of a mountain.

Sebastian was trying desperately hard to repeat the words from his spell building its power and allowing the wind around us to whip faster around the pentagram, focusing his magic on the chosen elements. I could feel the spell was coming to a climax and knew that I had one chance to make this work. Timing is everything, as they say. "Sebastian?!" I screamed as loud as I could.

"WHAT?!" he bellowed, showing that I had finally gotten to him.

"You shouldn't have killed Maurice," I said quietly so he could only pick out one or two words.

"What?!"

"I said . . . *"TINgyuh-onn mwin-EHduth!"*" I whipped up a hand that Sebastian no longer had control over. The swirling roots of my magic raced around my hand, matching the urgency of the spell, whilst Sebastian was too distracted to keep his mind focused on everything happening all at once. The entire deck of tarot cards came pouring from his hands like a Vegas dealer showing his shuffling skills to the adoring gamblers at his table as I called the cards to me. Only this time they landed in my open hand and not Sebastian's. All but one card was in my possession. And I knew exactly which card it was.

I had seen Maurice place it into Sebastian's trouser pocket as he held on to him, feeling Helsing's stolen dagger been driven into his stomach. Maurice kept his eyes on mine as the dagger was making its mortal wound, and what I had missed was his eyes flickering down. I thought he was taking in the fact that he had a dagger wedged in his bowels, but he wasn't. He was *looking* at something more than that; he was *showing* me something. I had been too distracted to see it clearly. Maurice slipped a tarot card into Sebastian's trouser pocket, but as he did, he held its face up so I could see which card it was, and at that moment I believed in fate, destiny, the planets aligning, or whatever you call it; everything was just right. Maurice slipped the card into Sebastian's pocket; it had the hand of a God coming through the clouds and was reaching to take the man who stood on the earth below, no doubt a sinner.

"You can't!" Sebastian shouted over the wind. "Your . . ." He was about to say ring, but as he looked at my hand, he could see that it wasn't on my thumb. He quickly turned, searched, and saw that he shouldn't have killed Maurice, as he gave him the opportunity to get close to both of us and slip my training ring from my thumb as he died in my arms, allowing him to die holding it for Sebastian to see as his world unravelled around him.

"JUDGEMENT!" I shouted out, calling the name of the tarot card. I thought that once I had taken the cards from Sebastian and had their power with me, I would be able to break the spell that Sebastian had started so I could bring him before the Court to answer for what he had done. I couldn't break the spell; either it had gained too much momentum or I just didn't know how to begin undoing a spell that was in full swing, and using so much natural power, it took me with it. "I CAN'T STOP IT!" I shouted as the wind was whipping around us so fast now that we couldn't see much outside the pentagram. It was a whirlwind that kept us within the five points, and as I turned to seek help from Sebastian, even after everything he had done, I saw that not even he could help me stop this uncontrollable magic. It was no longer his; the magic was running the show now, and we were along for the ride. He was being lifted into the air and being held as a point in the centre of the pentagram. He was shouting at me, and I could only just hear what he was saying. He wasn't asking for my help; he was showing me a side of him that I had never seen. He had kept this hidden to fool me into helping him destroy myself. Now the tables had turned, and he was showing me the serpent underneath. "WAYWARD! YOU TRICKED ME! YOU DID THIS TO ME! STOP NOW OR I WILL SEND YOU TO THE DEEPEST HOLE IN THE WORLD AND KEEP YOU THERE UNTIL I DECIDE IT'S TIME FOR YOU TO MEET THE DIVINES IN PIECES!"

"IT'S NOT ME, SEBASTIAN! I CAN'T STOP YOUR SPELL!" As soon as I finished speaking, I could feel myself being completely set free from his hold where I had been pinned to one of the plinths he called Adam and Eve. I stumbled forward, still holding the near-complete deck of cards in the air, although they seemed to be holding themselves up; I felt myself being picked up from the rocks like Sebastian had been and let out the same noise that everyone makes when they lose their balance. I was taken into the air, and I panicked because I had no idea what the spell entailed and whether I was going to come out in one piece.

We were picking up speed, turning around each other in the air, with Sebastian still telling me what he was going to do to me and how my family name deserved to be wiped off from the face of the earth. We were twisted around each other over and over, and I could just make out Bard holding Emilia, with Poet standing next to them. They knew something wasn't right and had gone wrong for their boss. They knew that I should have been a magic-less corpse on the floor by now that they could spit on, but I wasn't, and Poet and Bard, being the mercenary Mages for hire that they were, decided that they had had enough. I couldn't see exactly what was happening as the grit and moisture that had been picked up by the spell's whirlwind distorted everything outside of the pentagram, but I knew that the ball of blue light was another of those teleportation balls, and I could see the silhouette of the three pass through. To where? I had no idea, but I am sure that Emilia wasn't going by choice, as she was picked up by Bard's huge machine-like arms and was calling my name. "WAYWARD!" she was screaming, but her voice came through the whirlwind as the slightest whisper, and when the whisper had gone, I knew she had too.

Sebastian could see I wanted to get to her and knew that neither of us could stop the spell, so he just began laughing at me in a way I never thought possible, even for someone as twisted as Sebastian. I managed to pull some magic from the spell, most likely from some instinctual part of me, as I didn't know I had done it until it was too late to reconsider. I was forcing myself against the wind moving towards Sebastian, and when I got there, I collided with him, taking him off guard. My anger got the better of me, and I landed a punch right into his jaw, which sent the both of us spinning and shouting in the whirlwind of chaos. Static electricity was cracking inside the whirlwind, lighting up our magical death trap every few seconds. Sebastian was spinning in and out of sight. He managed to force his way to me, and I thought he was going to hit me, but he was reaching for the cards in my left hand. I was trying to hold them as far from him as possible. The wind around us was speeding up and no doubt reaching some kind of climax, and both of us were acting as if it was our last chance to get the upper hand, knowing that if we didn't, the consequences would be fatal. I was just managing to keep the cards from his hands' reach when he punched me in the stomach, and I doubled within his grasp where he threw both of his hands around mine, trying to pry my fingers off to get some leverage on the cards. "COME ON! COME ON!" he kept shouting in my face as he ferociously dug his nails into my hands, so I reacted accordingly. I pulled him in using his grip on my left hand and the cards he so desperately fought for and opened my mouth wide to come down on his ear. My teeth quickly found their way to meeting through the thin and delicate skin with his blood running into my mouth, forcing Sebastian immediately to scream and let go of my hand to pull me away from his now half-hanging and freely bleeding ear.

We moved apart from each other for a moment but still within arm's reach. Sebastian had tears in his eyes and two distinct streams of blood trailing across his cheek and down his neck, marking his bright white collar in dark red blood. "I CAN'T BELIEVE YOU BIT MY EAR OFF!" he shouted through the wind, and I could hear the pain in his voice. I saw a flash in his eyes and thought that I had beaten him, but at that moment, he gave me a darting look, reminding me of a wounded animal and how dangerous they can be. Before I had a chance to move out of his reach, he swiped his bloodied fist up into the air, hitting my left hand, exploding it into a shower of tarot cards being swept around the pentagram of wild winds. "WHAT ARE YOU DOING?!" I shouted.

"CHANGING THE GAME!" he shouted back with a hateful smile as he plucked one of the cards from the air. "WHOEVER HAS THE MOST CARDS WINS!"

"GOOD LUCK!" I shouted as I kicked out with my foot, just missing his private parts and connecting with his thigh, sending him and me into opposite spins within the cyclone. The wind was whistling with its own high-pitch scream as if it were in agony from the spell, causing me to cover my ears and fight for the cards. We both furiously started plucking as many cards as we could from the air, not caring which cards they were, just trying to be the one who ended up with the most when the spell came to its crescendo. I could feel the muscles in my arms and neck stretching to get the cards as I fired quick glances to see how many Sebastian had got. He was doing exactly the same with his arms and legs flailing in the air, trying to control which direction he turned in as if we were working in an aggressive zero gravity. I noticed at the same time as Sebastian that we were being pulled towards the Adam and Eve plinths, drawing him to one and me to the other. I saw it on his face and by how fast he began to grab all the cards around him; I knew the spell was coming to its big finale.

He swung out at me just as we were moving out of each other's reach to try to knock the cards from my hand once again. I acted out of survival and rapped my knuckles on his to force him to drop his cards back into the whirlwind we were trapped in. "NOOOOO!" he screamed.

"YOU REAP WHAT YOU SOW!" I shouted at him as we were pulled over to the plinths. I noticed this time that I was being pulled over to the opposite plinth than before, and Sebastian held his ear as his back met the stone, and I couldn't bring my arm down as my back met stone. The cards were holding themselves out in the air along with my arm. "I'M SORRY THIS HAD TO HAPPEN," I said as the wind started to die down.

"YOU WILL BE," his cold face spoke its poison-filled last words to me, and what I could see in his eyes was something I instantly recognised. It was a promise that somehow, someday he would get the vengeance he sought, and it would be worth all the pain and suffering that was about to happen to him.

Starting with the flame that was self-sustaining, each one of the elements began to react. Fire poured from its source and ran across the rocks in a line as if someone had drawn over the rock with petrol so the flames knew which direction to go in. After it had darted out to leave the pentagram, it darted back, heading towards the next element sitting as a ball of floating water. The flame hit the water and hissed but knocked it and used the momentum to let the water carry on its movement in an unnatural direction. The water shot out like the flames had, trailing across the rocks, creating another point that aimed away from the elements and then back towards the next, where the earth element shot out like the others, leaving a trail of dust, driving straight into the air pocket which left a stream of mist, creating the last point before getting to mine and Sebastian's feet at the bottom of Adam and Eve.

I could now see that the elements were creating the four points of a pentagram and that the final point was one of us. Sebastian began coughing, and I looked between him and the elements, which were now pulsating around the pentagram, stopping each time when it couldn't complete the five-pointed star. Sebastian groaned as if he had been winded, and as he coughed this time, blood came from his mouth and dribbled down his chin and neck, joining with the blood from his ear. His breath had become a rasp of air in and out, and in classic Sebastian fashion, he was muttering some half-attempted spell to himself that I couldn't quite hear. He looked as if he was meditating and trying to block out the pain that was so obviously clawing its way through his body. The occasional roar of pain left his mouth, but within a rasp, he was back to his mumbled words. I hated him for what he had done, but I wasn't sure that anyone deserved this, even if he had intended it for me.

This is when I saw the true power of magic and the price you pay when you mistreat it. Sebastian screamed in pain and forced his hands away from the plinth behind him, holding them out in front so he could witness his skin turning into a thick liquid which began dripping from his arms and soaking through his suit, turning it dark red, finding its way to a puddle forming at his feet. His screams of pain were unbearable, and I had to close my eyes and watch what happened next through glimpses, as I would have surely gone mad if I had watched how Sebastian Dove met his end. All the liquid from his body was draining the same way his skin had, leaving his muscles drying and twisting on to his skeletal frame into a bizarre and puppet-like form with eyes that had sunk back into its skull and hair that fell from its scalp, seeming to have grown as the muscles dried out and shrank, leaving teeth that protruded from their dried-out gums and fingernails that turned into claws with the lack of any flesh to pad them out. Before his entire life force had been drained from his corpse, he somehow managed to look in my direction, with his eyes no longer there to meet mine. He mouthed my name as his lips ran down his dried-up chin and into the Sebastian puddle beneath.

The drip-dried carcass that was Sebastian Dove dropped from its plinth at the same time I was released. I dropped to my knees and looked up to see Sebastian's puddle of flesh, the air, the earth, the water, and the flame all trickling their way into the centre of the pentagram, along with each one of the tarot cards being whipped up on the wind. There they bled into one another, creating a bubbling ball of all five elements steaming in front of my eyes; the cards melted into the liquid, and there was a surge emanating from it that was tangible, and I could sense raw power. Just as I had thought it, the ball consumed itself in an incredibly bright and retina-burning white light, leaving only a purple smoke in its wake. The cards were burnt, and the smoke poured over me and seeped into my skin, my pores, and my mind all within a few seconds, regardless of my attempts to swipe it away with my hands. I fell to the rocks in the middle of the pentagram, unable to move as my body locked with the smoke coursing through my being like fire water running through my veins. It didn't hurt; it was invigorating. I could feel Sebastian's knowledge of magic and his affinity and understanding how it works fill my mind instantly. In complete opposition to what Sebastian had wanted, he had now given me the keys to unlock all the spells of my ancestor, which still claimed their home tattooed to my skin.

The world was different and so was I, and there were so many things I knew I had to do.

CHAPTER THIRTY-SEVEN

Normalcy?

Sitting at the top of Tryfan accompanied with my grief and shock was a horrifying experience. Two people who had only recently found their way into my life and changed it so significantly were now my only company and they were both dead. Maurice lay where I had left him and where he had taken measures that would save my life and stop Sebastian from abusing nature's laws and magic. If he hadn't, then I'm not sure I would have gotten the upper hand over him. Sebastian's remains were propped up in a sitting position, which was the way his body fell against the plinth. His skin was gone, and the muscle underneath looked as though it had been squeezed dry of all the goodness and drained to the point where the muscle had cracked under the pressure of not having any lubrication for movement and had already rotted like long-forgotten and untreated split leather. In other words, he looked like an Egyptian mummy without the bandages wrapped around his body. The weird thing was that I could still tell that It was Sebastian as It still had his white suit on, although it was far from immaculate. It still had the same facial structure, just with no face to speak of.

I forced myself to my feet and over to Maurice. I needed family now that I felt so alone, and he was the closest I had. The next thought in my mind was what I was now capable of, since I had all of Sebastian's knowledge that he had spent his entire life researching and honing. As I got to Maurice, an overwhelming sense of guilt washed over me and took hold of my stomach with one thought playing over in my mind: *I should have saved you. I should have found a way, and I should have saved you.* I'm not sure how much time had passed before I wiped the tears from my cheeks and knelt down next to his body. I opened his hand and there it was, my iron ring of limitation. Even though I had the magic of my family at my fingertips and somewhere in my head was the knowledge on how to use it, I wanted to make sure that I didn't abuse the magic I had like Sebastian wanted me to. I owed it to Maurice. I was going to begin my new life as a Grimoire in control and that meant that I had to make sure I was making the right decisions, the first of which was to contain my magic by putting the ring of limitations back on my thumb, which felt like putting on a cold wet coat, dulling all my new senses.

With the ring of limitations firmly on my thumb, I left Maurice for a moment and turned towards Sebastian's remains. As I stepped carefully on the rocks over to the plinth It sat against, I felt that the wind had gone from the top of the mountain. I wondered if that was even possible, or if what we had done was the cause or void of nature's natural behaviour. When I climbed over to the plinth, Sebastian's remains were just below me, and I planted one foot on either side of It so I could hold my balance and be ready for anything. I had seen way too many horror movies to just assume that it was game over for Sebastian and that if his zombie body was going to attack, now would be the perfect time.

I brought my finger up to Its cold dead shoulder and poked It to see if I could get a reaction. Nothing happened. I poked It harder this time so that It couldn't pretend It didn't feel anything and would have had to have flinched or squirmed. Nothing happened. I lowered myself over It whilst keeping my legs straight and on either side of the remains. I wanted to look It in the eyes, or the holes where the eyes should have been, to see if there was even the faintest sign of life. What I saw was a void of life, emptiness where life should have been. It gave me a lone shiver running from the nape of my neck right down into my legs where I had to shake it off; otherwise, I wouldn't have had the nerve to do what I did next.

Bringing my hands in front of me, I felt my fingers twitching with anticipation, and I slowly pulled open the bloodied suit jacket of Sebastian Dove. I was like peeling back the wrapper from a gooey cough sweet that had been left in your warm pocket for way too long, and it had dried out, allowing for the jacket to peel back with an equally disgusting sound. The goo was at the stage of turning into decomposed dust, and as soon as the air got to It, It did just that. I leant It forward and Its dried taut muscular face landed on my shoulder, and my entire being went tight like an extremely well-coiled spring. *Perfect opportunity for a crazy magical zombie bite?* I held still, ready to launch into action should I need to, but nothing happened. I bravely moved on with my mission and pulled Its suit jacket down from his shoulders to reveal what I had been looking for. My fingers quickly found the two buckles that held my Helsing daggers around Its body and worked to unbuckle them. I had no idea how It had gotten these from Smoke and Mirrors, and right now finding out was not at the top of my 'to do' list, but I would want answers, and soon.

The buckles came free, and I slid the Helsing daggers and their leather sheaths and belt from the remains in front of me as I placed It back against the plinth, peeling Its face from my shoulder. Still, nothing happened. I quickly and tightly tied the belt around my own waist and shoulder, fastening the buckles, not ever wanting to lose them again so they could be used against me as they were. I made a promise to myself that the daggers would only ever be used *against* corruption from that day on and be drawn for the reasons they were given to me for.

I looked around the mountaintop and found that I was still confronted with the problem of how to get down and back to Smoke and Mirrors. *I could climb*, I thought. *What about Maurice?* I knew I had to take Maurice down with me, as I wanted him to have a proper funeral with the people who cared about him. Not that I knew any of them, but I still wanted him to have a send-off and be remembered for the man he was and what he had done with his last few moments on this world. Without moving my feet, I leaned over Sebastian's remains again and put my hand into his trouser pockets; there was nothing of interest apart from his wallet which had nothing in it except a few notes, and I wasn't about to rob a dead man. I moved on to the suit jacket that lay around his hips where I had dropped it, and after searching both pockets, I found what I was searching for. A magic lightning teleportation ball that I now knew was called a 'relativity orb', thanks to Sebastian's knowledge in my mind, because travelling faster than light and moving through time and space would break the laws of relativity; therefore, it can only be done with magic captured within tempered glass orbs containing the spell.

I took the relativity orb and knew what I had to do to realign its destination. Some of Sebastian's memories were finding their way to the front of my mind when they needed to be of use, and instead of seeing a memory of Sebastian, I saw myself in his place. I was thankful for my mind replacing me for him; I'm not sure I could have had Sebastian in my mind forever. I could see how I was supposed to spell the relativity orb. I could see how Sebastian, but also myself, had studied them for weeks within the inner sanctum of the Court and their libraries before testing one of my, Sebastian's, own creations in the training rooms miles below ground level. I pulled myself back into my head, and as I stood on top of the mountain, I gave Sebastian's remains one last look and said my goodbyes. "Maybe in another time and another life we could have been friends. I hope you find peace in the next world."

I held the orb up in the air and brought it gently down to rest on my forehead where I pictured the scene from when I last used a relativity orb, bringing Maurice, Emilia, and myself to this mountaintop. I wanted to be back in Smoke and Mirrors, and I gave the orb the memory of the exact place in the shop, allowing it to home in. The light in the relativity orb flickered and sparked to life as bright as the first one I had held in my hand. I moved over to Maurice's body and knelt next to him, pulling him up on to my tired legs where he was when he breathed his last breath, and I slammed the relativity orb into the rock that we sat on. The light, the tight internal feeling, and the pull through time and space happened as it did before. But this time when I appeared in the exact spot that we had left Smoke and Mirrors with Maurice in my lap, I didn't feel like throwing up. I felt a dizziness fall over me with one dry wretch and then I was able to let my grip on Maurice's suit jacket collar go. I slowly brought my vision back into focus to see Tamsin racing down the spiral stairs from my flat upstairs and Moon shouting up to her just repeating my name and saying, "He's here! Wayward's here!"

There was a good five minutes that I can't really remember as all the emotions I should have been feeling up on the mountaintop came flooding over me, and I cried more than I had ever thought possible, refusing to let go of Maurice. I have a faint image of Tamsin trying to take me away from Maurice, and when she realised that she couldn't, she hugged me and told me that whatever happened wasn't my fault and that swam around my mind, because I knew that it was. It *was* my fault.

When I had cried myself dry, I found that deep sudden breaths and sobbing took over; I explained to Tamsin and Moon what had happened step-by-step, play-by-play. They sat there and listened to everything I had to say, except for Moon making a pot of tea for the three of us in the middle of my tale of treachery and gullible fools who live up to their family name whatever they try to do. They didn't judge me or stop me to accuse me of acting the way I did once, and I loved them for that. When I finished talking, they sat there and kept silent, taking in everything I had said. I don't think they knew what to say to me, and I sure as hell didn't know what to say to them. I hadn't known either of them for more than a couple of days and yet I felt accountable to them for what I had let happen. Tamsin had finally managed to get me up from the floor, place a cup of tea in my hands, and sit me down behind the table that Moon had been using as his diviner post. "You seem different," she said as if it were just a personal thought that she had said out loud, not needing an answer, just wanting to say it. I took the bait as it allowed me to keep talking and focus my mind, helping to keep the shock I had so gracefully fallen into at bay.

"Different how?"

"She's right. You need a shower, a shave, and most definitely, a change of clothes," Moon added as he was nodding his head in agreement with his own personal judgement at my blood-and-mud-stained clothes.

"Not a physical change. It's your . . ." – she looked me up and down to try to pinpoint exactly what it was that was different – ". . . aura, your soul, or something. You just feel different." She could see the confused look on my face and spoke up again quickly as not to offend me in what was obviously such a fragile and bloodied state. "Not in a bad way, it's just that your magic used to swim in your aura as a deep blue colour and now it's more of an ocean blue, aqua colour," she said in a soft voice.

"You can see people's magical auras?" I asked.

"You can't?" she asked.

"I can't," Moon offered.

We found ourselves in silence again, and I knew that they were replaying the words I had spoken, explaining to them how I had let Maurice die and Emilia be kidnapped. I waited for one of them to shout and scream at me, but they didn't. I probably would have found some solace if they had cursed me and walked out, but they didn't. I couldn't quite believe what was said when Moon spoke to break the silence. "So what's the plan, boss?"

"The plan?" I asked dumbfounded.

"We're with you, Jon. Whatever you decide," Tamsin echoed Moon's sentiment. I stared into space as my mind raced through the options of what we could do, but there was one thing that kept coming back to me.

"We take Maurice to the Court for a proper funeral and make sure they know everything that's happened. I need to answer for my part in these events as much as Sebastian does, and they need to find Emilia and get their hands on Poet and Bard."

CHAPTER THIRTY-EIGHT

Enemy of My Enemy

I owed a debt to Maurice and Emilia that I could never pay back. It was all I could think about as I sat in the same bright white-walled room I had been in earlier this week when I was questioned by Bloyse, Morgause, and Bacon. Back then I had Emilia sitting on one side and Maurice on the other. I now sat alone.

I had gone through the events of what happened at the top of Tryfan, how I used a relativity orb to take us there, how Sebastian had staged his rescue of me from Poet and Bard to win me to his cause, and how he had most likely used the Servants of the Night to send Emilia out to me with my family grimoire. He needed me to have my family's magic before he could take it and why the hell not send me on a quest to find all of the tarot cards he needed to take my life and my memories as well.

Bloyse looked at me like I was some kind of Cold War spy who couldn't hide his Russian accent. Bacon had his usual wide-eyed look plastered across his face as if he was surprised at everything he heard, even when he was offered a glass of water from Morgause. She had a different expression upon her face, and I wasn't sure how I could look her straight in the eye. It was somewhere in-between curiosity, hunger, and caution, all hidden behind the gentle upturned corners of her mouth, showing a well-practised and formal smile. Apart from turning the chronicle on and squinting at the glowing light as it filled the room, no one showed any signs to let me know what I was in for.

Tamsin and Moon had brought me to the museum, but they knew that I had wanted to go in alone. Firstly, I wanted to make sure that none of the fallout landed on them for just being associated with me, which was something I couldn't promise, and secondly, I wasn't sure I could keep my calm and hold back the tears if they were there. I needed to hold it together in front of these three judicators and make sure that they received the whole story as truthfully as I could give it without an emotional bias one way or the other.

I had found the process of being interrogated physically and emotionally very draining, which I already had been before turning myself in. The shower and clean clothes had not helped restore me back to my fighting-fit state as I had hoped. What really wore me down my mental stamina was the fact that Bloyse had read my mind within minutes of my arrival in the building. In fact, he had commanded me not to say a word until he had read my mind so that he could check the two *versions* of events against one another. So even if I had wanted to bend the truth, which I didn't, I would have been caught out by Bloyse's memory-scanning magic trick.

Bloyse sat in silence with one of his hands gently rubbing his little beard, which I had also thought was strategically placed to stop him from saying anything that he shouldn't. I was getting a clear vibe from Bloyse, and it was that he was happy to use any sort of wrongdoing he could to hold me up in front of everyone to make an example of me. It was what he wanted, to have the Wayward family on trial for something and then, hopefully, they would get some kind of justice against them for all the slights that have been carried out in their name since the dawn of magic. If only I could've seen behind his iron gates in my mind's eye, I could have known for sure why he hated me and my family so much. Bacon watched everything; he watched me, he watched Bloyse watching me, and mostly, he watched Morgause ask me a question and wait to see how I answered, stealing a quick look at Bloyse to see if his face agreed with my *version of events*. Morgause was like a cat with an injured mouse laid out at her feet as she played with it and did whatever she chose. "Mr Wayward . . . May I call you Jon?"

"Of course." I had to keep my cool and stay on their good side; as much as I had been told that this was merely an investigation, I'm pretty sure that that was the Court's word for trial. "Just Jon."

"Jon, you have told us everything we have needed to hear, and we will adjourn to discuss our findings. Then we will reconvene, but before we do, I have one or two last questions that I would *love* you to answer," she said without breaking her predatory and, quite honestly, intimidating stare. I had no other play than to sit, smile, and answer whatever was coming my way. She asked her first question. "You were given false information and half-truths about the Court and its actions by Sebastian Dove, leading you to believe that the Court's goal was dominion over all those who practised magic across the globe."

"Yes."

"Is this a belief that you still hold to?"

"No. After realising Sebastian had dragged me into believing his lies and that it was for his own wants and gains, I could see that what he had said falsely accused the Court of what he himself wanted to achieve. It's why I brought myself before you and have asked to be tried for my actions."

"This is not a trial, Jon, this is an investigation into the events that have led to a Mage's death, an Alchemist's death, and the kidnapping of a Mage from the order of the Servants of the Night, involving two reported and wanted Mages of questionable character," Morgause said with what seemed to be practised lyrical verse.

"And the second?"

"We have ordered C.O.V.E.N. to send a team to the top of Tryfan, and they have searched extensively. You said that Sebastian Dove's remains were lying at the base of the plinths Adam and Eve. But we found no remains of him or of the tarot cards."

"What?"

"There were no remains," she continued.

"That can't be!" I protested, almost losing the cool attitude that I had worked so hard to maintain. "I left his body leaning up against one of the plinths. I took my daggers from his corpse and then searched him for a relativity orb. When I took Maurice's body from that mountaintop, Sebastian was still there, and the cards were disintegrated or incinerated during his spell!"

"That may be, but the fact remains that Sebastian's *remains* were nowhere to be found after you had left the site," Morgause said in the cool unaffected manner I wished I was using. "Our C.O.V.E.N. Operatives have yet to find anything."

"Ask Bloyse! If he has seen what I have seen, if he has read my memories, then he knows that I left Sebastian up there on that mountaintop." I was pointing at Bloyse and urging them to ask him to back me up rather than question me about it. Morgause turned to Bloyse with an open expression, and Bacon kept his usual gaze of puzzlement as he also turned to Bloyse.

"It's true," Bloyse said.

"See!" I drove the point home.

"What is true?" Morgause asked Bloyse without sparing me a glance.

"Wayward left the corpse of Dove atop the mountain and had no part in the removal of his remains," he said quite blankly and without making eye contact with me. The three of them had resorted to ignoring my presence.

They were acting as if they could freely decide my future in front of me rather than behind closed doors, which I would prefer, and as I was told would most likely happen. "He is in no way a part of or aware that he is a part of any deception or action that involves the disappearance of Dove's remains," Bloyse finished with his hand dropping from his beard to speak and then jumping back into its position, covering his mouth when he had let his tongue tell a tailored and formal version of what he was thinking. It was almost as if he were physically keeping his words from spilling out of his mouth.

I sat there in silence, waiting for one of them to say something, and just as I was getting comfy in the awkward silence, the three of them all stood together and turned to face me. I awkwardly brought myself to standing and could feel my aching muscle bruises start to settle in my bones. I knew it was not only the physical pain of being beaten across the top of a mountain and back but also the mental scarring which had left a permanent pain running from my belly button to the back of my spine. It wasn't my wound but Maurice's, and I knew it was my guilt that had kept it in my stomach wherever I went. Pushing the pain aside for a second and feeling the guilt that came with trying to ignore it, I waited to see what was happening with the Archmages and whether I should be doing something.

Morgause could see the look of patience on my face and knew that I was waiting. Her very practised and formal smile broke for a flash, showing me something a little more human, or at least Archmagish. "We will adjourn until we have reviewed all the evidence provided. Jon, you will wait outside if you would be so willing, and you will be called back in to discuss our verdict," Morgause said with her very elegant professional voice. Without further ado, I bowed my head to each of them respectively and made my way into the corridor where someone had put a wooden chair out for me to sit in. Painted white, of course.

I sat on the uncomfortable chair with no one in sight and wondered whether they would be cruel enough to find the most uncomfortable chair that they could find and set it out for me whilst I waited to hear what my fate held in store. I spent some of the time out in the corridor that seemed dull in comparison to the bright white room, thinking about the Archmages' decision and what I would do depending on what they decided. If they came back to me and demanded that I turn myself in for imprisonment or even execution, I wasn't sure that I would try to stop them. I could run or I could take off my limiter ring and fight my way out or die trying, but I was not sure I wanted to. I wasn't even sure that I believed that I deserved to live, let alone be free. If they wanted me free, then I would spend the rest of my days making up for letting down Maurice and Emilia, but I would never let myself be controlled again, not by anyone, including the Court.

I spent the rest of the time outside the white interrogation room, recollecting everything I had said to the Archmages and making sure that I hadn't left anything out. I wanted to make sure I had explained everything as honestly as I could, whether it was in my favour or not, to the best of my memory and for the memory of a good man.

The door to the white interrogation room opened, and Bacon appeared in the doorway. They had obviously decided that the more oblivious of the three should be the one to come and get me. His open and wide-eyed expression gave nothing away as he spoke. "Would you like to come back in, Mr Wayward. I believe we have come to a conclusion." His voice was soft and unthreatening, but I knew there was a reason he was an Archmage, and I was sure that it wasn't because he was a pushover.

"Of course," I said and followed him through the door, having to squint my eyes as we entered the bright brilliance of the room. My sympathy pain for Maurice resurfaced in my stomach, and my nerves went into overdrive. I had to work a lot harder now to try to keep a cool exterior. I was reminded of that old saying about a swimming duck and how they seem so calm and collected on top, yet underneath they are paddling like a madman or mad duck in this case.

I walked back over to the chair I had previously sat on and took my place. Of course, now that I had sat down, none of the Archmages did, and it looked either extremely rude or extremely brave of me to sit whilst they all stood to deliver their verdict. I'm not sure which one it was either.

When Bacon had rejoined the other two, Morgause, who seemed to be in charge during this *investigation*, began speaking on behalf of the three. "Jon Wayward, after much deliberation, we have come to the conclusion that your version of events is truthful and exact in detailing your actions and choices leading to the death of Maurice Talpidae, the supposed kidnapping of Emilia Nótt, and the disappearance of Sebastian Dove. We have also concluded that during your time in aiding Sebastian Dove, an agent working against the Court and the betterment of magical kind, you were under false impressions and tricked to work against those who you now *know* to be allies. You may leave this Court free of any judgement for your actions as long as certain conditions are met as you develop your skills as a Grimoire within this Court's jurisdiction. We will also be passing our recommendations to all Courts in case you decide to travel."

"Conditions?" I asked, waiting to bring up her wording on the *supposed* kidnapping and *disappearance* of Sebastian after I had found out what I was agreeing to.

"Condition one, you will begin your training with Ms Blight as soon as possible and continue to train with your assigned Alchemist until she informs us that you are capable of controlling your Grimoire magic and using it responsibly," Morgause explained.

"Fair enough. I accept," I allowed.

"Condition two, you will make yourself available to the Court should we require you, as all Grimoires have been blessed with the rite to inheritance imbued by the power of the Court. Therefore, you are sworn to uphold and protect those the Court protects and holds dear."

"I will serve the Court to the best of my ability," I said, knowing that at some point in my life, I would have to choose between what the Court thinks is right and what *is* right. Odds are I'd be dead before I would have to make that choice, so I nodded along, knowing I wasn't going to be let out without agreeing to these conditions. "What's the last condition?"

"Condition three," Morgause offered with a raised eyebrow, "you will leave all further investigation into the matter of Sebastian Dove and the Seals of Thoön to the Court and the Counter Occult Violations of Ethereals and Necromancy. You will not pursue this matter, is that understood?" I nodded but took note that she referred to the tarot cards as one of the *Seals of Thoön* and not as some random magical artefact. "Jon?" Morgause said, and I raised my eyes to meet hers. "I want you to say that you agree to the third condition, and I'm afraid we will require more than a nod." She waited for me to say that I agreed, and I didn't disappoint.

"I agree to your third condition." I hadn't thought it when coming into this *investigation* as I knew I was making up for my failures, but I was beginning to feel dirty with all the conditions I was agreeing to, and I just wanted to get back to the shop. I think the Archmages could sense I wanted to leave, and by the looks of them, they didn't want to be in this room any longer than necessary. "Now that I have agreed to your conditions, may I leave?"

"You may," Morgause said, "as long as there are no more questions." She looked at Bacon and Bloyse, both of whom shook their heads. "Then you are free to leave with the blessings of the Courts of the world."

I got up from my seat and walked out of the interrogation room, thinking on the conditions I had just agreed to. I felt bad that sooner or later I knew I would break one of these conditions, but until then, I had other matters in my life to occupy my time and begin to make amends. One thing the Court and I had in common was my training with Tamsin; we were both keen for it to begin, and that was exactly where I was heading – home.

CHAPTER THIRTY-NINE

Start at the Beginning

Smoke and Mirrors was a welcome distraction from the world of conditions set by those you are apparently accountable to *and* letting down the people you care about by allowing them to be kidnapped or die in your arms. We're not all perfect, and to be fair, some of us are less perfect than others. At least I can say that I tried, and that is something I had to keep reminding myself of on a regular basis if I was to make it through the next week or two without falling further into a depressed and isolated state. Tamsin and Moon were doing a brilliant job of keeping me distracted, always giving me a new job to do or something else to pick up around my own shop. I hadn't noticed until a few days after my unofficial date with the Court, but business was booming, and I couldn't remember a time when Smoke and Mirrors had seen so many customers and customers who actually spent money as well!

We had the usual lost soul coming in through the shop door not really knowing what to expect, but generally, after a while, they worked out that we didn't sell *normal* antiques and that the rest of the customers in the shop weren't your average crowd. I wasn't sure how they had done it, but Tamsin and Moon had gotten word out to all their magical contacts, and when I was running through the receipts for the last two days, I couldn't believe what our profit margin was. My grandfather George would have been proud, and I think in his way, he would have approved of my new staff and the heavy flow of magical folk who had come to see the Wayward business up and running at full steam. I'm not sure he wanted to see me accept the Grimoire inheritance, but it's like I said: no one's perfect.

There was something about people who used magic; they just seemed to give off a certain aura that let others who use magic know that they are of their kin. As I was filling up the shelf above the *Field Guide to Imbued Jewellery*, which was a good seller to new magical folk, I overheard two young magic users who were talking about Sebastian Dove and how he was one of the most skilled Alchemists the Court had ever known and that Wayward Grimoire had killed him in cold blood because he wanted to leave the Court and live a normal life. "So Wayward, like, took him up to this mountain in Wales or somewhere and held him over the edge to scare him," the long-haired greasy teenager said.

"I heard he threw him off the edge!" said the shorter and plumper one.

"No, he didn't! Coz if he did, like, Dove'd be dead, idiot," said the long-haired one.

"He is dead!" said the shorter plumper one.

"Yeah, but not from falling off a cliff. Wayward gave him one chance to y'know, like, keep working for the Court." He quickened his story.

"And what happened?"

"To show he was serious, Wayward even killed one of his own guys! He's a total badass!" said the long-haired one. This created a pit in the bottom of my stomach, which didn't show any signs of being temporary. *Is this what people really think of me? Do they really think that I could kill those who are closest to me?* I thought, remembering my life before taking over my grandfather's shop and how I didn't really have anyone in it. I knew what loneliness really felt like, and I had just got used to it. I didn't know at the time just how lonely I was, but once people come into your life, they start to mean something, and sooner or later you mean something to them as well.

"No way! That's epic!" said the plumper one. "So how did he do in Dove?"

"He used a spell that drained him of all his magic, like, and his blood! Drained him dry and left him to rot, like," said the long-haired one with relish and affection for the word 'like'.

"That is savage!" the plump one said in awe of his friend's tale.

"The worst thing is, like, that no one knew Wayward is like, working for . . ." the long-haired one trailed off, and even I was on tenterhooks now as I was desperate to hear who I was supposedly working for.

"Come on, who?" said the plump one.

"He's working for . . ." the long-haired teen looked up and down the aisle and saw people at either end. They were too far to earwig into his conversation as he said his next two words carefully and slowly, mouthing each syllable much bigger than he needed to. He did not realise I was no more than ten inches behind him in the next aisle. *"A-k-t-o-r T-h-o-ö-n."*

"No way!" the plump one said in amazement. "That can't be true, can it?"

"Come on! Everyone felt it when he broke the first Seal. Like why would he break the first Seal if he didn't like, want to break the rest and set him free?" asked the long-haired one.

"This is unreal," squeaked the plump one.

"I'm telling you, the Waywards have, like, always done what they wanted. My dad said they are just out to get more power and that they will, like, stop at nothing. Wayward probably thinks that Thoön can, like, give it to him," said the long-haired one to the plump one who was lapping up every word he said. Well, I had something to blow his tiny little mind, and it was about time that these two teenage punks were put in their place, in a non-violent way, not that they knew that.

I walked to the end of my aisle, and just before I turned into theirs, I indulged in a few of the more visual side effects that I had found whilst training with Tamsin over the last week or so. I turned my eyes red and pulled flaming balls into each of my clawed hands, swirling with my family's magical signature, roots twisting and growing around and in-between my outstretched fingers. Taking in a deep breath, I moved into their aisle where they turned at exactly the same time to see me taking slow and determined steps towards them. After I had held my breath for long enough and had heated my lungs, turning the moisture in my breath into steam, I let it out slowly as I began to speak, so it looked like I was breathing smoke and flames. "You dare talk of me in my own home!" I bellowed across the aisle, knowing that the rest of the customers would hear as well. It was worth it. "Holy crap! It's him!" said the plump one who turned and ran down the aisle and out of the front door, immediately letting the bell ring on the door.

"Just one left," I said, turning my head on its side in true inhuman horror-movie style. "Still enough for me to get my teeth into," I said in my creepiest voice as I widened my eyes and opened my mouth fully like the monsters who had tried to scare me in the past. I allowed the steam to pour from my mouth and show me in a truly visually terrifying light. The long-haired boy screamed and followed his plump friend out through the shop's front door, letting the bell ring out again. Before any of our other customers came into the aisle, I swiftly dispersed any side effects, and within a second or two, I was back to normal. This was just in time for a man in an orange-and-red robe, matching turban with a beautiful gemstone sitting in it above his forehead, stepping into the aisle to see what was going on. I held out my hand. "Hex bag, sir?" I asked with my practised customer-service voice. He looked with a furrowed brow for a moment, realised there was nothing going on that interested him and shot back around into the aisle he was actually interested in. One thing I do love about magical folk is that they are always too wrapped up in their own business to care too much about yours.

I put the hex bag away and thought on what those boys had said and wondered if that was what everyone was thinking. *Was it only Tamsin, Moon, and the Court who knew the truth?* I thought and hoped that it was not the case, but it wouldn't surprise me. I didn't care too much about what people thought, especially as the Wayward name couldn't really drop any further than 'war criminal-turned-traitor', although 'cold-blooded killer' did have a certain ring to it. What I *did* care about was being called something that I'm not. I can't change what my ancestors have done, and I can't change what I have done, but I will not let my throw of the dice with the Wayward name be as bad as those that have made us infamous among the Grimoires of the world.

I carried on with menial tasks until the end of the day, and when Tamsin had served our last customer, who bought the twin to the shaman staff I had previously used to implode a Lamiac's head into the pinewood flooring, we went upstairs. I kept the other behind the counter now, so it was easy to grab in those common shape-shifting lizard demon encounters. I asked Tamsin and Moon to follow me after Tamsin had locked up the day's takings and Moon had pulled his divining table back into the corner and stacked his chairs up. I poured three glasses of red Rioja, as a glass of wine at the end of the day had become a regular thing as business was doing so well, and I sat on my rocking chair in the living room, facing the coffee table, looking at the two empty seats of the sofa. As I waited, I thought about how I was going to say what I wanted to say and how I would need to ask both of them to listen to me completely and how difficult it was going to be until they understood my motives and why I had to do what I was going to do.

Tamsin and Moon came up the stairs one after the other, Moon after Tamsin, as was his preference. They came in talking about the Shaman staff, telling each other the story of how I used its brother to bludgeon a Lamiac to death, even though they had both heard it from me a hundred times. They sat on the sofa, picked up their glasses of wine, and Moon swallowed a large gulp, leaving Tamsin who smelled the bouquet before having the smallest taste, savouring each sensation. They were completely different, but they worked side by side with me, never complaining and never finding fault. They were always happy to work together, and I knew I was just about to throw a stone through our blissful glass house.

Tamsin and Moon sat there enjoying the feeling of a hard day's work and the glass of wine they held to confirm it. "A toast, to the three of us," I said as we all raised our glasses. "You two have held me together this last week and that has been no easy task. I don't think I would be as healed, both

mentally and physically, as I am without your care and comfort. To you."
We clinked our glasses together and sipped at our wine. Moon finished off
his glass and poured himself some more as he spoke.

"Well, boss, ya're a good man, regardless of what some may fink, and
I'd stand by ya no matter what," he said, offering the loyalty I was about to
test in full. Tamsin followed his lead.

"Jon, you are a kind man still finding his way in the world of magic,
and Court or not, I am honoured to be your Alchemist," she said and gave
me one of her beautiful smiles that instantly drove my nerves away. I had
to speak up; knowing I was about to ask them to do something they would
morally disagree with was killing me.

"Since losing Maurice, you brought me back from the brink and made
what could have been a pit of despair into a refuge, and for that, I am and
will be eternally grateful. But there is one matter I need to discuss with you,
and I will need your answer today." Moon and Tamsin looked from me to
each other and back. "In my conditions from the Court, I was told I couldn't
investigate the Seals, that I had to carry out my education into magic and
be at hand should the Court need me. Technically, I will not be breaking
any of those conditions, but the lines of right and wrong may become a little
blurred from here on in."

"What are you talking about, Jon?" Tamsin asked.

"I'm going after Emilia," I said and carried on talking before either of
them could try to dissuade me. "It's my fault that she was on that mountain,
and I wasn't able to stop Poet and Bard from taking her. Who knows
where she is and what state she is in. The Court sent a representative from
C.O.V.E.N. to try to find her, but the Servants of the Night stonewalled
them and told them nothing. I can't let her waste away in the hands of those
animals," I finished my little speech and waited to see what their reaction
would be.

"So where do we start, boss?" asked Moon.

"Seriously?" I questioned, thinking I was about to get a lecture from
both of them about the Court's ruling.

"Like you said, Jon, *technically*, we're not breaking any of the conditions
set by the Court, and as long as you keep me by your side, we can continue
your training," Tamsin explained calmly and in complete opposition to what
I was expecting from her.

"So you're going to help me? Both of you?" I asked, and once again,
they exchanged a look to each other and turned back to me and answered
at the same time.

"Yes."

"Right then," I said, not really expecting to start looking for Emilia straightaway, as I imagined I would be convincing them for a good few hours. An image flashed up in my memory. It was what I had seen when I had first met Emilia, what I had seen clearly for the first time: the hooded man and my prophesied death. The vision didn't scare me like it had done before; I now saw that it offered me a chance to change what would happen to me. A chance to change how I would die . . . My eyes drifted to my rolled-up sleeve where the Wayward oak tree stood in bold ink, its roots reaching down my flesh, reminding me of the promises I had made in my family's name. "I guess . . . we start at the beginning."

Jon Wayward will return in . . .

'SCION'
A Wayward tale

Lightning Source UK Ltd.
Milton Keynes UK
UKOW04f0101040215

245645UK00002B/132/P